MW01294066

LITTLE
MOVEMENTS

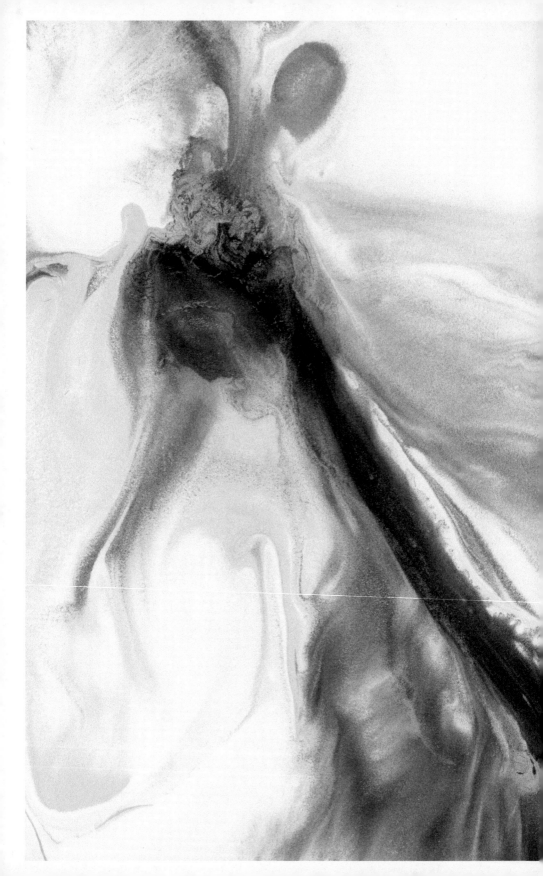

LITTLE
MOVEMENTS

A Novel

LAUREN
MORROW

RANDOM HOUSE

NEW YORK

Random House
An imprint and division
of Penguin Random House LLC
1745 Broadway, New York, NY 10019
randomhousebooks.com
penguinrandomhouse.com

Copyright © 2025 by Lauren Morrow

Penguin Random House values and supports copyright.
Copyright fuels creativity, encourages diverse voices, promotes free speech,
and creates a vibrant culture. Thank you for buying an authorized edition
of this book and for complying with copyright laws by not reproducing,
scanning, or distributing any part of it in any form without permission.
You are supporting writers and allowing Penguin Random House to
continue to publish books for every reader. Please note that no part
of this book may be used or reproduced in any manner for the purpose
of training artificial intelligence technologies or systems.

RANDOM HOUSE and the HOUSE colophon are
registered trademarks of Penguin Random House LLC.

LIBRARY OF CONGRESS CATALOGING-IN-PUBLICATION DATA
Names: Morrow, Lauren author
Title: Little movements: a novel / by Lauren Morrow.
Description: First edition. | New York, NY: Random House, 2025.
Identifiers: LCCN 2025012073 (print) | LCCN 2025012074 (ebook) |
ISBN 9780593736753 hardcover acid-free paper | ISBN 9780593736777 ebook
Subjects: LCGFT: Novels
Classification: LCC PS3613.O77848 L58 2025 (print) | LCC PS3613.O77848 (ebook) |
DDC 813/.6—dc23/eng/20250401
LC record available at https://lccn.loc.gov/2025012073
LC ebook record available at https://lccn.loc.gov/2025012074

Printed in the United States of America on acid-free paper

1st Printing

First Edition

BOOK TEAM: Production editor: Cara DuBois •
Managing editor: Rebecca Berlant • Production manager: Samuel Wetzler •
Copy editor: Hasan Altaf • Proofreaders: Alissa Fitzgerald, Dan Goff, Jennifer Sale

Book design by Elizabeth A. D. Eno

Title page art: Artlu/Adobe Stock

The authorized representative in the EU for product safety and
compliance is Penguin Random House Ireland, Morrison Chambers,
32 Nassau Street, Dublin D02 YH68, Ireland https://eu-contact.penguin.ie

For my mother. And for everyone trying to begin again.

If a person does not invent herself, she will be invented.
—Maya Angelou

PROLOGUE

The problem was, I had only ever considered what *not* to be. Who *not* to become.

As a girl, on weekday evenings, before my mother started working overtime to pay for dance classes, we'd watch Ricki Lake, Jenny Jones, and Maury Povich together. Teen moms proudly proclaimed their promiscuity or boasted of their babies' endless appetites while the audience booed. Years later, I finally understood what my mother had been teaching me—*don't satisfy the expectations of everyone around us by ending up like that. They'll blame it on our Blackness, our poorness, our godlessness. And if you do, for some godforsaken reason, become a teen mom, don't become the sort who goes on national TV to curse in Daisy Dukes. Who feeds your toddler pounds of bacon and Oreos. If you become a teen mom, be the sort who keeps things quiet, works hard to get through school, then gets a dull but steady job because nothing matters more to her than her child. Be the sort who turns her life around, gets married, has another child, and moves into a flimsy suburban house with a gray kitchen and a living room full of accent pieces from HomeGoods. But to be on the safe side—and you should always be on the safe side—don't be a teen mom.*

It wasn't an issue. At my Missouri school, the few Black boys found me standoffish, while the white boys found me Black. Fine by me.

Still, fear remained a cornerstone of my life. Guidance from my mother and all the other authoritative voices around me.

Don't get fat! A mortal sin. There was such extreme blame placed on the fat. Aunts, uncles, teachers, and friends of the family all went through a WeightWatchers phase and came out on one side or the other—either miserable, slim, and smug, or prepared for a life filled with equal parts self-deprecation and daily pleasure. There was never talk about the health risks—just as there was never talk of the risks faced by the girls at my dance studio who'd learned to move the food around their plates just so, whose bones showed through their chests like washboards, who didn't seem weak, but whose insides were clamoring for any nutrient they could find—only talk of the inability to fit into a pair of favorite jeans. My teen years were all Lean Cuisines and George Foreman–grilled chicken breasts. Shirtless in front of the bathroom mirror, I sucked in, searching desperately for even one ab. Nothing, but at least I hadn't begun to inflate.

Don't end up with less than you started with. Not so hard considering where I came from. Still, every risk increased the chance of failing on this count. Drugs and alcohol could ruin a person from the inside out. But the real cautionary tale was ambition—too much ambition, too much faith in oneself, could land a moderately intelligent and talented person in a lifetime of debt and regret. Dream enough, but not so hopefully that it ruined your life. Dream medium.

Avoid being alone at all costs. Evading all of the above, I'd been taught, would help with this (though some of the girls on *Maury* saw point one as a remedy, however temporary). My father died when I was young, and my mother, who was single from that point on, was desperate for me not to be. It was essential to find someone to experience all of life's ups and downs alongside, even if you weren't particularly fond of each other. It was helpful if the other person also had a mastery of areas in which you lacked, so that they were more than just a warm body. Fix the toilet, hem the pants, etc. Only then could you circle back to the idea that had first been a warning but was now a mandate. Now you could become a mother. Now you *had* to become a mother. You could hope there was still enough time. That the universe—and your body—wouldn't betray you. Then you'd never be alone.

I'd spent a lifetime dodging missteps rather than following my gut, or my heart, or whatever other world-making forces tangled within me. I'd been paying such close attention to the dangers that I couldn't see all that shimmered in the slivers in between. Even my occasional risks—college on scholarship in New England, a move to New York City for work—were relatively safe. I'd never taken a true leap of faith, had been so concerned with what not to do that I'd never determined what *to* do. What I wanted. Who I was. Until now.

PART I
SHOW. BUSINESS.

//

SEPTEMBER–DECEMBER

We talk too much of black art when we should be talking about art, just art. Black composers must be free to write rondos and fugues, not only protest songs.

—Alvin Ailey

CHAPTER 1

I thought about giving up before I'd even begun. After the five-hour drive, I found the key beneath the doormat and shimmied it into the hole. But the little blue house wouldn't let us in, no matter how cleverly I twisted the knob or torqued the key. It wasn't until Eli shoved his body against it three violent times that the door popped open with an exhale.

He fell inside, but I just stood there, hesitating still. It would have been easier had the door never opened. We could have gotten back in the rental, driven home to Brooklyn, and when people asked what happened with that big thing I was supposed to have done, I'd shrug and admit I simply couldn't figure out the door key.

But easy was the opposite of the point. And now that I was inside the house, really taking it in, I felt that tickle in my belly I'd felt all my life at the start of something new. That first-day-of-school feeling. That glance-from-a-crush feeling. This felt so much bigger than all those other firsts. Big enough to silence me for the last half hour of the drive through those rural, winding roads. Big enough to change everything.

The house had an incoherent mix of art styles and trinkets sprinkled throughout. Clashes of color and texture. A cute that teetered just this side of tacky. From the entryway, I saw the living room to the left, the kitchen at the end of the long hallway, a small washroom just to its right, and the stairs that led to where we'd later find the bedroom and bathroom. More than enough for one person accustomed to New York City living.

"This whole place is ours?" asked Eli, walking up the staircase, looking around.

"Just this half. It's a duplex. The landlord, George, is on the other side."

Eli had been saying *we* and *ours* all day, but I was the choreographer-in-residence. Technically these things were *mine*. He'd only be here for a week, to help me settle in. After that, I'd be alone to create—there was no prospect more thrilling and terrifying. We hadn't been apart for more than two weeks since we'd started dating eight years ago.

At the top of the stairs, Eli placed his butt on the wooden banister for a moment before thinking better of it and simply running back down. This was a glimpse into the sort of child he'd been—an unruly, bone-breaking boy. He still looked like the childhood photos scattered across his parents' Iowa home, only his hair was more brown than blond now, his green eyes newly puckered by crow's-feet but still twinkling with mischief.

I'd been the opposite sort of child in every way. Careful, introspective, anxious from the start. My coarse curls had been relaxed for years, pulled back into a bun, an attempt to go unnoticed. To disappear. Now, decades later, I was finally letting my natural hair out—tight curls and twisted updos. I was finally ready—willing—to be seen.

But I was overwhelmed by it all—the house, the responsibility, the attention, the solitude.

Eli wrapped his arms around me and kissed my forehead.

"Why don't you lie down? I'll start bringing stuff in."

"There's too much to do," I said. "I don't want to lose momentum."

"I'll take care of everything," said Eli. "Stretch your legs. Rest your eyes."

I appreciated the permission, though I knew I wouldn't be able to relax, so I made my way to the living room. Unlike the cream walls of the entryway, these were covered in an awful wallpaper, yellow and green stripes. A tan, crushed-velvet camelback sofa was pressed against the far wall, beneath a window. I tried to get comfortable, but this wasn't the Midwestern La-Z-Boy furniture of my childhood. I closed my eyes and listened to the sounds of Eli moving around outside, then entering the house, grunting with each drop of a bag, each stack of a box.

Packing light had never been my forte, and the fact that I'd be here for nearly nine months hadn't helped. There was so much I didn't know about this place, these months—when the weather might shift, where the nearest Black beauty-supply store was, where I might find an 80 percent dark chocolate bar flecked with chili, what events I might attend. I had to be ready for anything, to bring as much of myself here as possible.

Finally, Eli closed the front door and sighed, sounding more sad than exhausted. Now that everything was inside, I was one step closer to having an existence far away from home. He was having a harder time with the change than anticipated. That much was clear from the last few weeks in New York—sullen, prickly, tainted with misplaced spite.

His feet padded my way, and he crawled on top of me, said, "Make room." I scooted, and he slipped an arm beneath me, the other around. His chest beat against my back. I began to drift, but never reached sleep, just felt our bodies sync until it was impossible to tell whose breath was leading whose.

The summer had started with a bang—the offer from Briar House such a jolt to our lives that I was sure they'd made a mistake.

"What if they meant to invite Leela Smark or something?" I said, re-reading the email from my phone as I sat on our living room couch.

"No one is named Leela Smark," said Eli. "They want you, Layla Smart. You've worked so hard for this. Everything is finally coming together."

Then came the question of long distance. It didn't make sense to give up seven hundred square feet of rent stabilization, for both of us to up-root our lives, including his job, for nine months, only to start over again in Brooklyn. When you had a good thing going in a city so expensive and competitive, it was best to hold on.

By July, Eli was smothering in his affection—kissing me as I finished work assignments, squeezing my hips in the night, our skin sticky with sweat. I'd inch away, he'd inch closer.

The trouble came in the last two weeks. I had begun to stash things in piles, small collections of my life accumulating in corners of the apartment. Shoes, clothes, books.

He'd already lost so much. We both had. The little thing we'd rested our hopes on last winter. The tiny life we would build our world around, gone before it even arrived. Before we'd told a soul. Better that way. It happened all the time, I told him, partly to convince myself. But Eli couldn't grasp the normalcy of it. Couldn't understand my swift, tidy mourning. The way I refused to let it halt my life. The way it only made me want to live more.

We'd created this home together—Wayfair chic, peppered with flea market finds, cluttered with books and plants. Now that I was leaving, it didn't matter how homey the place was. The piles were monuments to my imminent departure. Eli was hurting, and his sadness looked a lot like anger.

By August, my words and actions were all wrong in his eyes. Shoes left in the doorway; a bell pepper sliced in the wrong direction; a jar of pasta sauce made with high-fructose corn syrup; *LaCroix* mispronounced; a purchase from Amazon rather than a local business.

The night I changed our dinner plans was when Eli lost it. He claimed we only ever did what I wanted. But hadn't he always liked what I'd wanted? What *I* wanted was what *we* wanted. After eight years together, two years of marriage, I'd suddenly become a sitcom nag, a stand-up punch line. *Wives, amirite?*

He stormed to the bedroom, pulled off the kerchief he'd just tied around his neck—the kerchief I'd insisted several times over the years was *a lot*—and slammed the door.

Maybe I should have left him alone. When I met him in the bedroom, he spewed anger like I'd never heard from him. He stared at me, something hard inside of him—shards of it had crumbled off sporadically over the years, but now it was breaking off quickly, in chunks.

Anger and fear tangled inside of me.

"Just tell me if this isn't what you want," I said. "Say what you're really getting at. 'Don't go or else go for good.'"

He looked into my eyes. "Why would you even say that?" His voice was soft before it broke into sobs. His tears flowed, his shoulders shook.

"It's what you were thinking! It's what you want!" I said.

"How could you possibly know what I want? When did you ever even ask?"

We'd never been so cutting with each other. So cruel. While Eli cried, I refused to. My throat, nose, and head were tight with the tension of holding it all in.

Eventually, I went to the kitchen and drank glass after glass of water from the tap as though rehydrating for the tears I hadn't let come.

Eli came in to drink too, his eyes red rimmed, glassy.

"I don't want you to go," he said. "But I know you have to."

We held each other then, for what felt like hours. Until the sun went down. Until the night went quiet.

Things cooled after that, perhaps the power of catharsis. By the time our rental car, packed to the brim, crossed into upstate territory—high-rises and billboards replaced by lush trees and glimmering water—the spell had broken. Maybe all we'd needed was to leave the city. Nothing I would ever say out loud. Our little corner of Crown Heights felt more like home than any place I'd ever lived—never more than a few blocks away from the most beautiful brownstones, the cutest coffee shops, the loudest block parties, the most flavorful foods. A utopia, if you could live with the corgi-sized rats, the occasional gunshot, the harrowing rent.

We rolled down the windows and cranked the music. We sang to every Top 40 song from before 2020—when pop music began to evade us—that crackled through the speakers. We let the smack of wind cleanse us.

After unpacking and eating the sandwiches we'd grabbed at the exit nearest the house—perfect for the cheddar that was, indeed, better than any in New York—I insisted we have sex. We had a week left together, six weeks until his next visit, so there was no time to lose. I squeezed his butt as we finished the dishes.

"Right now?" he said. "You don't want to have that ice cream?"

"I don't want ice cream. Not right this second."

"First time for everything."

He hoisted me onto his back, turned his head just enough for a quick kiss. It felt like the early days, when we were young, nimble, and fearless. But now I tensed as he carried me, fearing one wrong move would send us tumbling. It wasn't the time for a break or sprain.

Eli climbed the creaky stairs with belabored stomps, and in the bedroom, he dropped me like a sack of potatoes. The mattress sang a chorus of springy moans. He crawled on top of me as I eyed the room. Like downstairs, ornate paper covered the walls. The bed was an old four-post cherry piece shrouded in deep maroon bedding. A bureau stood against the wall, above it a massive pastoral painting. Eli rolled to his side.

"How old do you think this house is?" he asked.

"I don't know, eighty, ninety years old?"

"No way, this place is at least two hundred years old," he said.

"Why'd you ask me, then?"

"You think old-timey people fucked here?"

"Of course," I said. "Old-timey people stayed fucking. All those kids they used to have!"

"So wild to think about." He shook his head.

"Can we not think about, like, colonial settlers boning?"

"They probably wouldn't have been settlers—"

"Shut up," I said, covering his mouth. "Just stop."

I pulled him toward me and kissed his neck. He closed his eyes and found the zipper of my jeans. We kissed softly as he slipped his hand between my legs. It was perfect, the weight of his touch, the feel of his lips. We knew each other completely. It wasn't the same as when we were new to each other, but there was comfort in the guarantee. No questions, no surprises. Our clothes were on the floor. I was on top of him, he was inside of me. We kissed fiercely until he told me he loved me, our mouths still pressed tight, both of us bursting with relief.

I draped my arm and leg across him. The room was stuffy, the air heavy with sweat. So I opened the window, let in the cool night air. The moon was almost too close, too bright. And then there was the endless flicker of diamond light.

"Look outside," I said as he curled into me. "There are so many stars here."

"There are so many stars everywhere," he said, dragging a finger over the hill of my hip, tilting his head toward the window. "It's nice to actually see them."

The day should have exhausted me into a night of deep sleep. That and the comfort of having Eli with me for a little longer. But adrenaline swam through my veins. I kept thinking about all the bodies the bed had held. All the artists that house had seen. Successes and those forgotten to time. For every one who'd made a career for themselves, there were twice as many who hadn't. Just because I didn't know their names didn't make them failures. But I wasn't naïve. This was how it worked. Every opportunity had the potential to be a last stop. The end of the road before shifting to a more stable life. Would the person lying in this bed five, ten, fifteen years from now know my name? Would I have the courage to push myself all the way? There was a lot that might go wrong.

My journal was still tucked beneath our bed in Brooklyn. Forgotten. At first, I'd kept it private from Eli out of embarrassment—it had felt girlish, like I might as well have been writing my thoughts in glitter gel pen rather than the utilitarian Bics I preferred. But then, it felt important to have something of my own. For years, I'd written down my anxieties in the minutes between him brushing his teeth and coming to bed. But my choreography journal was the only notebook with me now, and cross contamination wasn't an option. So I held my thoughts, felt the pressure in my temples as they piled and piled.

CHAPTER 2

There's nothing like the disorientation of waking up in a new place for the first time—that split second of having absolutely no idea where you are. The possibility. Your life can be anything at all. I'd felt it on my first morning in Connecticut, dizzied by my place in the top dorm-room bunk. On that nervous, jet-lagged morning in Perugia, Italy, the study-abroad foreignness mixed with hope and juicy risk. With each New York apartment—the sound of the street sweeper in the narrow Chinatown alleys, the stench of my roommates burning eggs in Bed-Stuy, the feel of Eli's weight beside me that first morning in Crown Heights.

It took a moment for things to come into focus that Monday morning in Vermont. *Home,* I told myself, looking around the strange room—almost stately save for the inexplicable Homer Simpson nesting dolls on the oak dresser.

I dressed quietly while Eli slept, then ground coffee beans and listened to Vermont Public Radio—switching my home station from WNYC in the NPR app. It was important to get acquainted. To be here now.

How strange to be entering this new phase at thirty-three. For all those other wakings, I'd been so young. So free to experience a whole-bodied new start. Arriving at a place like this years ago would have been nice. But I'd been confounded by how to build a creative life in New York. I had romantic visions of the city: sweaty studios, bohemian parties, endless performance opportunities. But I didn't anticipate rent hikes, the lack of general interest in dance, the destructive pleasure of brunch.

For my first year in the city, I shared a one-bedroom with Ashley, a friend of a friend. We separated the large, carpeted Financial District bedroom with a floral curtain from Lot-Less. Every weekend, I pretended to sleep on my side of the curtain while Ashley enthusiastically bounced atop some Lower East Side bartender.

An internship in the publicity department at Brooklyn Academy of Music helped to supplement a babysitting job that paid more but was slightly demeaning (at BAM I never received the finger in unison from sticky six-year-old twins). Three promotions in two years, each bump inching me closer to a living wage and boosting my ego. My colleague Josefina took me under her wing—showed me how to craft a perfect pitch, how to please our boss, the artists, the press. The satisfaction of getting a press bite, seeing the final feature or a glowing review, was intoxicating. And those promotions were lifeblood for my bank account, helping me land my very own bedroom in a shared Brooklyn apartment— farewell to Ashley and all her carefree fucking.

There was comfort in the security of work. Perhaps I was meant to promote other artists rather than be one myself. I pushed choreography aside, found peace in letting it go.

My nerves spiked when Eli, the BAM IT assistant, first came by to fix an issue with my Outlook. The following week I put in a ticket for a PDF problem. My desk phone was *acting funny* the week after that. Of course, everything was fine by the time he came by. Maybe he was good luck, I shrugged.

We moved in together after a year of dating and staggering our work entrances in the morning to deflect suspicion. And now that my love life was steady, it felt like the right time to make another change. Old friends had been asking about my choreography, email blasts announcing submission periods and grants flooded my inbox. Work was starting to numb me, but quitting wasn't financially viable. So I rebuilt my artistic life bit by bit. Saturday mornings in front of my bedroom mirror moving, gingerly at first, but with more freedom each time. Soon, I'd twist and spin, jump and drop. Eli came running into the bedroom after a turn gone wrong. He helped me clean up the shards of a mug that had flown from the dresser and scattered across the hardwood floor. *Don't hurt yourself.*

Before long, those falls became choreography. A show here and there. Solos at first, but eventually I found dancers who performed for free, just as I had been inexplicably willing to in those post-college years.

After being highlighted a few times in blog reviews, I started applying for fellowships and residencies. But nothing came through. It felt like I'd forever be on the bottom rung, showing at small outer-borough black boxes, never quite reaching that elusive *emerging artist* stage. And then Briar House came calling.

I kissed Eli on his sleeping forehead and dashed out the door. The mile walk to Briar House was a grassy path dotted with wildflowers, lush green hills rolling in the distance as far as the eye could see. It was obviously all real, but something about those hills seemed impossibly pure. How had a place remained so untouched?

The path ran along a main road that saw a car only every few minutes—each slowing as it passed, the driver squinting through the sunlight, staring, smiling, nodding. I smiled too, hoping to look less like a strange wanderer, more like a friendly new neighbor. There were small signs in the grass for shops and farm stands—a weaving-supply store, a dairy farm, a winery. A house up a hill boasted Pride and Black Lives Matter flags.

Eli was likely just now getting up. He seemed comfortable here already, though I couldn't be sure if he'd come to terms with the fact that *my* creative work had brought us here, not his. When we'd met, Eli had been an aspiring filmmaker. He left BAM after three years there, bounced between part-time jobs, worked on screenplays. After a year and a half, he took another full-time IT job at a different nonprofit—managing the company server, building databases, troubleshooting complex issues. If his IT work was as intrusive as my publicity work had been—always on call, constantly available to artists, managers, the press—he might have been eager to get back to Brooklyn.

But he wasn't, and here we were, and there it was. Briar House was three stories high, the original redbrick house nestled within the expansion—a modern façade of black brick and sleek floor-to-ceiling windows on the south side of the building.

In the lobby, a young white woman with blond dreadlocks introduced herself as Mia without looking up from her phone. She told me Margot Mattenberg—Briar House's director—would be late for our meeting because of traffic. I told her I'd heard on the radio that the Green Mountain Men, a local conservative group, were blocking the highway in protest of . . . something—the coffee grinder had roared over the details.

"Those boomers are out of their minds," Mia said. "When I was growing up, they were pissed about Briar House's expansion. They canvassed, tried to get signatures, but, like, know your audience, dudes. This isn't New Hampshire."

"That's bizarre. Briar House is such a nice asset to the community." And one that seemed to care about local artists as much as those it brought in—the corkboard of flyers outside the co-op suggested a disproportionate number of string bands and ceramicists for a town this size. "Besides, this building isn't huge. It's not like they built a mall."

The only parts of the original building that remained were the exterior bricks and benches, plus the concert posters that decorated the walls. I'd read that the place had been gutted in the early aughts, tripled in size to create more studio and performance space. The residency program expanded as well, taking up most of the year.

"Those guys don't care about art," said Mia. "They care about the land, which sounds nice at first. But it's really just about hunting. And there's a lot less space for that."

As we chatted, a few people walked by in linen and Tevas. Administrative staff who'd remain anonymous to me, confined as they were to their third-floor office space.

Then an older woman walked through the doors. A salt-and-pepper bob, slim body swimming in Eileen Fisher. Her tortoiseshell glasses balanced delicately on the bridge of her aquiline nose. She was stunning.

"Margot," said Mia. "This is the new choreographer, Layla Smart."

"Right!" said Margot. She pressed her glasses up to take me in. Sunspots dotted her tan face. "Welcome, Layla! I hope you weren't waiting too long."

"Not at all," I said. "It's a pleasure to finally meet you in person."

We'd corresponded over email all summer. Margot had shared the requirements: an evening-length piece set on a pickup company we'd select, a detailed proposal of the project—from concept to music to design—a preview event in February, a premiere in May, appearances in their promotional materials, and interviews at their communications director's discretion. I'd said yes to everything.

We took the stairs to Margot's second-floor office, which was sleek with dark wood and brushed metal, the shelves adorned with glass awards. Even her achievements were chic.

"We're thrilled to have you here this season," said Margot. She offered me a coffee, then put a pod into the Keurig that sat on a shelf in the corner.

"We've welcomed some wonderful international artists the past few seasons," Margot said as the machine purred. "Pilar Godoy set a beautiful tango-inflected modern piece last year. Olga Semenova brought us contemporary ballet. And of course, there was a stunning Tanztheater work by Søren Janssen a few years back. A nice global roster."

She handed me my coffee, along with a pod of half-and-half and a few Stevia packets. I ignored the packets, watched the white swirl delicately in, stirred until the coffee was a creamy brown.

"This year, we wanted to celebrate Americana! Each artist-in-residence is from the States. The composer grew up in the hills of Appalachia, the visual artist is from Wyoming—she's doing some really exciting work with watercolors. And then there's you."

Americana. A strange category to throw me under. I'd always felt fickle about my Americanness, tried to escape it however I could. I'd spent a semester of college trying and failing to incorporate berets into my look, another twisting my hair into what I thought were Bantu knots but that my friend Kofi—the only other Black dance student in my class at Connecticut College—informed me were simply not. *Baby girl,* he'd said, *go to a salon!*

"I first saw your choreography at Montrose back in 2019," said Margot. "A revival of your original solo show?"

I appreciated the term, as though my work had taken Broadway by storm. I'd had no idea she was there that night. It was a mixed bill, and she'd likely come to see another artist who was on the rise. I'd originally performed the solo, but set it on another dancer for Montrose. It had become clear that my body no longer carried the movement in the way that I, or anyone, wanted.

"The angst in your movement reflects what a lot of people are feeling these days. It was put together beautifully with the text and the soundscape. The duet at the Palmer Center was also quite moving. I loved the power dynamic, with the woman doing all the lifting. A striking commentary. You're going to bring something powerful to our stage. I hope you're thinking about where you fit into the canon."

"The canon! Wow. That's so flattering. I'm truly just working out my five, six, seven, eights at this point."

"You should start viewing yourself through a canonical lens. Situating yourself among the greats. Alvin Ailey, Bill T. Jones."

"Martha Graham," I said jokingly. "Merce Cunningham."

"Camille A. Brown," she said. "Ronald K. Brown."

All the Browns. All the Blacks. I loved these artists and their companies, of course. Had seen them at BAM and other major theaters across the city. Ailey was undoubtedly an influence—sharp, explosive movement, intricate musicality, the sweet marriage of hip-slip and debutante posture. But so was Cunningham, his experimentations with rules and randomness that made each performance a game—something fresh, new. Graham, the mother of modern dance, whose raw surrender birthed a movement. Pina Bausch, who brought glamour, humor, and flirtation to the world with her dance-theater. Every underappreciated choreographer who'd made a music video move in the past thirty years—all bombast, and sex, and swag. But I wasn't a purist. Influence and inspiration were different. My style was guided by dozens of choreographers—it was difficult to pinpoint exactly from which family trees I branched. Placing myself beside any of them felt like a premature act of arrogance.

"I can't wait to see what you do," said Margot. "Especially with everything happening in the world now. Everything that's happened in the past. The *pain*. The *injustice*."

My breath lodged at the back of my throat, preparing for what might come next. A chant of *Black Lives Matter*. A performance of "We Shall Overcome" by a gospel choir waiting in the hallway. But Margot just stared at me, the next great hope of the Black dance canon.

"Well," I said. "I'm excited to get moving in the studio. Can't promise I'm going to crank out a *Revelations* redux, but I'll see what I can do."

"Do see!" said Margot. "Don't sell yourself short. Your work was moving even when you were working full-time. Now the possibilities are endless. There's a phrase in Swahili that I learned during my time in Tanzania."

I pressed my lips together in what I hoped looked like a smile.

"You may know it."

I squinted.

"Haraka haraka haina baraka." She stared at me. "Do you know it?"

"I don't know any Swahili, no."

"It translates to *hurry, hurry has no blessing*. The greatest things take time, dear. You've got that here. And money! Ask for what you want, and there's a strong chance we can make it happen."

What I wanted was to be known. For artistic directors and funders around the country—around the world—to see my name and not have to wonder. I wanted them to want me, to give me funding, stages, and respect. Margot could make that happen. Briar House was part of the Vermont Institute of Ideas, one of the best-funded multidisciplinary programs in the country. The institute was at the forefront of environmental science, public policy, and tech, so Briar House was hardly the centerpiece program. Nonetheless, it was connected, with a powerful board to boot.

Margot turned to her computer.

"I've got a meeting in ten, and I want to get through some logistics with you."

I'd be paid $3,600 on the first of each month—a sum that would have seemed painfully low if not for the fact that they were covering housing and, I could tell already, there was little to spend money on in this town. Briar House closed fully for three weeks at the holidays and into the new year.

The dancers would arrive this week. I'd meet with Jason and Amy, the composer and the visual artist, next week.

I finished my lukewarm cup of pod coffee.

"Communication is key. If you have a problem, if you need something in order to take the piece to the next level—funds, labor, feedback—reach out to me. We're all working together to make this thing great. Too many missed signals, and it all goes kaput."

"Understood," I said.

"Friday!" she said, tossing her hands into the air. "I'm having all the artists-in-residence over for dinner at my house. It's nice to get the collaborators together early on. Partners are welcome. I don't like to pry. Some people have them, some don't."

"I'll bring my husband," I said, glad for her to know I was lawfully wedded. "And I'm glad we got to talk. I'm really excited to be here."

"Me too, dear," said Margot, following me to the door. I held out a hand as we stood in the doorway. But Margot pulled me in for a hug. Her scent was soft and expensive, her hair like silk against my face.

CHAPTER 3

Before my first ballet class, I cried in the car. My mother bribed me with chocolate Ensure—a strange treat I'd discovered during visits to my grandparents in their final years. She'd caught me sneaking them and figured that if the chalky drinks were good for dying bodies, they were fine for growing ones too.

The first few classes were a struggle—itchy tights that sagged at the crotch, strange new words paired with unnatural movements, the fact that I, at five years old, was expected to do only one thing for an hour straight. Most of us were in despair. One girl cried for the entire class, even while executing the moves, her lips trembling as she fluttered her feet across the floor to a jaunty *Nutcracker* tune.

There were no other Black students at that two-room strip-mall dance studio, tucked between a Little Caesars and a rent-to-own furniture store. The other girls were doused with hairspray, mouths rimmed with Hawaiian Punch, their princess panties bunched beneath their leotards and tights. The hefty bangs of the mothers, the stale stench of the gray lobby carpet.

It had been hard, but there was such satisfaction in finally grasping the terminology: plié, tendu, chassé. In my body obeying my command to move against its greater instincts.

"Beautiful, Layla!" the teacher shouted one day as I completed a stable series of chaîné turns across the floor. My favorite combination of words from that moment on.

Tap and jazz came next—the holy trinity of dance for the American girl. Each skill learned and compliment earned filled me with a glowing warmth. I craved the studio with its worn wooden floors, portable steel barres, and harsh fluorescent lighting.

By my second year, we were given the assignment of choreographing a three-minute dance routine—a ridiculous task for children who'd only recently mastered tying their own shoes. We could choose our own music, a newfound freedom. I'd just gotten my first CD, Whitney Houston's *My Love Is Your Love*. It was filled with songs about love and heartbreak I wouldn't understand until years later, but I listened to it constantly anyway. For me, back then, music was all about voice, and Whitney's gave me chills. Even at six, I knew feeling mattered most of all.

In my pink-carpeted bedroom, I practiced to the title song—only after my mother vetoed "It's Not Right but It's Okay" and "Heartbreak Hotel," claiming they were inappropriate for class, though I could listen to them at home as often as I liked. I didn't know what she meant, but I liked this one well enough, so I didn't mind. I played sixteen counts and created moves to match. I restarted the track, repeated the moves to be sure they fit. If they did, I moved forward, if not, I closed my eyes and listened to the music again, moving until things fell into place. By the time of the studio showing, I was prepared, confident. Families sat in folding chairs along the studio mirrors. My body pulsed at the click of the cassette tape, the first beat of the song.

The dance was full of shoulder-rolls, turns, and leaps to match the energy of the song. Certain lyrics earned more interpretive gestures. When Whitney sang about love, I pulsed my hands above my heart. Circles had been a big part of our training—competition judges loved a good shape—so I cartwheeled around the perimeter of the studio as she sang about the years passing by. That had seemed appropriate. For the finale, I slid into a slow split, my arms raised, as Whitney's voice soared.

There was instant applause, an internal rush. The parents nodded, impressed. Everything was so simple. It was only a matter of piecing things together bit by bit. Shapes, sounds, and rhythm. My mother's eyes were wide with pride as she jumped to her feet. Something worth one hundred *beautiful, Layla*s.

My mother and I applied for and received a scholarship to a better dance center closer to the city, farther from home. No more sequins, no more competitions. At eleven, I took my first modern dance class, where I relinquished the austerity of ballet, the flashiness of jazz. We rolled on the ground, we rolled on each other. We *felt* instead of counted. We invented our own vocabulary.

It was a challenging transition, and I gravitated back to ballet—clean and certain. The teacher at the new dance center was a woman with thin gray hair and frighteningly bony hands. She taught complex variations, while the jolly accompanist banged on the piano like he was a soloist at Carnegie Hall and not playing for a bunch of preteens. I loved it. And when the recital arrived that year, my family could tell. They expected me to be good at jazz and tap, but I was stiff and tense, far from a young Savion Glover. I started coming around to modern, though I was still working toward that crucial release. In those days, ballet still held my heart. My cousin Bria ran up to me in the hallway after the showcase with a grocery-store bouquet.

"Girl, you was really doing it in the 'Beef. It's What's for Dinner' dance!"

"Thank you!" I said, still breathless from exiting the stage, cheap makeup caked to my face. "It's actually the *Rodeo* suite by Aaron Copland."

"Chickadee," said my mother, bending beside Bria to hug me. "That was amazing. You were wonderful in everything, but you really stole the show in the ballet number. So beautiful!"

The compliments made me feel high. Infinite.

A couple of years later, the ballet teacher poked at my bulges. I wobbled on my pointe shoes, tipped in crushed rosin, not because my ankles were weak but because everything else, I was told, had grown too big. And without sticks for limbs, without ribs slicing through my leotard, my lines were no longer right. The teacher stopped correcting me. I wasn't even worth fixing—my first sign that there was no future for me in ballet.

Dance was all about adaptability. Changing shapes, changing course.

The body could be controlled to an extent, but it was nothing without the mind. Dance would never hold a singular meaning for me, a simple, clear purpose. It would continue to reveal itself in thin, peeling layers.

But I never forgot the itchy pink tights, the flashy routines, the Copland springing my body to life. The lagging rhythms and pokes to my fatty parts. The pressure coming from all sides. I still wanted it, despite the pain—inside and out.

The Briar House dance studio had a high ceiling and wood floors covered in fresh black Marley. Afternoon sun spilled in through the windowed walls that faced the woods. Deer pranced by as I warmed up. With the delicate bounce of their gait, the shock of their tawny fur against the green, they were beautiful, simple. But perhaps their lives had been made more complicated by buildings like this, by people like me. Artists who came here for a dash of the space and clarity the deer had been born into. The deer didn't need clarity. They just existed. Lucky things.

I began to move, appreciative of the perfectly sprung floor—just the right amount of give. The musicians in the upper studio played for part of my warm-up—where I shoulder-rolled and hip-rocked, pointed and flexed, bent and stretched—but they stopped midway through. So I paired my phone with the sound system and let my music shuffle—Nina Simone, Nils Frahm, FKA twigs. My body was warm, buoyant, ready to create.

Instead of looking at the notes I'd written over the past few weeks, I decided to lead with my body. Eyes closed, I began to circle my wrist. It crawled up my body until it passed my face, grazing it before reaching for the ceiling. It pulled out to the side, where I chased after it, feeling a rush of air as I ran, a drop in my stomach that halted as I stopped just before colliding with the windows, then tilted on my heels. I stumbled back a few steps, before my left foot slid into a lunge. Slowly, I melted to the floor, then curled into myself before stretching my limbs like a starfish. My chest lifted, my legs crossed, my hands slapped the floor, and all in one motion, I sprang into the air, then landed with a supple bend of my knees.

The eyes of a tall, black-haired man caught mine from the opposite side of the glass door, and I screamed before I could stop myself. He jumped too. I covered my face with my hands. He mouthed *sorry*, tossing his hands up, ashing his cigarette in the process. I found the door latch hidden in the corner of the glass wall.

"My bad," he said. "I was taking a break and caught you. That was great."

"I was just messing around," I said, crossing my arms to cover my belly peeking out between my oversize crop top and loose sweatpants.

"I'm Jason." He offered a hand. "The composer. You're the choreographer?"

"Good eye," I said. "Layla."

We shook, his grip slightly too firm. He smelled like my childhood summers—uncles' houses ripe with Newport smoke. It was only now, close up, that I could see, despite the last name in the welcome packet—Mitchell—that he was Asian. The first person of color I'd seen since arriving in Vermont. What a relief that I wouldn't be the only one.

"Great to meet you, Layla. I won't keep you. Don't wanna disrupt your flow. I know how that is. But I'll see you soon."

"Definitely," I said. "Friday at Margot's, at least."

"For sure. Good luck in there."

I nodded, but my concentration was broken, my psyche shaken. In performance, *good luck* is bad luck.

CHAPTER 4

Dancers know their bodies, push them to their limits without fearing sweat or pain. Dance isn't about sport or dominance; it's about creating something magical with one another. I'd never felt properly dancer-like in this way, had always been too hesitant, too doubtful of my body. Walking into the studio that Thursday to see my four dancers warming up, I was reminded of this fundamental truth. I might not be able to dream for my own body, but I could certainly dream for theirs.

Creating alone in the studio was one thing, but working with a new group of dancers was another entirely. They were polite, greeted me kindly. Two wore frayed T-shirts and baggy pants, warmed up flat on their backs with isolated movements. The others wore crisp leotards and neat buns, completed a perfect ballet barre.

My pulse throbbed in my ears, my hands shook. These were professionals, not the recent college grads I was used to. They'd worked with the best choreographers. Their lives were dedicated to performance. They knew what they were doing, so I'd have to pretend I did too.

I fiddled with the sound system in order to turn away from them, place a hand over my chest, take slow, deep breaths, scan my body from head to toe—a stress-relieving technique I'd learned from an app I deleted from my phone for storage space.

After another look at their lithe figures, I grabbed an oversize sweat-shirt from my bag and pulled it over my tank top, suddenly reminded of my arms and stomach. A softness that had quietly made itself at home over the last few years.

I turned back around to see them clustered in pairs—stretching, chat-ting. They stopped at the sound of my voice, and I was shaken by their attention.

"Welcome, everyone!" Their eyes stayed glued to me. I had not con-sidered the fact that I'd be stared at for the better part of a year. For most of my life, I'd worked toward the opposite.

"I'm so excited to be working with you all, but honestly, I'm also a little nervous."

"Us too," said Jade Freeman, a dancer I recognized from BAM. She sat casually in a center split. Her hair was barbered short, her body roped in lean muscle, her warm skin adorned with tattoos, draped in loose clothing.

I spoke about the piece, how the themes were still emerging, how there was a fragmented nature to it. A sort of collage. They nodded—although how often had I feigned comprehension with no clue what was truly being said?

They introduced themselves, neck-rolling and hip-stretching to keep their muscles warm. I took notes.

Jade spoke first, her voice deep as she explained her eclectic dance background in Philadelphia, occasional trips to her mother's home coun-try of Jamaica, the yoga teaching that paid her bills, the doula training that fed her spirit. She'd found moderate success in the dance scene but needed a reset—space, and nature, and consistency.

Terrell Diop was tall and slim with a ruby nose ring and tidy corn-rows. He'd studied modern dance in the Bronx and learned Sabar during family trips to Senegal. I recognized his face from the New York dance scene, though from smaller companies and venues.

Ava Martinez was petite with bright skin and a neat low bun. She'd trained in ballet in New York, studied at Juilliard, and danced with some notable junior companies. As she spoke, legs outstretched, she pointed to reveal an impossible arch, her toes reaching all the way to the floor.

Courtney Lee-Edwards was a ballet dancer from Boston. She had a deep complexion, long box braids rolled into a topknot, and dimples just beneath her eyes that peeked through when she smiled. Her confidence didn't ooze like Ava's, but her fingertips swam when she spoke, her posture never wavered.

I'd watched fifty audition videos and given Margot ten options—of those, seven were Black, and here were four of them. It would have been fine otherwise—it wasn't relevant to the piece—but this felt like a gift. An opportunity.

"It's great to see some familiar faces. And new ones too," I said. "I can't tell you how excited I am to be working with all of you."

"Did y'all know we were all gonna be Black?" asked Terrell.

"Definitely not," said Jade, laughing along with everyone else. "Especially here, of all places. I just assumed that, aside from Layla, I'd be the only one."

Briar House hadn't had a Black choreographer in nearly two decades—a shock considering the number in the industry. This had not been lost on me when I applied. Briar House boasted a progressive mission and needed someone like me as much as I needed them.

"This is wild," said Courtney. "I've never even been in a room with all Black dancers."

I hadn't either.

"First time for everything!" I said, standing. It would be easy to get sucked down a rabbit hole of stories and experiences of what it was like to be the only, or one of few. But I needed a strong, authoritative start. We were there to dance, and that was what we'd do.

"You're all warm, but I'm not. So, bear with me. I'll teach you the first phrase, but everything should be a little bigger than what I'm doing."

I moved through a simple section—gentle enough that I wouldn't pull a muscle, but energetic enough that they could see the intention behind the choreography, and I'd in turn get to see how they moved. Some followed along, but others simply watched. Often a better technique.

My arm stretched across my body, one foot crossing in front to walk around myself, then a chassé toward the mirror, a quick spiral in reverse.

Ava, trying to move along with me, sighed.

"Maybe just watch this first time," I said, still in motion. "We have time."

I dropped into a deep second position, then swayed back and forth, eyes closed, hands cupping an invisible orb. I washed the orb over myself and brought my right leg into my left, leaning into that side, then slid across into a run.

"These are bigger, prettier," I said, circling them with stag leaps, one leg bent in front while the other stretched behind me. There was a time when I soared through the studio, gliding on air. Now my leaps were lower, heavier, my legs angled downward rather than parallel to the floor as I imagined. Still, I was dancing, full-out despite myself—my arms grasping for some imaginary thing just out of reach. My lungs cursing me. I finished with an inward turn that melted into itself, until I lay still and quiet, limbs splayed, on the ground, panting. The dancers clapped.

"Don't gas me up," I said, blushing. "I probably won't be able to walk tomorrow." I wiped the sweat off my face with my sleeve. "Let's go through it all slowly."

There were only a few verbal cues—*turn, leap, schwoomp, badada*—those requisite sound effects that take on meanings all their own.

The dancers followed, but then came the questions.

"What are the counts for the turn?" asked Ava.

"I'm not sure. Just feel it. Feel the energy of the others around you."

"Where are you looking for the *schwoomp*?" asked Courtney.

"Let's see." I did the move three times, my gaze in a different direction for each. "Do whatever you want for now. I'll watch and see what looks best."

"How are the arms for the leap?" asked Ava. "I can't tell if they're bent or straight."

She meant: *Your technique is weak, be more precise. I'm better than you.*

"Bent," I answered. I needed to appear decisive and in control. "And your foot is relaxed in the hop that comes next," I added, "not pointed."

We moved through it until it felt smooth. Until it looked like dancing. They ran it a few times to a classical track, and it looked nice. But when I turned on a Victoria Monét song, they rolled their hips and sang along, except for Ava, who stood stiffly.

"This is just for fun. Not necessarily what I'm using. But, good. Get into it."

They loosened up, and the movement deepened, even if it wasn't quite what I'd envisioned. They were all better dancers than me—better than I'd ever been—and stood out in different ways. Jade was soulful and buoyant. Courtney's leaps were gorgeous moments of suspension. Ava's lines made her limbs seem infinite. Terrell was both rooted and weightless, like some outside force was in control of his body.

The dance world was cruel. It made no sense that these dancers—as beautiful as any I'd ever seen onstage—were here with me, in Vermont. When making my selections, I'd figured Jade at least would be out of the question, scooped up by a proper company. She'd probably made it to the final round for everything, been cut for arbitrary reasons. The same was likely true for the others. What kept them from being in rehearsal studios with larger companies or Broadway productions? Fear, chance, timing, one person's opinion? In any case, I was grateful.

The dancers made their way to the picnic benches outside for lunch. It was warm out, and the sun might have done me good. But I craved solitude. Teaching was like performing—I had to be *on*. If I was expected to last another four hours, another nine months, I needed to preserve myself.

In the sterile gray conference room, I picked at leftovers and wondered if I should employ some new diet during the residency—go vegan or keto—then immediately decided against it. There was no reason to try and inch my body closer to the ones around me, or even to what mine used to be. I was healthy, I only needed to acclimate to moving so intensely and consistently again.

I needed a break from myself, from all this, so I pulled out my phone and scrolled through Instagram. My cousin Bria posted a video of her two kids eating the oldest child's birthday cake like ravenous beasts. *Heart.*

My closest friends were from Connecticut College—Dahlia and Kofi. Dahlia and I were in the anti-racism club freshman year. We'd met at the group's Talib Kweli concert, the only two at the snack table rather than elbowing our way to the front. Kofi and I had met in the dance program, where he quickly eclipsed us all—no one could compete with his athleticism, speed, and charm. The three of us all moved to New York after graduating, separately but intertwined. Now Dahlia was a children's rights lawyer and Kofi was a touring choreographer. They'd figured themselves out.

They'd both shared a photo of a sunset at a rooftop party from the weekend. *Heart.* Kofi, as always, shared more. He was guest-choreographing for a mid-tier company, and there was a clip of the dancers rehearsing, and one of them all doing a silly dance, Kofi leading the way, so at ease with them. *Heart.*

My phone buzzed with notifications from Briar House.

Please join us in welcoming our newest choreographer-in-residence: Layla Smart. The Brooklyn-based choreographer's work will debut in May. Stay tuned for more!

The post featured a stoic headshot Eli had taken of me with his DSLR in front of a graffitied brick wall in our neighborhood—a photo I now found unbearably cheesy—followed by shots from my previous dance shows. It had one hundred and fifty likes, and I had eighteen new followers. A few comments of enthusiasm, led by Kofi.

Is it just me or is this the most gorgeous choreographer they've ever had?!

Only one negative comment, someone saying my presence was the work of the *woke mob.* Obviously.

I tapped the heart beneath the photo, then tapped it again, to unlike. Was it self-aggrandizing to like something like this? Should I comment instead? Should I repost? That would be best, but I'd need to come up with a caption that was gracious while also being true to my own voice. There were only ten minutes left before I'd need to head back to the studio, and these things never came easily to me. So I buried my phone in my bag, where I might not hear it buzz. Might not feel the vibrations of all the lives orbiting mine.

The next section of choreography was a duet. Two people navigating each other's bodies was precious. There was no room for error.

"Partner up," I said, giving them a moment. "Everyone will learn both parts eventually. Let's say the person on the left is—" I paused, thinking.

"Carmen de Lavallade. And the person on the right is Geoffrey Holder."
Only Jade and Courtney chuckled, and I was reminded of their youth—
Jade was the oldest at twenty-six.

With Courtney as my partner, I showed how Carmen wrapped around
Geoffrey's torso and let her legs float away from the ground, while Geoffrey spun her gently to the other side, before the two fell into a deep
lunge, holding each other's forearms. Carmen stood as Geoffrey slipped
out into a fall, then was pulled up by Carmen. It went on like this, a
catch and release between the two. A slipping away. There were gentle
lifts, pliant jumps into each other. And here, more than in the other sections, there was stillness. Moments where both bodies were frozen, or
where one was and the other moved around it, under it. When hands
crawled over a face, a torso. These stillnesses would make or break the
section.

First they practiced all together, then I watched each pair, Moses Sumney's almost–a cappella as the soundscape. There were some near drops,
some stumbles, some missed connections. All so confident individually,
they were somewhat shy with one another. I stepped back, gave them
time, watched as they found their way.

Some moments were trickier than I'd imagined. I'd created the movement alone, of course, the other person an imagined figure. I had no idea
that the positioning of one person's legs made it impossible to lift the
other person. That they would nearly kick each other's faces at one
point—exciting to watch but frightening to dance, according to their
yelps. But they adjusted, made it work on living, breathing bodies, not
just the partner I'd been dancing with in my head.

The pairs performed in rotation. Jade and Courtney were balanced,
cool, and light, but almost too relaxed. Ava and Terrell, to my surprise,
partnered beautifully.

Ava's head stopped at Terrell's shoulder, but she was a pillar of stability
as she carried his weight. Terrell's body floated around her, lifted with
unbelievable ease. More importantly, they took their time. In the still
moments, the only movement was the blink of their eyes, the breathy rise
of their chests. They made the moments last and moved again only when
it was time. Somehow, they always knew. Terrell closed his eyes as Ava's

hands crawled over his body, and when his eyes opened and locked with hers, they collapsed into each other in a way that felt rich, desperate. With a hook of their arms, they spun in a circle, Ava's feet lifting effortlessly from the floor before running to the opposite end of the room while Terrell spiraled to the floor. They fell apart and came together. Lifted, tossed. And finally, at the end, they rocked to silence, eyes straight ahead, until they were still. Until they were through.

The others clapped. It took a moment to realize they were waiting on me. That this was choreography I'd created, not the story of two lives moving forward in real time.

"That was perfect," I said, taken aback. They'd created a sensation I hadn't known I'd craved. "Just beautiful."

Their faces were sweaty, pleased, a little afraid. The rest were waiting for something, direction. The tick of the clock caught my ear. We were ten minutes over.

"Oh god! I'm so sorry. We're finished. Go, be free!"

They clapped and pounded the floor with their palms, thanking me and one another by sending a rumble through the studio.

"Thank you so much for what you brought today," I said.

"We have to take a first-day pic!" said Courtney. "Somebody get what's-her-name."

Jade went into the hallway and came back with Mia. I handed her my phone.

"Could you take a few on this one too?" I asked.

The dancers crouched behind me. Mia held up one phone, and then the other, snapping a flutter of pictures on each as we all smiled, shifting from pose to pose. I adjusted tentatively—unlike every other millennial, I'd never learned my face, my angles.

I scrolled through the pictures as they left the studio. Something was off in every shot. Blurry limbs, closed eyes, faces caught mid-shift. I didn't post a single one.

Eli was stirring tomato sauce in the kitchen, his torso partially covered by an apron. He'd once been obnoxiously firm all over, and it comforted me

to watch his body give along with mine. My arms slid around his soften-
ing middle. He wasn't wearing deodorant, and his funk was sharp against
the tomato sauce. I didn't mind.

"Affection, eh?" said Eli. "What do you want?"

"Nothing, jerk. You're not going to be here forever, that's all. Holding
you while I can."

Eli was quiet. He didn't like to talk about leaving, but I knew the
meals he made each night were gestures of love.

This was hard for me too. I'd never loved another man. My father
existed for me only in bits and pieces of memory—his thick mustache,
the smell of Old Spice, his bass holler.

When I was younger, love from a man was all I'd wanted, though I
knew it was a foolish desire. Men were selfish, crude, perhaps didn't even
have the capacity. Distant relatives had lingered too long in their hugs, let
their eyes skate over my blooming body. Boys in high school had ignored
me, and though I had a few encounters in college, even those who'd
slipped their tongues down my throat in dark corners at parties or franti-
cally poked between my legs on extra-long twin beds would avert their
gaze in the dining hall the next day.

There had been only one real boyfriend before Eli, a kind biracial
waiter I'd flirted with at the spot near my first apartment. He was fine,
but he lived in Weehawken, had no real goals, and still listened to a lot of
New Found Glory. It never would have worked.

Then I met Eli, and drinks with co-workers turned into late dinners,
just the two of us—jerk chicken with rice and peas from aluminum containers, eaten on Eastern Parkway benches under the glow of lamplight
and summer moon. Natural and easy. I was wide open, sentimental. The
sort of person I never thought I'd be. The sort of person I laughed at now.

"Dinner is almost ready," Eli said, snapping me back into the room.

"Smells zesty."

"I figured you probably worked up an appetite. How'd it go?"

I told him about the dancers—how they moved, the moments that
shone, the anxiety. How it had been a long time since I'd been surrounded
by quite so many young, beautiful people, and for just a moment, I'd felt
like a complete ogre.

"Don't be ridiculous," Eli said, kissing my cheek. "You're beautiful, and you know it. Stop fishing."

"I'm not! It was just strange. A lot came up."

"It sounds like it's going as well as it can," said Eli. "I'm really proud of you."

"I was so eager to get here, and I know it's going to be great once we're in the groove, but I also can't wait until it's over."

"That's kind of what life is. Hoping for something and then dealing with what it means to actually have it. Everything takes work, especially the good stuff."

Sometimes his clarity surprised me.

"Try to enjoy it while you're in it," he said. "It's an amazing opportunity. I'd kill for something like this."

He'd applied for, and been rejected by, several screenwriting programs years ago, resigned himself to an eternity of nine-to-five. I could feel his hope for me, but could also sense his envy.

We ate quietly. Eli had put some misguided herb in the sauce. Dill? He sometimes did things like this. *Experimented.* It wasn't awful, but it was nothing I'd ever want to eat again.

I reminded him that tomorrow we'd be having dinner at Margot's.

"You'll want to wear a shirt," I said, tickling his nipple beneath the apron.

"Do I need to look *nice* nice?"

We had this conversation every time we went to a decent restaurant or the home of someone slightly more sophisticated than we were.

"Black-and-white striped shirt and black pants. But iron them. Clean sneakers are fine."

"Roger that."

"And maybe give it a snip snip," I said, grabbing his chin.

He looked unreasonably handsome with a five-o'clock shadow, but he hadn't trimmed since our arrival and his beard was growing in unwieldy patches. He'd nearly broken my skin when we kissed the night before.

He'd been enjoying the break from his real life up here in Vermont. His parents were evangelicals—an engineer and an office manager who required clothes to be ironed, tables to be set, hair to be neatly brushed, flyaways to be tucked. Even in New York, there was a measure of present-ability to which he still subscribed. Vermont had allowed him to be un-ruly and free. But now, Margot's dinner.

We carried our dishes to the sink. He placed a hand on my lower back.

"When can I see what you're working on?"

He knew I didn't like sharing anything until it was complete. Dance required the right ingredients in certain measure. I feared letting anyone taste anything that wasn't fully cooked, properly seasoned. There was al-ways the risk of random dill.

When Eli was still writing, he would share scenes with me as he wrote. I'd scratch out whole lines, question themes and half-formed ideas. He was never offended, didn't waver in his confidence. It either was there or it wasn't. Of course, now, it wasn't.

"They're making me show for all the moneybags on February first. An invited rehearsal thing. You can come to that."

"February?"

"I know. Black History Month. A little on the nose, right?"

"That's five months away! Maybe I can sit in on rehearsal when I come back in October. Or when you're back home in December. You could film a rehearsal and show me."

"Maybe."

"I'd really like that," he said.

He pulled me in, and I pressed my lips to his, let my chin be scratched. A little pleasure, a little pain.

CHAPTER 5

Ava was out.

"The project isn't a good fit for her," Margot said. The morning light beamed in through the office window, taunting me. "She came up to chat after rehearsal yesterday. She was expecting something different and feels her time would be better spent auditioning."

I was embarrassed, though not entirely surprised. Her skepticism of my teaching style, her request for counts that didn't exist, guidance I couldn't provide. I understood—had my body not precluded a future in ballet, I might have followed that strictly structured path.

"Ava and I have known each other for years," said Margot, leaning in. "I was on the board of the School of American Ballet when she was a scholarship student. It's nothing personal, she just has a different style. I wanted to tell you before rehearsal."

"Did she say anything specific? She took on the choreography beautifully."

"Well, you know. She's a wonderful dancer but comes from a traditional background, so was expecting something"—she lifted her fingers for air quotes—"'more professional.'"

"Margot, would you like to watch rehearsal today?" I asked, anxious at the thought. "There's nothing unprofessional happening."

Margot placed her hands over mine on the desk. I hadn't realized until then how close I'd gotten to her face, or that sweat was pooling in my armpits.

"I trust you," Margot said, smiling. "Ava just wasn't the right fit."

"Without her, there's a gap in the piece. It's a quartet."

"It'll be tough to find another BIPOC dancer that can move up here on such short notice."

I felt an internal squirm—maybe because of Margot's open admission that this place was aggressively devoid of color. Maybe because of the way she'd said *BIPOC,* like she'd just learned the term in a mandatory DEI seminar.

"I never requested Black dancers," I said. "I'm fine with anyone from the long list, as long as they're capable and open." A slight betrayal of the camaraderie we'd built yesterday, but perhaps it wasn't as sacred as I'd thought. Ava obviously hadn't thought so.

Most of my other top picks had landed different gigs. Margot said she could ask someone who'd performed in their show last year and taught at the Vermont Ballet Academy. Apparently I'd seen her tape and liked it. But she was white. Margot wanted to be certain I was fine with that.

"Unless you'd prefer just three dancers?"

"I need four. I mean, I think I do. All summer I was conceptualizing the piece for four dancers. Once I see them move again, I'll have a better sense of what'll make sense."

"You creatives and your *process.*" Margot bobbed her head. *Silly chore-ographer.* "We'll talk later."

She watched me walk toward the door, and I sensed it then—her first kernel of doubt.

The other dancers said they had seen Ava's departure coming. They called her icy, shady, a bunhead to the core.

"We don't need to get into it," I said, though I wanted them to spill, to drag her to filth so I could feel relief at her absence rather than offense. "Just wanted to fill you in. Someone new may be joining, I'm not sure yet. For now, let's work on the first section from yesterday."

Rehearsal moved forward, but I felt the tug-of-war I always struggled with. I was desperate to please too many people, a deep-seated tendency. I wanted to impress the critics, but also my family and friends. The dancers should be as proud to perform the piece as Margot and the institute would be to present it. Letting anyone down was upsetting. And I'd already done that.

I moved with them—jumping, and spinning, and sliding to the floor—my muscles alternately knotting and throbbing, but in a familiar, almost comforting way. Four dancers were necessary, and here I was, doing it all, leading the way, even if I was a bit sore. It had been years since I'd danced onstage. I didn't love the way my body moved anymore—effortful, heavy, stiff—but with months of training, and against the bouquet of the others, I might be able to pull it off.

Others I'd studied with in college had been intense. Kofi, like the Briar House dancers, pressed his body to unthinkable limits—until muscles pulled, nerves pinched, joints twisted. Ice and rest, and he was back at it again, throwing himself wholeheartedly into the choreography. I'd been timid, careful. Sure, I'd pushed myself, felt the thrum of possibility spread through me when the dance extended beyond my limbs and into the atmosphere. When a teacher shouted their praises. But my lungs stung when a choreographer called for one more run, thighs ached as they demanded a deeper plié. My stomach dropped as I tossed my body into flight, catching horizontal stasis for a split second before rolling into the ground with the bang of my hip bone to the Marley. The strain in my calves as a choreographer commanded higher leaps. The sharp splitting of skin beneath my pinky toe after too many barefoot turns. The click in my knee when I landed slightly off. But for the choreographers, it didn't matter. *Again! Again! Again!*

Then came the cognitive torture—*reverse, invert, retrograde.* Turning everything upside down and inside out. There was also the matter of my face. It needed to look like I wasn't being tortured. Effortless, powerful, happy, flirtatious—something new each time.

The shift to choreography felt right—encountered so long ago but abandoned along the way. It wasn't an escape from dance that I'd needed, only a more civil relationship to it. I learned to embrace my body and its instincts, to explore the architecture of it all. That's when I was noticed again. That's when it all began to make sense.

When I moved away from the stage, I thought it would be for good. But if there was ever a time to reintroduce my body to pressure and performance, it was now.

I made my way home through the shortcut—an isolated route that saved ten minutes and boasted a trio of massive pines, a constant hum of insects, and the occasional scurry in the grass that caused me to jump every time. My mind churned with ideas for getting back in shape. It was so quiet in Vermont, so devoid of the normal distractions. Unless I found myself deep in the knitting community or with a sudden interest in hiking—neither of which seemed likely—I'd have more than enough time to retrain my body. To do what I needed to keep up. Once Eli left, it might be good to have another layer of purpose.

Margot lived in a large colonial home tucked away at the top of a hill, fifteen miles south of Briar House. A perfume of herbs, spices, and meats wafted down the path to the doorway. It smelled like wealth—the sort I'd first encountered visiting high school dance friends in their homes near Washington University, where their tenured parents led the cozy, intellectual lives I came to dream of. And later, going with college friends on long weekends to their homes in Massachusetts and Connecticut, where their parents crafted luxurious spreads and—to my surprise—let us drink glass after glass of wine.

Under the porch light, I flashed my teeth at Eli. There was a fine line between sophisticated and clownish when it came to red lips, but he gave me the thumbs-up. I adjusted the straps of my black slip dress to make sure my tiny breasts didn't make an appearance. We hadn't even rung the bell when Margot opened the door wearing a navy caftan and strappy sandals. Her wrists were stacked with bangles, and she held a glass of white wine between her slender fingers.

"Layla!" She hugged me, then turned to Eli. "You must be her husband."

"Eli. Pleasure to meet—" he said. Margot was hugging him, his arms hovering awkwardly over her body. He was freshly trimmed and ironed.

Margot smiled as she stepped back to get a better look at him, not unlike the way the catcallers on Nostrand eyed me on summer days.

She led us through the foyer, its gray walls lined with abstract paint-ings, to the sparkling kitchen, where a marble-topped island held trays of food. She rattled off drink options as she looked around the massive stainless-steel refrigerator that, for whatever reason, spoke—with a Brit-ish accent, no less. Eli and I gave each other a quick look at the sound of the robotic voice, then quickly turned away. We were prone to the church giggles, had once wiped away tears at a war documentary Q&A when the stodgy moderator kept pointing to people in the last row and saying, *I'll take it in the back.*

From the list Margot offered, I asked for a glass of Sancerre—it seemed the most expensive. Eli took a bottle of the local IPA. The refrigerator didn't object to either.

"How are you finding the area?" Margot asked as we clinked our drinks.

"It's cute," I said. "Definitely a big change from Brooklyn."

"I'm from Vermont, about an hour north, but lived in Manhattan for years before returning. It's a transition, but a lovely place. People are quite passionate about the community."

"It's great," said Eli. "Small towns are nice."

"Yes," said Margot. "Sometimes simple is good."

Loud stomps came from the hallway stairwell.

"Is it party time yet?"

Margot rolled her eyes playfully, then welcomed a man who looked like a country club Larry David into her arms.

"My husband, Arthur."

Arthur waved and poured himself a glass of wine.

"Honey, meet Layla, our new choreographer-in-residence, and her husband."

"Nice to meet you, Layla and her husband."

"Lovely to meet you, Arthur. Thanks for welcoming us into your beautiful home."

"This old shack?" he said as the refrigerator reminded him to close the door all the way. He elbowed it shut. "Glad to have you here. You're city slickers too, so I imagine you'll get tired of these hempseed-chomping, Birkenstock-wearing hippies soon enough. Come over anytime. We have Roku and a Peloton."

"People love those things, huh?" said Eli.

"Jess is the only thing to get me out of bed some mornings."

"Well, you have a *job*," said Margot, clearly tired of hearing about Arthur's Peloton crush.

"But do I look *forward* to the job at six A.M.? It's not the same."

He grabbed a tomato from the salad with his fingers and left the room as the doorbell rang and Margot dashed off to answer it.

"Cider Hill catering did a great job with the food," Eli said, pointing to a bag behind the recycling. We caught each other's eyes again, laughed without making a sound.

"Layla," sang Margot, returning to the kitchen. Eli and I turned to her with bright, forced smiles. "Meet Amy Van Buren."

Amy was a petite, freckled young woman with strawberry-blond hair twisted into milkmaid braids. A gray sackcloth dress, no makeup or jewelry.

"Your dances are great," she said in a delightfully raspy voice. "The duet was my favorite. Really subversive."

"Thank you," I said. "Your artwork is amazing. Really striking."

I couldn't recall any details from Amy's paintings. Links had been sent over the summer, but I'd been overwhelmed wrapping up work, preparing to move, everything with Eli. I had reviewed everything passingly. A selfish move, in retrospect. What I'd seen had been nice, I was pretty sure.

"Mm-hmm, thank you," said Amy, seeing through my bullshit.

"You're from Wyoming?" I asked, grateful to remember at least one detail.

"Born and raised. But I went to college in Minnesota. Went back home to work and save up for a year. Now this."

I shuddered. Amy was moving into her first dorm room the same year that I got my IUD strategically placed, ready to hold until I turned thirty-two. The arbitrary age we'd had in mind to start trying. I visited my ob-gyn last fall, and she pulled it like a splinter from my uterus. Easy peasy, save for the two-second metallic bite at my organs.

"Dinner will be ready shortly," said Margot, who was moving food around on the countertop behind us as though everything hadn't already been prepared by the good folks at Cider Hill.

She herded us into the dining room, which appeared to be lifted from a Restoration Hardware catalog, though the massive oak table might have been designed by some high-end local furniture maker. There were brass wall hangings, masks, and vaguely ethnic symbols—perhaps collected on the same trip where Margot had learned her treasured Swahili adage.

"I was hoping we could dine al fresco and enjoy the sunset," she said, placing the tray of baked ricotta on the table, "but the mosquitoes have been a nightmare this week."

"A composer got West Nile a few years ago," shouted Arthur from the study across the way. "You wouldn't believe the paperwork. Guy didn't even get that sick!"

The bell rang again, and Eli, Amy, and I grabbed at the tiny honey-doused mounds of ricotta before Margot returned with her arm wrapped around Jason.

"We're all here!" said Margot. "Five more minutes and we'll sup on boeuf en daube."

I hadn't eaten red meat in so long that it sometimes made me ill.

"And seitan en daube for the vegetarians!" she added from the kitchen entryway, as though reading my mind.

"Everyone's favorite," Amy said.

"You're a vegetarian, Amy?" said Jason. "I didn't know you could be in Wyoming."

"You can care about animals and the environment anywhere, Jason," said Amy. "And I didn't grow up on a dude ranch. My parents are doctors."

"Doctor parents?" he said. "Must be nice."

I'd heard people say that doctors didn't make that much money, but it always came from people who didn't know how little money could be made. Who had never felt the lifetime that can stretch between two paychecks. Who never counted their toilet paper ply by ply on a Thursday before the direct deposit hit on Friday.

It was obvious Jason and Amy had met already—the music and art studios were next to each other on the east side of the second floor. I was tucked away on the west side of the building on the first floor. Their tension could have been competitive or flirtatious. It was fun to remember those days of play and uncertainty.

"Layla," Jason said. "Good to see you."

"You too. This is my husband, Eli."

Eli stood to shake Jason's hand. Eli was slightly shorter, not nearly as broad. Jason had a barbell-set-in-the-garage sort of body. Unusual for a composer, but what did I know?

"Soup's up," said Arthur, returning with the stew. It smelled incredible, and even though Margot was right behind him with a vegetarian option—seitan that looked like pan-seared insulation—I'd dip into the sauce. A spoonful wouldn't give me the high blood pressure, diabetes, and heart disease that plagued nearly every member of my family. I read an article in college that had sealed the deal for me, though it hadn't mentioned the weathering that tolled us too. The external stressors and cellular trauma we carried with us. But there wasn't much I could do about that, so cutting out red meat had seemed like the best option, despite my mother's objections.

Arthur refilled our wineglasses as the dishes circled the table.

"Before we dig in," said Margot, raising her glass, "I'd like to toast our newest artists-in-residence." We all lifted our drinks. "Amy, Jason, Layla," she said. "What an honor it is to have you at Briar House. A talented and diverse trio! May your creations be rich. May your connections be deep. May your hearts grow fuller by the day."

"Hear, hear!" said Arthur, taking down the dregs of his white.

We clinked glasses, then dove into the food, Eli gleefully scooping boeuf en daube onto his plate.

"Let's all share a bit more about ourselves," said Margot. Conversations of this sort pained me to my core. The performance of it all.

It was difficult to pay attention as she spoke about her Burlington upbringing, Vassar, a move to New York to work for a classical music label, followed by a shift to nonprofit development work. My mind was preoccupied with what I would say. How to present myself in an interesting and worthy way.

"When my mother got sick," said Margot, miraculously still talking after what felt like twenty minutes, "I came back to Vermont to take care of her and eventually move her into a home. I started at Briar House thinking it'd be a two-year stint. And that was, what?" she said, turning to Arthur. "A decade ago?"

"Eleven years," said Arthur, as though he'd been counting the days.

Amy talked about how she'd started painting as a child in Wyoming, where there was so much nature to capture. She painted the same tree every day for a month in ninth grade and was astounded by how each painting looked exactly like the tree but nothing like the other paintings. I wanted to die.

She spent the subsequent summers in France, perfecting her skills, exploring her artistic urges. It was the sort of thing I'd heard college classmates mention, as though it were standard and not an immense privilege.

Jason talked about how music funding was cut from his school, but his mothers had old banjos and dulcimers they taught him to play when the violin was no longer an option. I felt clarity at the mention of *mothers*. I'd wondered how someone like him had found himself in West Virginia, even earning a slight accent along the way.

"It was kind of a relief, actually," he said. "I loved the violin at first, but once I learned it was stereotypical for Chinese kids, I wanted to drop it."

This wasn't unlike the way I intentionally missed shots during the PE basketball unit or restrained myself from rapping along to songs when students chanted them in the hallway, even when I knew all the words. And I always knew all the words.

Jason returned to traditional instruments when he got a college scholarship. He now played six.

The room quieted. It was my turn. I felt feverish at the thought of speaking. I hadn't studied art abroad in high school, didn't play a single instrument. I only knew how to do one thing, and until now, almost no one had deemed me remarkable even at that.

"Where to begin?" I put my lips to my empty glass. "I was a very shy kid. An only child. But I started taking dance classes, and something clicked."

I didn't share that my kindergarten teacher had been concerned about my debilitating shyness in those first months, had asked my mother if I participated in any activities at our church. My mother had explained, as I flipped through a book on the alphabet carpet, that we didn't go to church. This was unheard-of in our town, and I felt the teacher's silence like a grip around my neck. But after a moment, she recommended options. Dance seemed the most sophisticated to my mother, who had always envied Katherine Dunham and Judith Jamison. She took on a few extra overtime shifts and signed me up at that dingy neighborhood studio.

Everyone was getting antsy, tired of the formality of what Margot had placed before us, so I jumped ahead.

"By my early twenties I was more interested in choreographing than performing. Especially after auditioning in New York and realizing I was never going to become a dancer."

"Why?" said Jason. "You must be good to be where you are."

"Good at choreographing, I suppose. A lot of people are good dancers. But I never had the body type they were looking for. Not thin enough, not athletic enough. My confidence got pretty shaky."

"The patriarchy knows no bounds," said Amy, chomping on seitan.

"I was working full-time. Got out of shape."

"BAM, I hear?" said Arthur. "Fine institution. Weird shit."

"Weird indeed. Three-hour Kabuki, subtitled Dutch operas. You name it. I got rusty and self-conscious about dancing. I didn't want to perform, but I was still drawn to choreography. I got back to it. And here I am. I can feel my muscles reawakening. I'm coming back to life. It feels good."

Eli took my hand beneath the table, rubbed his thumb over mine.

"Life is so full of twists and turns," said Margot. "And you're all so young! I can only imagine what's in store."

"A baby, we hope," said Eli.

I turned to him, heat rushing to my face, his tightening in regret. He'd barely said a word all night and this was how he chose to chime in?

"I'm really focused on my choreography right now," I said. "My mind is on the movement!" As though this would erase the image of the two of us fucking with purpose.

I grabbed the nearest wine bottle and filled my glass.

"I want to have, like, ten kids," said Amy.

"Ambitious," said Arthur.

"Not naturally, of course. I imagine my partner will carry, though I guess I should probably discuss that with her, when the time comes." She chewed as she spoke, and I had to turn away from the sight, though the sound was no better—wet and gummy. "I mean, I should get a partner first. We can adopt if she doesn't want to carry. Probably a better idea anyway. Too many people on the planet as it is."

"Do you two have kids?" Jason asked Margot and Arthur.

Margot's face stiffened. "No. We don't."

So often Eli didn't think before opening his mouth. Maybe we should all go through our medical histories, reveal our greatest hopes, our deepest struggles.

"Margot, Arthur," I said. "You have such great taste in music."

Bossa nova I'd mostly heard in hotel lobbies had been floating through the dining room all night.

"Aside from peeking in on Jason and his musicians in the studio, where can we go for good music around here?"

I had no interest in their taste in live music—especially if the loop of "The Girl from Ipanema" was any indication—but we needed safe territory. Eli mouthed *sorry* at me as Margot and Arthur described a wine bar in Manchester with a jazz night. It was probably like stepping into a scene from *La La Land.* I certainly wouldn't be visiting.

Soon, it was late. Margot brought out dark-chocolate-covered figs, which seemed like a fake dessert, in the way that the twins I babysat after college were each allowed a piece of fruit after dinner. But when I tasted the figs, I couldn't figure out how I hadn't been finishing every day with such a treat. Rich and chewy. There was no option to speak—a perfect ending. We let our fingers grow sticky.

The car ride home was quiet at first, save for the soft rock on the radio, the hum of the tires rolling over the road as we crept along. There were no lights, only occasional yellow signs warning of sharp turns and moose—signs that appeared nearly too late.

"Never do that again," I said.

"Jesus, Layla." Eli's voice was louder than I'd expected. "Is it such a big secret? Is it such a shock that two married people would want a child?"

"I can barely deal with our parents asking us about when we're having a kid, much less my new colleagues. My boss!"

"It was a party! I was making conversation! If I didn't know any better, I'd think you didn't actually want this."

"Don't be ridiculous," I said. "You don't get it. You're not constantly being asked when you're going to have a baby by every person in the goddamn world. You have no idea how stressful it is. Especially after what happened."

There was the memory of my legs covered in blood, the small knot of flesh that had pressed its way out.

"It happened to me too, you know."

"No, it didn't! It happened to *me*. You were a part of it, but it happened to me. My body."

"Our baby."

"I don't want to talk about this anymore. Not right now."

His face was tense, eyes glassy. I suddenly felt very hot, so I rolled down the window, stuck my head out like a dog. But he drove slowly, so there was no wind, only the chill of night air. The headlights piercing through the darkness—we could barely see what was right in front of us.

CHAPTER 6

I hadn't felt drunk at Margot's but woke with a pounding head, a sour stomach. Eli and I drove to a nearby diner for breakfast—a quiet ride, neither of us quite ready to apologize or double down. It was Eli's last full day, and we both knew there was no point in pressing things any further. Aside from asserting that we needed two full orders of hash browns, my only other demand was that we get the food to go. My body couldn't be trusted, and I resented the way they asked us separately where we'd like to sit, assuming we weren't together. Just like at the diner in Missouri where our families had first met six years ago.

That Christmas, Eli and I visited my mother in St. Louis, and his parents decided to drive through the city on their way to see family in Louisiana. We met at a diner not far from the interstate to make the detour more convenient for them—I was relieved that we wouldn't host them at my mother's modest home. That I wouldn't have to feel any waves of shame about the plumbing problems or my mother's obvious disinterest in homemaking.

Eli's mother, Beth, a small woman with a graying bob, had shouted the entire time, a smile never leaving her face. My mother—tall, sturdy, calm—had flinched as Beth approached and hugged her tight.

We squeezed into a red booth, flipped through the laminated menu, ordered omelets, pancakes, bacon, waffles. Beth had a fruit cup and hard-boiled eggs. She wouldn't shut up about how good her fruit was—*so fresh!*—closing her eyes and wiggling her shoulders like those particular chunks of honeydew were rocking her world.

She called me a doll. Well-mannered. Sweet as could be. And my mother said she was right, that I'd always been a good kid. I wanted Eli to chime in and say that I was also smart, and talented, and driven, but he was face-deep in his lumberjack plate.

We talked about our holiday plans—dinner at my uncle's house, some movies here and there.

Let me guess: Harriet! *We've been meaning to check that out. I mean, what a tough gal, Harriet Tubman,* Beth said.

I closed my eyes, as though I might will the moment away.

We're seeing Parasite, my mother returned.

I don't know that one!

Surprising, said Eli, before asking for the check. *We're gonna be late for the movie.*

Jack and Beth hit the road in their Audi, and the three of us got into my mother's banged-up Nissan. Eli apologized for his mother's stupidity. My mother shrugged, saying she'd experienced much worse. Beth didn't know any better. She hadn't left the town where she'd grown up until meeting Eli's father and moving thirty miles away. How was she supposed to know that sometimes Black people watched foreign films? That we, occasionally, sought entertainment that didn't represent our history?

But as we'd pulled onto the highway, I couldn't stop thinking of Beth and Jack being introduced to a little brown baby and saying, thinking, doing, all the wrong things.

On the car ride back to the Vermont house, I ate my hash browns, delighting in the satisfaction of salt and crunch, and we finished the rest of the food in the kitchen, silent and focused. Eli suggested a walk to the water. The landlord, George, had given us a map to a nearby swimming hole, drawn on a napkin.

Bugs buzzed against my skin, sweat pressed through my pores. About a mile from the house, Eli and I approached a stream. He dipped in easily. I flinched at the touch of cold water on my skin.

Entering was meant to be the hard part. It was supposed to feel better once I was in. But my teeth chattered as we treaded water, the balls of my feet timidly gliding over the slick rocks.

My calves relaxed, my heels flattened. I felt more stable, but still uneasy. When I was fifteen, I'd earned a scholarship to a performing arts camp in Colorado—my first time away from St. Louis alone. I trailed through the hills and creeks behind the others, dancers and musical theater kids who had no control over when they might start belting "Seasons of Love." They had reveled in treks into the woods and waters, but I'd been certain death was somewhere under the creek's surface or slithering through the high grass. I felt quite the same now.

"So relaxing, right?" said Eli. "I could stay out here forever."

We craned our necks to see the tops of the firs. Between the lush leaves, dotted with birds, a perfect sky peeked through.

"It's cute," I said. "But you know I'm not trying to live in the woods."

Places like this had never been anything but eerie to me. Isolation felt ominous. I preferred lights and streets—where someone would hear my screams.

Eli shrugged, then sank beneath the surface, doggy-paddled my way. He hooked his arm around me from behind. He didn't lift or splash me, as he probably would have liked to. I was grateful that he recognized my irritable state. That he wanted to make the best of our last full day together.

I closed my eyes as our bodies pressed close, slick with fresh water. His hands crawled into my tight curls, my shoulders loosened. The water babbled, the birds sang, and the air was clean and still. Maybe Eli was right. Maybe it would be better to stay right there forever.

But we didn't. We got out and stretched our bodies across towels over the scratchy grass. Eli lit the joint he'd rolled at the house with the weed he'd brought from New York.

"Sure you don't want some?" he asked. "You seem tense."

"Hard pass," I said. I was bad at being high, didn't know how to relax into it.

"I wish I could stay," Eli said.

"Me too. But Ellen needs you at the office. You'd get bored, anyway."

"I'd hang out with Jason. I'd ride Arthur's Peloton."

The truth was, he would. He'd never had trouble making friends. Not that I did, exactly, I was just less eager to, more comfortable in solitude.

We took each other's clothes off on the couch, went one last round. We drank tea and made dinner, dragged ourselves upstairs. I feared getting into bed. We'd close our eyes, then open them, and the next time we closed them, we'd be sleeping in separate beds, hundreds of miles apart. But we couldn't stay awake forever.

Eli had transformed this strange house into a comfortable home. He'd replaced some of the old paintings with photos from our trips, lined the shelves with thrift-store bookends and handmade candles in intricate jars, placed plants on windowsills, hung them from the kitchen ceiling. Now he sulked through the house, saying goodbye to it all. I'd cried for two weeks straight before leaving Brooklyn—during my office farewell party, at a final dinner with friends, taking in our apartment that last morning. At least I could blame time and memories. We'd only been here for a week.

Outside, we ran into George. Eli made him promise to take care of me. George said he would, shook Eli's hand, hopped in his truck. I shook my head at their antiquated agreement.

Once we could no longer hear the gravel crunch of George's tires, Eli pulled me in.

"Goodbye, my love."

"I'll see you soon."

"Six weeks. Not so bad."

We kissed against the rental. I felt a pulse run through my body as I blinked out a pair of tears. His eyes were red too. He was a horrible crier—unabashed, full throttle. He was trying his best not to unfurl now. We stood for a moment, holding each other.

"Call me when you get home," I said, running a hand along his face.

"Love you, schatzi."

It was a German word he'd learned in Berlin, the trip where he'd pro-posed. *Dear.* He'd been trying to make it work ever since. It never sounded quite right, but I said it back.

Eli gave me one last kiss, then got in the car. He backed out of the gravel lot and made his way to the main road. I stood there for a long time, expecting him to turn around. I was sure he'd forgotten something. He often did. But he didn't come back. He had everything.

CHAPTER 7

When I was a child, my mother left for work early and came home late, so I spent weeks of summer days alone with my library books and the buzzing living room TV. It was in that house—all carpet and floral wall borders—that I learned to be content with myself. My thoughts. I'd thrived in solitude. Being with Eli had startled me in the beginning. He was always there, looking at me, saying things, wanting something.

Even as I swallowed two melatonin pills that night to slow my racing mind, I expected to hear him rap at the door. But he was gone.

The melatonin was hardly the sucker punch I needed. I lay awake for an hour, my ears listening for a hint of Eli's presence, startled by occasional creaks. The house teasing me with its settling.

Was this whole thing—the risk, the distance—a mistake? Was Eli losing his mind alone in the apartment? Would he skip work tomorrow to stay home and wallow? Would he skip work all week? Would he lose his job? Would we go from comfortably middle-class, finally, to below the poverty line? As a child, when other kids dreamed of becoming veterinarians and firemen and athletes, I simply dreamed of the middle class. No penny-pinching. No sacrificing small things for other small things. But taking this residency paused all that. It was up to Eli now, but could he hold us until I returned? Until I landed something bigger?

Just as my spiral neared its apex, the crickets outside the open window driving me mad with their songs, Eli called. He was home. Had been for hours. Our bed felt too big without me. He hadn't known what to eat for dinner, so he ordered Thai food, but only had a few bites. No appetite. I thought of the cost—twenty-five dollars with fees and tip. And he'd barely touched it.

He decided he'd drive back up the following weekend. It wasn't necessary, but he said it might be. For him. I calculated the cost of the car rental, the gas, but I said only, *Wait out the week and see.* We kept talking. And though I comforted him, I couldn't help but feel resentful too. My mind was overwhelmed, and I wouldn't get the rest I needed to be sharp for rehearsal tomorrow. Which was now today.

CHAPTER 8

I was ready to join the dancers. To awaken muscles that had long been dormant.

But there was someone new in the corner, in leggings and an oversize tee, leg stretched over the barre, a brown ponytail resting at the nape of her neck.

The other dancers gathered, whispered. Their eyes shifted between the new dancer and me.

"Hi? I don't think we've met," I said, smiling politely. "I'm Layla. The choreographer."

"Rebecca," she said, with a limp handshake. "Margot called me on Friday. I'm so excited to be here!"

"Nice to meet you, Rebecca," I said. Then, to the group, "I have to take care of something upstairs. Keep warming up, and maybe go over the group section if I'm not back in ten."

Margot's door was ajar, and I poked my head inside.

"Can I come in?"

Margot beamed, threw her hands up in the air. "Come, come!" she said. "It was lovely to meet Eli on Friday. What a handsome couple you are!"

"Thanks for having us." I sat. "It was really lovely. But I actually wanted to talk to you about something else."

"Becky?" Margot smiled. "Can you believe she was able to start today?"

"We never decided on needing another dancer or not. I wanted to bring it up at dinner, but there wasn't really a good time."

"You wanted someone to fill that spot. I could see it in your eyes. But you were afraid to ask. Don't be afraid to ask for what you want, Layla."

"I *do* want four dancers, but I was going to step into one of those roles. I figured it would be easy enough, since, you know, I'm creating the movement. And it would save Briar House some money. We could use it for something else. Costumes. Even pay increases for the dancers."

"Don't be silly," said Margot. "You don't need to worry about dancing *and* getting back in shape on top of everything else." I crossed my arms, attempted to shrink. "Just focus on making something brilliant for us! That's what you're here to do—create!"

"It's just. I haven't seen her move. The new dancer. What if she isn't a good fit?"

"You saw her video and liked it! Becky's a real gem—trained with Boston Ballet and Gallim. *That* company's doing some interesting work! She was in last year's show here with Pilar. A fantastic dancer. Trust me. Unless the issue is that she's white?"

She raised her eyebrows, her face somewhere between accusation and camaraderie.

"No!" I said. "I don't care about that."

"Good. I didn't think so. Remember, I want this to succeed as much as you do."

Success probably looked different for each of us. But maybe Margot was right. It might be best to keep a bird's-eye view of the piece and not have to manage the dual pressures of choreographing and dancing. I'd woken up each morning last week feeling like my body had been smashed between two brick walls, just from marking. And Becky was already here, warmed up, ready to go with just a weekend's notice. There was something to be said for that sort of dedication.

"Let's see how rehearsal goes today," I said.

"Becky's signed her contract." Margot tapped a paper on her desk. "When things fall through, you have to move quickly."

Heat rose from my fingertips up through my ears. But I couldn't blow everything up. I needed Margot on my side as much as the dancers. And they were waiting for me, eager to learn and work.

Margot's phone rang. She looked at the number that flashed on the screen.

"Board member," she said. And with a wave of her hand, "Would you mind closing the door on your way out?"

I wanted to slam it, leave Margot's office quaking, send a rattle through all of Briar House. But I only closed the door with a little extra force—I'd never been much of a slammer.

We circled up for a fresh round of introductions. Courtney had been more formal last week—she'd probably been constantly told to adjust herself by ballet teachers. Her leotard had been replaced with a Ntozake Shange T-shirt, her fingers wrapped in silver rings. Terrell was the most transformed. He had not only taken out his cornrows but shaved his hair close and dyed it white-blond. Jade was the same—always exactly herself.

"My name is Rebecca Allen, but I go by Becky too. Either's fine."

"We'll call you Rebecca," Jade said.

"I'm from the Middlebury area originally, and I teach at the Vermont Ballet Academy in Manchester. I was in last year's show here, and I've trained and performed in Boston and New York."

"Okay, lovely," I said, sensing the group's eagerness to move on, their disinterest in hearing more from her. "Let's get going while you're all still warm."

We reviewed material from last week, and Courtney made a special effort to catch Rebecca up. I gave them time to improvise or work on their own movement. I loved seeing the way they moved when the music played and the others weren't looking. Terrell's shoulders and hands had an effortless slip. There was something unique in the quick work of his feet, his gravitational resistance. Courtney was all long lines and effortless grace. Jade's body fell into abstract folds and collapses, striking in their strangeness. Rebecca moved in a loose, spontaneous Gaga dance style—a technique I'd always admired but never learned.

I thought of joining in, letting the music speak through my body, feeling my impulses burst through. But that wasn't the point. The point was to learn them through their undirected movement. To get a sense of their natural strengths and tendencies, to build from there.

As we left the studio for lunch, Courtney whispered to Terrell, "We should've known Briar House wasn't about to go full Wakanda."

"Homegirl seems nice, but we need to loosen her up," said Terrell. "Give her a shot of D'ussé and some cornrows."

"Please don't!" laughed Courtney. "Oh my god, what if she pulls a Dolezal!"

The two of them screamed in snarky delight.

"She'll figure it out," said Jade, who'd been stretching in the corner. "We did, right?"

I knew what Jade meant. We'd all figured out how to speak, move, and be in order to fit into various spaces. We'd learned to pick up cultural references and look up what we didn't understand. Would Rebecca be able to learn to move her neck, and shoulders, and hips in a way that matched the energy of the other dancers—something I hadn't choreographed but that had emerged naturally? What would be worse, if Rebecca couldn't find a way to master their style, or if she tried it on and found that it fit like a glove?

The group section was sharper and more technical than what I'd taught last week. The dancers picked it up quickly, even Rebecca, but they weren't moving as one. Some were too delicate, others too forceful. The steps were there, but the texture was amiss. It didn't help that I was indecisive. All the dancers did the movement differently. I liked each version but wasn't quite convinced of any of them.

Exhausted by my indecision with the group section, I craved the satisfaction of the duet for the final hour of rehearsal. But with Ava gone, I might never see it shine the same. I paired Terrell with Rebecca. The two danced well enough together, but there was no spark. Lovely, but nothing more. They needed some anguish—a scrape to the skin, a punch to the gut. Rebecca moved like life was easy. Like things always fell into place. Like she slept well at night. A peace I'd never known.

CHAPTER 9

My mother called to ask about New Hampshire. Never mind that I was in Vermont. Fair enough. I'd never met anyone from New England who could find Missouri on a map.

My mother had always been supportive of my commitment to dance, though she preferred musicals and hoped my move to New York might land me on Broadway. But when I told her about the one show other than my own I'd performed in—a site-specific exploration of depression where we crawled around outside of the Department of Health and Mental Hygiene offices reciting Sylvia Plath poems, clad in nude underwear—she stopped asking.

Now that I'd gotten a residency, she could see Broadway in the distance. Still, we only talked about dance for a moment before switching to Eli. She wanted to make sure I was doing okay. She couldn't believe we'd made the choice to live apart for so long.

Eli was the only man I'd ever introduced to my mother. I'd been nervous before that trip home for my cousin's wedding. I knew he'd adore my mother—her wry humor, easy warmth, near-constant output of baked goods. But I was unsure what she, or anyone in my family, would think of Eli. Of us.

I taught Eli the Cupid Shuffle in our living room—I knew he'd be clowned on the dance floor either way, but if he could keep up with this, he'd earn the respect of my cousins in their Fashion Nova, my aunts in their bedazzled suit-dresses, my uncles in their pinstripes and Stacy Adams shoes. And he did. My mother couldn't stop talking about how impressed she was by his rhythm. I told her that was condescending, but she just shrugged, made her way to the dance floor, stepping and swaying alongside him.

Within a few days she was teasing him.

"Look at those tiny little pants you got on!" she laughed when he walked out of the spare bedroom—a generous name for what was once my *playroom*, littered with VHS tapes and board games, but now held a trundle bed and framed paintings from HomeGoods—in skinny jeans. "I could barely get one leg in those things if you ripped 'em at the seams and made one big pant!"

They laughed as he kicked his scrawny legs around.

She treated him better than me when we visited—relegated to separate bedrooms thanks to a sliver of conservatism that had been in her since her rural childhood. She bought his favorite foods, made sure the place was stocked to his liking—more oat milk and Clif bars than I'd ever seen. Avocados by the bag, because we were *health nuts*. The house had been held together by rubber bands and safety pins for most of my childhood, but now she fixed the wobbly kitchen cupboard door, had a plumber unclog the shower drains. She wanted Eli to stick around.

In the beginning, I didn't think about it, but later, I'd wonder why my mother had gravitated to Eli so quickly. Would she have been as fond of any decent man I introduced her to, because it meant I was happy, or was there something about Eli's personality? Jovial, kind, helpful. He had family from the South, so country as she might be sometimes—our Mississippi roots deeper in her than in me—it was familiar to Eli.

She'd laid out a path for me before I was even born—the move from St. Louis city to Millwood—our dreary, conservative-curious, sepia-toned outer county. I'd accomplished a lot in my life, but maybe for her, Eli was my biggest achievement. With him, I'd finally made it.

But now he was gone, and my mother could hardly deal. Wasn't I scared up in New Hampshire all alone? Wouldn't I get lonely? What if something needed fixing? I assured her I'd be fine, could occupy my mind, my body, my time. There was Google, YouTube, a landlord.

My mother couldn't fathom having a man and letting him go, even if only for a while. She didn't understand modern relationships. She had, reasonably, been scarred by her past. Despite my deep and complicated love for her, there was always an undeniable pleasure in proving her wrong.

Of course it baffled her, my being here, taking a massive pay cut, risking so many elements of the security that she'd wanted. I was breaking the rules, whittling at the box of a life she had helped me build—making it into something that better fit my reality. She'd worked her whole life to barely get by. She picked blackberries at age ten for a nickel a bushel—a fact that sounded so horrifically antebellum I tried never to think of it. She sold fragrances at Dillard's after high school, then landed a typist job at General Electric, worked both for a period, and held on to the latter for dear life, taking incremental promotions until retiring four years ago, after forty years with the company. A choreographic residency existed in a different universe.

Still, my mother was grateful for my ease. She'd worked her entire life so that I might have it. And I'd make something of the residency, I was sure. Larger stages, more opportunities, perhaps even a tour that would bring me through St. Louis. She was already proud of me, but nine months from now, I hoped we'd both understand what it had all been for.

CHAPTER 10

People lost their minds over the *leaves turning*. Kofi, Dahlia, and I once took the Metro-North upstate to pick apples and wander through an orchard drinking cider like a Hallmark movie throuple. It was nice, but there were no fewer than a hundred other New Yorkers equally desperate for rural charm—we kept bumping into loud girls in carefully curated flannel outfits, couples trying to find the light for their selfies.

Here, I could actually take in the beauty. I cracked the window above the kitchen sink and let the breeze swim in, watched the burnt-orange leaves flutter on the commanding tree just outside, a brilliant pop against the still-green grass. Farther beyond, birds of prey circled above the expansive woods. And in the Briar House studio, with its massive glass walls, I appreciated the land peppered with trees in alternating reds, oranges, and yellows, the mountain peaks in the far distance.

But I never quite felt alive in it, like I was moving inside a painting. The air was so clean and crisp, but there was no one to breathe it with. On weekends, just George and me. Aside from the day when he wore a red hat, his presence brought me comfort. It had only been a Red Sox cap, but I'd remembered the story I'd heard about the Green Mountain

Men on the radio. The town's quiet conservative corners made it impossible to see the place as simply quaint. To feel safe moving through it.

When I wasn't in the studio, Vermont was a pastoral. I admired it from inside the house, listening to public radio, drinking coffee, grateful to experience this beauty and quiet but also to return, eventually, to the city that was more suited to me. A place filthy with energy and life.

And while leaves fell and the temperatures dropped, things bloomed in the studio. Rehearsals ran smoothly. A few bumps and stumbles, but nothing that wouldn't be remedied. The dancers had come around to Rebecca, helping her through the brief sections of choreography they'd learned before her arrival. She picked up the movement quickly and was working to relax. Though I'd never admit it to her face, Margot had been right.

The Briar House development and communications director's office smelled of bergamot and gas station cappuccino—an oddly comforting combination. Taylor had fair skin, a blond pixie cut, and enviable natural pink lips, and sipped their cappuccino through a metal straw as they swiveled in an ergonomic chair, piles of file folders and newspapers cluttering their desk.

"So," they said, "I hear your piece is about the modern Black experience? Love that."

"What? No. Margot keeps pushing that, but it's not *about* anything. It's abstract, more concerned with shape and musicality than specific themes. I want people to take from it what they will."

"Noted." They scribbled a note onto a steno pad. *Dance NOT Black.* "Any other angles? I want to make sure I'm positioning your piece properly. What themes should I keep in mind?"

"I hate to disappoint you. I was a publicist before this; I know how much it helps to connect a piece to larger issues. But right now it's truly just movement."

"I think that's the story. What you just said. You were once in my shoes."

"Is that interesting?"

"Not especially," Taylor said. "But we can make it interesting."

"Sure."

Taylor would spin it. They thought I was cool, brave, even. They thought thriving in a place like New York City, like BAM, was something to be proud of. They thought giving that up to be here was even better. They were building the story before my eyes, and to my surprise, they didn't have to exaggerate. I sounded much more interesting in their words.

"I'm just grateful that you're doing the legwork," I said. "Publicity isn't easy, especially in performing arts."

"Well, I basically have two jobs now. Since the development director left over the summer, I'll be pitching you to donors too. Rolling your narrative into the organization's larger story."

"Godspeed."

"You can send me a list of media names, or reach out to people directly, if you want," they said. "Just let me know who, so we don't double up."

"I will not reach out to a soul. Far be it from me to step on any toes."

For years, I'd wanted to be relieved of these pressures, and I finally was. No way I was going to thrust myself back into that world.

"Got it. Just let me know if you change your mind."

"I won't," I said, standing, my body on a new clock since arriving, eager to move.

"We're gonna make you a star, Layla. They're going to love you!"

My breath caught in my throat. There was a thin line between love and hate.

In late October, as the trees continued to undress, Eli told me that a colleague had quit, and there was a big website overhaul. Ellen, his boss, needed him to manage the project. He couldn't visit.

It was disappointing, but I was grateful he'd stepped up at work. We could use the extra income if Ellen moved him into the position permanently. Eli had always resisted professional progress in a way only the privileged can. He thought advancement was selling out.

On the phone, Eli said it made him sick to think about waiting until Christmas to be together.

We'd be okay, I assured him. It would be good for him to focus on work, take his mind off his loneliness. We'd talk every day, and the anticipation would make the December break that much more special.

"The good news is I got to see Charlotte's kids today," he said. "That was nice."

"The Frenchies," I said.

He'd been helping a colleague pick up her children after school. I'd met them over the summer at their apartment in Greenpoint. The kids went to a preschool not far from us, in Prospect Heights. Now he tried to cheer me up—or maybe himself—by sending photos of the smaller boy. Dark curly hair, rosy round cheeks, and a serious face. Eli had picked him up today while Charlotte got the other. They'd all played in the park after, then gotten ice cream.

"New job potential. Fathering. You're a real adult at this point."

"It's like we reversed roles."

"What does that mean?" I asked, eating chocolate chips straight from the bag.

"You're making dances and getting drunk every other night."

"The one time I got drunk, you were here, and I blame it mostly on that tragic seitan."

"Still, you can't tell me you're not having the time of your life up there."

His romanticization of the residency annoyed me. But he was far too sensitive for me to call him out.

"I'm working. It's beautiful here, but I only ever see people in the studio. My life is small. It's weird."

"I want to figure out a time to come see you, it's just tricky. Let's talk tomorrow and iron it out."

We hung up, and I sat in the silence—the silence I was getting used to. Whether I could stand it for another two months was another story. But if I was having a hard time, I knew Eli's time was harder. He'd grown up in a full if tightly wound house, had always lived with roommates or girlfriends, had never spent more than a few nights on his own. The residency was for me, but he would grow from it too.

CHAPTER 11

The visit to Charlotte's apartment in August was a night I'd turned over in my head many times.

Charlotte, her husband, and their sons lived in a narrow rail-road apartment in Greenpoint. I couldn't figure out how they managed a place smaller than ours with twice as many people, but it was a neighborhood where people had become desperate to live. They'd make any situation work to be near the boutiques and restaurants on Franklin Street, the bars of Manhattan Avenue. A delicious, white, quietly luxurious Brooklyn.

There were toys and books all over their apartment, which made me feel better about the clutter I sometimes let build. The clutter Eli couldn't stand. Their bathroom was barely big enough for me to squat above the toilet after my protective toilet-paper strips—two little boys and one grown man, I was no fool—floated into the bowl.

Charlotte wasn't the frazzled middle-aged woman with Cheerios dangling from her hair that I'd hoped for. She was my age, petite and curvy with shiny hair and smooth fair skin, dimples and a wide smile, a loose T-shirt dress and a silver nose ring. While she wasn't quite beautiful, she was attractive and cool in a quintessentially Parisian way.

Her husband was in Argentina visiting his mother, who was very sick.

"They don't expect her to make it much longer," Charlotte said in a slight accent.

"I'm so sorry. It must be hard with the boys all alone."

I'd grown up knowing more single mothers than married, so while the statement was true, I felt no outsized pity for Charlotte, who was only managing this temporarily.

"It's a lot," Charlotte said, opening the bottle of Vinho Verde we'd brought. "Eli has been so helpful. I don't know what I'd do without him."

"I'm sure you'd do fine."

Charlotte poured for us all, then raised her glass. "Tchin-tchin!"

I hooked my arm in Eli's as the smaller of the two children ran up and grabbed my leg.

"Hello," I said, bending over to his cherubic face, his mischievous smile.

"Hello," he said, in a higher-pitched voice than I'd expected.

"What's your name, mister?"

"No," he said. "I not mister."

"Well," I laughed, "what *is* your name?"

"Paolo," he said, like it was a secret.

His brother came running in. "My name's Emilio!"

"Hello, Emilio. Pleasure to meet you. I'm Layla."

"Mister!" Paolo repeated.

I got on the floor to meet them at eye level. The boys were laughing, though I couldn't tell if it was at me or with me. I got close to Paolo, squinted in his face. He squinted back.

"Tell me about yourself, Mister," I said.

He leaned forward, then gently rubbed his nose against mine.

Eli and Charlotte laughed, and I did too, feeling myself melt. I wanted to hold him, cradle him, take him as my own.

"Okay, mes petits choux," Charlotte said. "Time to get ready for bed."

They hugged us good night, and Eli ruffled their hair. Charlotte corralled them into the bedroom.

"Cute, right?" said Eli.

"Very."

"Charlotte's a good mom."

"How's this cheese?"

I sliced into the pungent, gooey triangle. Before I knew it, I'd eaten much of the cheese and crackers she'd plated and was pouring more wine to balance things out.

"I can't believe they all live in this tiny place," I said.

"I know," Eli said, lowering his voice. The lights had dimmed in the back, and Charlotte was singing them a lullaby in French. "Weird layout."

"Our place is actually a nice size and layout. More open. We could turn part of the living room into a nursery," I said. We'd talked in the spring about starting to try again, but the residency had put that on hold. We'd bumped our timeline, would wait until the curtain closed on Briar House before moving with intention this time, scheduling sex based on ovulation. An idea I found horribly privileged and boring, if completely necessary.

"We'd just need to move the bookcase," said Eli.

"And hope the child never grew very big."

"We wouldn't feed it much."

Charlotte emerged, her long hair now piled atop her head, perfectly messy. My bun was tidy at the nape of my neck. I loosened it just slightly, casually pulled out two tendrils, hoping to look more French, but—upon a glance at my reflection in the fingerprint-covered mirror—achieving *quirky* at best.

Charlotte rolled a joint, and she and Eli smoked beside the open kitchen window. My head was swimming in wine, and my eyes followed the joint as it passed from her lips to his.

"You want some?" Eli asked.

"Yeah," I said.

I took a long pull, hating it, handed it back to him while looking at Charlotte.

"I thought you didn't smoke?" Charlotte said.

"Not normally," I said, feeling judged, and annoyed that he'd told her this. "But tonight, I'm feeling fun."

"Good! You've been working hard, finishing up your job and making dances in the living room. You have a big autumn ahead of you."

How did she know so much?

"Autumn," I said instead, laughing. "The residency is this mysterious, looming thing. It's nice to be here and spend some time with Eli before we hit the road in September."

I leaned into him and kissed his cheek, tipping my glass, spilling wine onto the high-top table.

"I'll clean that up," I said. "Paper towels, paper towels."

"Use the dish towel," Charlotte said, pointing to a rag that hung over the sink. "We don't have disposable products."

Grabbing the towel, I dabbed at the spill, then washed my hands and dried them on my jeans.

The night spun forward until it was too late, and I was too drunk.

"I guess we better head out, huh?" Eli said.

"Yes," I said, fighting for enunciation. "We should definitely be going."

"I'm glad you came over," said Charlotte.

"Same, girl," I said, opening my arms for a hug, smelling her—citrus and wood. Eli followed suit, and as I clomped down the rickety stairs, I uttered a clunky, round "au revoir."

We stopped at the pizza place around the corner, and I ordered a plain slice. I covered it with red pepper flakes, ate it so fast I burned the roof of my mouth. I licked at the peeling skin, swallowing myself, bit by bit.

The next morning, I was still in my clothes, mouth dry, pillow covered in mascara. I let out a bottle of Vinho Verde and a half pound of cheese into the toilet. Eli knocked lightly on the door. Asked if I was okay.

I couldn't say.

Charlotte was so different from me—sweet, petite, cool. And Paolo and Emilio were cute, funny, chubby cheeked. Everything I craved.

Alone, in Vermont, was I jealous that Eli was getting in low-commitment kid time while I was experiencing the opposite? Was I jealous of Charlotte, who in that moment had so much of what I wanted?

Were they getting too close? What if, when I stopped taking the pill—a stopgap between the IUD removal and the end of the residency that I remembered to take *most* of the time—I couldn't get pregnant? Or what if, after the residency, I determined I didn't want to be a mother? It was hard to disentangle my desire for children from the fact that I'd been told since childhood that I would one day be a mother—a cruel brainwashing for little girls, in retrospect. But I hadn't thought about children since Eli left. There were none around. There was nothing to envy.

CHAPTER 12

Jason and Amy came in to observe. It was important for them to know what they were working with, especially Amy, who'd be designing backdrops and collaborating with Briar House's wardrobe manager on costumes. She moved around the studio, watching them dance from all angles, jotting notes and making pencil sketches in her Moleskine.

During the hour-long breaks in our rehearsals, I mapped out spacing, sequencing, groupings. The dance felt like an equation, and while math had never been my strength, I was sure this was a problem I could solve.

But increasingly, I went to the conference room tucked in the back of the ground floor, laid my head down on my hands, closed my eyes, let everything shut off until my phone alarm sounded. Every part of me was exhausted. Perhaps it was the intensity with which I was working, the amount of newfound authority the work required.

The weekend that Eli had planned to visit arrived just as the dancers and I hit our stride. I was grateful to keep the momentum going, to push through without breaking for him. And to continue sneaking my precious naps. But the night before he'd been scheduled to come, I couldn't sleep. The extra space in the bed left a chill in the room.

Eli called. Said he missed me like crazy. Work was only making things worse. I told him to come here for Thanksgiving. But his mom would cry through the phone about how her children didn't love her, he reminded me. It was what she'd done when he hadn't come to her birthday party in August and each time we didn't spend Christmas in Iowa. Eli couldn't bear to hear it more than once a year.

"I could come next week," he said, "stay for a week, fly straight from there to Iowa."

"If that's what you want, sure."

"I miss sleeping next to you," he said.

"I do too. But you've got a lot going on. A lot to keep you busy. It's good! If you don't start feeling better, maybe you should see a therapist."

He grunted. He'd always been resistant to therapy, despite how much it had helped with my anxiety in my late twenties. His family had gone as a group when he was a kid, and hearing the truth about one another, learning the truth about themselves, had pushed them further apart. His older brother didn't talk to his parents. *Call me when someone dies,* he'd said to Eli two years ago, leaving for an ashram in Bali.

"I'll be fine once I see you," said Eli.

"Take the week," I said, wondering how much I could get done in the next five days. "Once the website launch is over, you'll feel fine. Let's talk tomorrow."

I hung up. It was like his sadness had somehow seeped through the phone and morphed into sickness along the way. I ran to the bathroom and lost what little I'd eaten that day into the toilet.

It suddenly felt so difficult for the two of us to be on the same page. Eli's depression took such a different shape than my anxiety. This felt like years ago, when we were first painfully out of sync.

Eli wanted to go to plays and events all week, parties all weekend. I was working more than ever—at the office, choreographing, rehearsing with dancers and coordinating with venues anytime I was lucky enough to land a gig—and craved hygge when I had downtime. In the beginning, I thought I had to be there with him for every moment. Then I realized he didn't need to sit in the living room while I read Toni Morrison, and I didn't have to stand beside him at dark Bushwick bars or experimental film premieres. He had friends. Friends were important too.

I'd get annoyed if he came home early, right at the start of a chapter or episode, or just as I was falling asleep. He always had a story to share from the night, a word-for-word replay of a conversation or scene, like he needed to prove that he'd been in the world. He'd seen people, and they'd said things. To him! I'd nod and half listen, and he'd accuse me of not listening, and I'd tell him I was listening, and we'd play Tell Me What I Just Said. I always could, because it's possible to hear without really listening. This pissed him off the most, and he'd storm to the bathroom like a child to brush his teeth. The smell of IPA would linger on his breath, so I'd turn away in bed. He'd pull his arm back and turn away from me too.

Too ashamed of my dissatisfaction even to tell my friends, I started journaling—releasing into the little notebook I'd tucked beneath my side of the mattress.

I wrote that while I loved Eli, I wasn't sure I liked him anymore. The click of his keys in the door sent a wave of disappointment through me. The feel of his fingertips on my body had, more than once, made my skin crawl. He was senseless with his choices, failing himself. Did I want to be with a failure?

I'd asked him to talk: about his writing, his goals, our future. I suggested he make a plan, and I felt a tinge of heartache when, days later, he came back with nothing. He wanted to be a screenwriter but hadn't finished a script since college. If he wanted something enough, he usually got it. Exude charm, say the words, and poof—there it was. But not this. So he let it go for the moment and lined up three IT job interviews for the next week.

It was a difficult choice for him, but he'd committed to making a change. And so could I. I could listen to his boring stories, let his hand rest on my shoulder and not recoil. I could change my image of him—easier now that he was digging himself out of his hole. Easier because, despite sometimes not liking him, I always loved him.

That had been one of the great challenges of my life. Some people loved and were loved easily. For me love was bone-deep and rare. I couldn't imagine ever caring for someone the way I cared for Eli. So I would work to like the man I loved. I wrote the words in my journal. A declaration.

I ripped out the earlier, angrier journal entry, tucked it into my work bag, and ran it through the shredder. As though the feelings could be destroyed with the words.

CHAPTER 13

Jason's band was playing at the Rusty Rail. I'd spent one too many Friday nights on the couch scrolling through movie options, watching trailers, reading reviews, only to decide I was too tired to get through a whole film. Besides, the dancers would be there. I was overdue on bonding, had already passed on a hiking invitation and a distillery tour. It was now or never.

I didn't expect to feel so comforted by being in a bar—the low lighting, the loud music, the constant rumble of laughter. This place was somewhere between the cocktail bars of Brooklyn, with their mustachioed bartenders and eighteen-dollar drinks, and the sports bars of my hometown, with their four-dollar you-call-its and the ever-present smell of mozzarella sticks and cigarettes.

The dancers and I slid up to the bar and caught the shots the bartender slid our way, on the house. Apparently they were known here.

"To Auntie!" said Courtney, raising her shot glass.

"Is that what you call me?" I asked, feeling my ears growing hot with embarrassment. An auntie was middle-aged and thick in the middle. Wore a housecoat and curlers inside, heels out of the house, but never without complaining about how much they hurt her feet.

They pressed their lips together, holding back laughter.

"Yes," said Jade, who didn't drink, but squeezed a lime into her tonic and cranberry. "We call you Auntie, because everyone loves their auntie. Right?"

"You think I'm old."

"No!" said Rebecca. "You're so young and beautiful."

"To the young, beautiful Layla!" said Courtney.

They all repeated, lifting, clinking, drinking. This was more embarrassing than anything, their pretending I was one of them. I took down the tequila shot quickly, hoping it would relax me, but nearly gagged as it hit my throat and tried not to let it show on my face. It had been years, but I kept it together, eager to prove something. I was more a big sister than an auntie.

Jason and his bandmates arrived, and the dancers went over to chat with them while I ordered a glass of white wine. The bartender asked if I wanted a six- or a nine-ounce pour. I settled on nine and lowered my expectations.

The band finally went on. Only one song was familiar to me—a track Jason had shared—the rest were new. The dancers began twirling one another with the first chord. The other patrons swayed until they'd drunk enough to dance.

"This one goes out to my Briar House crew," said Jason. The dancers whooped and hollered, and when the song began, they danced even harder.

Standing at the bar, I told Jason his band was great. It was true, and not just because it'd been too long since I'd seen a live set.

"We've been great every weekend this month," said Jason.

"I know, I'm sorry!" I said. "I've had a lot going on. I've been focusing on my work."

"I'm glad you came tonight. You want another drink?" Jason asked, pointing to my empty glass.

The heavy pour coupled with the shot had caught up with me. Another drink might change the night, but I needed neither excitement nor hangover. I was a married auntie.

"I'm good," I said, just as the bartender began pumping music through the speakers—something familiar and trappy. Something, I imagined, he'd learned only since the dancers had started coming. "Gonna get in one last dance with them."

"You need a ride home?"

"I'll get a car," I said, backing up onto the dance floor, ass-first, the dancers cheering.

I stayed for the full song, unable to stop myself from twisting and turning, from dropping low. I'd ache in the morning, but for now I let my head swing, my shoulders roll, my hips sway. We sang the words. It had been a long time since I danced simply because it felt good.

The song ended, I blew them all kisses, tossed Jason a peace sign. Near the door, I requested a Lyft and was shocked to see that it would be twenty minutes. But of course, this wasn't New York City. It would be strange to rejoin the group, so I stood in the vestibule and watched as they moved, letting the bar know exactly who they were.

Amy arrived as I zipped up my jacket, offering me a quick wave—hands splotched in paint—before grabbing Jade and giving her a quick but tender kiss on the lips. News to me and only me, it seemed.

Finally, my car arrived. The driver pulled onto the road, and I noticed the Green Mountain Men keychain dangling from the ignition. My first time in a car with a right-wing militia member. There was no doubt he was clocking my skin, my demeanor. We were on the road. Too late.

"You're that dancer," he said, his heavy blue eyes catching mine in the mirror. "From Briar House."

"Um," I said, only half-shocked that he recognized me from the local paper coverage. "Yeah. I've had such a great time here. It's a wonderful place."

I suddenly felt carsick, but there was no way I'd ask this man to stop on the dark, isolated road. I tightened every part of my body until the car pulled into my driveway.

"Best of luck to you," he said.

"Thank you," I managed. "Have a great night."

I watched through the peephole as he drove away, less nauseated but slightly shaken. He knew where I lived. He knew who I was.

CHAPTER 14

If it had just been the nausea, I might have chalked it up to dehydration, nerves, a dramatically increased consumption of cheddar. Might have pinned the fatigue on my stress levels, or working from dawn until dusk, conceptualizing music sequences, lighting, arc, and emotionality. There were also the applications—the residency ended in May, so I was beginning to research and apply to opportunities for the following fall.

Of course I was tired, anxious, nauseated. But there was more—nasal congestion, piercing headaches, a sudden aversion to non-starchy foods, breakouts I blamed on my carb-heavy diet. There was the sour taste in my mouth. At one time in my life, I might have passed off all of these as symptoms of cancer or an autoimmune disorder—among my many interests was self-diagnosis. At least twice a year I was certain I was dying.

But then there were my breasts. My modest, uneventful breasts. The breasts for which my cousin Bria elected me president of the Itty Bitty Titty Committee in the summer of 2004. They were tender and big. As plump as I would've begged for them to be in my late teens.

This was what sent me to the pharmacy in a Lyft—driven by a young stoner with a Bernie sticker, thankfully—on a Tuesday night in November. This strange collection of bodily complications was familiar, from this time last year.

Just as the pharmacist was preparing to lock the doors, I found a box of pregnancy tests. At home, I peed on the plastic stick and waited. Dual waves of relief and panic as the lines formed. I wasn't sick. I wasn't dying. I was multiplying.

I swallowed one of the prenatal vitamins I'd purchased—just in case—from the pharmacy, then got in bed and called Eli. He didn't pick up, but texted me back immediately.

About to leave a tech panel for work. I'll call you when I get home.

It's okay, I typed, unbearably sleepy. *I'll call you tomorrow.*

A strange mix of calm and panic washed over me as I lay alone in bed. It was finally happening, and yet I'd been here before—filled with hope, only to have it burst in an instant, like a pin-popped balloon.

Perhaps there was nothing I couldn't do with a baby growing inside of me that I could do without one. Maybe I could continue to live my life completely. I'd once had a dance teacher who'd spun and leaped energetically until the day before her delivery, even performing in a few shows in the preceding weeks. But I'd also had a colleague who'd walked around the office with a cane in her third trimester, who had gone on her coveted maternity leave two weeks early so that her body wouldn't break to pieces.

These were delicate weeks. My doctor was in New York, so I went to a nearby clinic first thing in the morning. A bright, white place full of young girls beside their mothers, women nearing menopause, partners holding hands, rubbing bellies, some faces gray with dread, others hopeful. The doctor was swift but kind, told me I was six weeks along. Nothing more than a lentil. She called the thing inside me *Baby,* dropping the article as though that were its forever name.

She gave me a pamphlet, and I scheduled my next visit with the receptionist as a teenager behind me cried into her friend's shoulder. There was a small crowd of protesters outside. I was grateful not to have to walk through them, that I could run straight to my waiting car—the same Bernie bro as before—though I hated that I wanted to explain myself at all.

The last time, it had all happened so quickly. The knowledge of the pregnancy came so late, the loss arriving a week later. Nine weeks. Now was a chance to do things right.

But I feared it would happen again. One of the worst parts had been watching Eli fall apart. He'd finally gotten the promotion at work. It felt important that he rebuild himself rather than be confronted with a potential emotional roller coaster. So, as I lay in bed, I decided to wait a bit longer to tell him. Until the second trimester, when everything was on the up and up.

It was strange knowing while Eli didn't. Maybe he could sense it. Maybe something in him flared up, an alert. It wasn't likely—I had barely known, after all, and the lentil was growing in *my* body. How strange that something so central to your life can be real, can exist in the world for weeks without your knowing. How strange to live your life as though things are normal when everything has already changed.

CHAPTER 15

My kitchen window had been broken for weeks, but I didn't realize it until the cold came slicing through. George found me shivering in my coat, eating oatmeal and drinking coffee at the kitchen table, when he came by to fix it.

"How's your husband doing?" he asked before beginning to drill. In my experience, most men didn't know how to be alone with a woman without talking about the man closest to that woman. Perhaps it was an attempt to establish a clear boundary, to not be a creep. Or maybe they just couldn't see us completely on our own.

"Good," I shouted over the blare of the drill. "He was supposed to come up a few weeks ago but had to cancel his trip because of work. But I'm excited to see him in December."

"What?" said George, after he stopped drilling.

"Good," I said. "My husband is good."

Winter in New York was sloppy and gray. In Vermont the world went soft and clean but brutal. Getting dressed for my walk each morning became an event, and any other socializing was out of the question.

The chill affected me and everything I held inside. I'd only told my mother, who'd claimed I *sounded pregnant* over the phone, a comment I found both offensive and nonsensical.

It felt absurd to keep it from Eli. But it would be better to reveal it to him after crossing that precarious threshold, when things were more certain. When he wouldn't have to live each day with the fear of losing it, the way I did.

As soon as we returned from the break, the dancers and I would hit the ground running. The preview on February 1 meant that donors, the board, and other dance presenters would come in to observe all that we'd created so far. I needed to do as much as possible while I could. As I neared the end of the first trimester, I found myself with a renewed energy and determination.

"We need to get this choreography tight, but please, take care of yourselves. Make sure you're eating well, drinking plenty of water, getting plenty of rest."

Even as I said the words, I knew they sounded silly, like I was reading from a pamphlet. I'd never received such wholesome advice when I was a young dancer—a college ballet teacher had recommended we suck on a hard candy to remedy hunger. And it felt elitist to suggest that everyone might be able to achieve eight hours each night. All but Rebecca lived in shared apartments provided by the Vermont Institute a mile north of Briar House, and I didn't imagine rest came easily in a place full of twentysomething artists, even if you were one. Plus, most of them worked supplemental jobs—Terrell was bartending in Manchester, Jade taught yoga in Bennington on the weekends, Courtney had taken over Rebecca's evening classes at the Vermont Ballet Academy. If not for Eli, I'd be doing the same, considering the Briar House pay. I couldn't deny how much freedom simply having a supportive partner allowed—I could focus on my art, create from a place of inspiration rather than desperation. Sure, the dancers were young, hustle still an expected part of their lives, but I feared they'd burn out.

Margot would be looking for weak spots when she visited rehearsal on Thursday, so I watched with a razor-sharp eye, noting every mistake. Terrell's feet weren't pointed during the leaps in the group section. Jade was looking the wrong way for part of the trio. What was happening with

Rebecca's face during the slow section? Courtney was doing three rotations while everyone else was doing two.

"It's a double turn," I said sternly. "Don't show off, just do the choreography."

Courtney nodded, looking at the floor. Fearful. Something in me writhed. Courtney was the sweetest among them. Cruel of me to cut her down like that, but it was in service of the piece. Everything was in service of the piece.

In the more tender and sensuous moments, I stepped onto the Marley, got so close that the dancers nearly sliced through me with the whip of their arms, the kick of their legs.

"I need you to feel it," I said so that only the dancers nearest could hear. "To need it."

Was I growing into someone new? Someone solid and single-minded? I rushed to the conference room each day during the lunch break, writing notes, mentally moving things around. New eyes meant new possibilities. New anxieties. I'd seen enough choreographers rise, enough fall, to feel the weight of what was to come in every inch of my body.

By the Thursday before the break, the dancers had drilled the movement into their bodies. I was undergoing an entirely different physical transformation, fitted clothes replaced by oversize pants and sweaters. I pushed the dancers but was gentle and wary with my own body—something that might have appeared lazy and inequitable from their perspective. I'd read up, knew that exercising was important, but also that anything too strenuous was dangerous. I'd seen one too many movies where a single trip was the end of that storyline.

The dancers were growing frustrated and fatigued, so I called everyone together that morning.

"I know this has been an intense period, but I want you all to know how grateful I am for your hard work. You're all incredible dancers. I ask you to do something, to fix something, and you do it like that," I said, with a snap of my fingers. "You've shown me what you're capable of. You can do anything."

The dancers' eyes stayed locked on me.

"Obviously, Margot's visit this afternoon is important. She's going to be talking to the board members, the institute leaders, and a few other presenters over the holiday break. I want her to appreciate this piece, but also how amazing you all are individually. She's got connections all over the Northeast, all over the country. So, this matters. Not just for me, but for all of us."

"The piece is coming together," said Jade. "And all of you are absolute beasts." She looked to the dancers. "But our bodies are fucking tired. My hamstring is a mess. Courtney's sciatica is flaring up. Terrell did something to his ankle. We're all at a breaking point."

I'd been so concerned with myself that I hadn't thought twice about their occasional flinches, hobbles here and there, gauze-wrapped joints. I remembered the days of pushing—the adjusting, overcompensating, smiling through the pain. Risking more than you realized for those few moments before an audience. This was another reason I'd stopped dancing—an unwillingness to tear my body to shreds for a career that would likely be over before I hit forty, sooner with one wrong move, one bad landing.

"The good news," I said, "is that after tomorrow, you'll have three weeks of rest."

This didn't inspire relief in the way that I'd hoped it would. My ears burned, and my pulse thumped through my body.

But we were so close. We needed to push just a little bit further. I had them mark at first, to preserve their bodies. They danced gently through the first portion of the group section, moving in and out of spaces, turning and jumping around one another so that we could see where the problems were—where one person was angled slightly askew, or moving during a still moment, or sinking in a turn when they should have been rising. We reworked things. We compromised.

It was finally time for the dancers—bodies tired, desperately drinking in sips of air—to run the entire piece full-out. We'd been doing the sections independently over the last two weeks, but hadn't strung them together since early November.

The music began, and as the dancers sulked toward their places, I noticed Courtney's shoulders begin to shake. Soon she was sobbing. Her face pained, her teeth chattering.

"I can't," she whispered, her hand on her lower back as I stood over her. "It hurts so bad."

Jade grabbed an ice pack from the first aid kit and placed it above Courtney's sacrum. The cold immediately soothed her, and her eyes found mine.

"Okay," I said. "Let's all just take a break. I'll see the three of you back here at one."

Jade, Terrell, and Rebecca stared at me coldly while Courtney lay back, the ice pack beneath her.

When the three of them left, I noticed Moses Sumney was still singing through the sound system.

Am I vital if my heart is idle? Am I doomed?

Taylor made an appointment with a local physical therapist, and I drove Courtney's car to the facility. Courtney emerged from the exam room revealing the diagnosis—a pinched nerve—just as I was texting the dancers to begin afternoon rehearsal without me. She'd be fine but needed to rest over the break.

"Not the worst timing," I said as we left the facility.

Courtney just stared ahead.

Jade was rehearsing a section with Terrell, a part that Courtney normally danced but needed to be filled while she was out. They were still stepping up without my asking.

"Let's walk the group section to make sure we're good without Courtney," I said.

The dancers marked through the movement and caught all the choreographic and formation gaps her absence left. There were sections with gaping holes, and I considered reworking it all, making it look neat for Margot, for the camera. But the dancers protested. It was one runthrough. Had things been different, I might have jumped in myself. But my courage was gone, and it wasn't just me anymore. Besides, I needed to see it all flow. We left the choreography as it was, gaps and all.

Margot and Taylor entered the studio, kicking off their shoes. Taylor knew of Courtney's injury, but I explained things to Margot as well, so that she'd understand any bumps and gaps along the way. I needed to prepare them for any imperfection.

Margot sat in one of the folding chairs that lined the studio mirrors, and Taylor assumed a squat in the far corner, a camera slung around their neck. I was grateful for the sunset that shone through the windowed wall. The dancers looked gorgeous already, strips of light cascading across their bodies.

The opening went smoothly, the dancers sharp and focused. Next was the duet. I held my breath for the entire five minutes that Rebecca and Terrell danced. It held no emotional weight, but they each made it through in one piece. Jade's solo was next. She'd been careful and tired earlier in rehearsal, wary of a pending injury, but she danced full-out now. Still, her passion had already packed its bags, left for the holidays.

Finally, the group section came, less impressive without the presence of a fourth. The dancers moved with certainty and strength. The harder one danced, the harder they all danced. They weren't rehearsing anymore. They were performing for the first time.

I glanced at Margot, who nodded and tapped her fingers on her lap. I exhaled. She was happy.

I smiled and shifted my focus to the dancers. The music swelled and Terrell mistook a cue, running right into Jade. Her hands caught him just before their noses might have smashed.

"Fuck!" she shouted, pushing past him to get to her next spot.

My entire body clenched. *Fuck* was not in the piece. *Fuck* was not what Margot came to see.

They kept dancing, but it was over. Every few moments there was a misstep or collision. Terrell and Rebecca ran toward each other, but both stopped, marked the lift half-heartedly, Rebecca rolling her eyes on her way offstage. There were more *fuck*s, a few *watch it*s and *Jesus*es. Could I sneak out the door before Margot noticed I was gone? Walk to the house. Crawl under the covers, maybe even the bed, and hide for the rest of the day.

But I was their leader, and so I remained, numbing with each mistake. It was a disaster. A gorgeous leap or a strong moment of unison wouldn't change that. The piece was a blazing mess.

It ended in utter anticlimax, the dancers slowly sliding to the floor or walking directly to their water bottles the moment the music stopped. Taylor clapped enthusiastically, while Margot looked over the bridge of her glasses—which were at the farthest point of her nose, hanging on for dear life—smelling something rancid.

Margot stood, looked from dancer to dancer, then walked out of the studio without so much as a glance my way.

A sudden rush up my gullet. I made it to the bathroom just in time.

I splashed water on my face, rinsed my mouth, and ran back to the studio.

"You have plenty of time," said Taylor. "It's only December. May is forever away. It's going to be amazing!"

I shook my head. "The last thing I need is a lie."

Briar House artist-in-residence Layla Smart rehearses her stunning new work, premiering in the spring.

Taylor posted a series of photos on Instagram: One of me by the mirrors, speaking to the group. One of Jade beautifully pained in her solo, arms and legs outstretched. One of the duet, the dancers caught in midair. One of the full group, each of them tilted with a leg pointed toward the sky.

This was my work. My catastrophe. But Taylor knew about angles, about timing, about positioning. With the right lens, the right crop, anything could look like art.

I was supposed to fly to New York in three days. Eli and I would head to St. Louis for Christmas with my mother. But I couldn't wait that long. The day had devastated me, and I was nearing the end of my first trimester.

I sat on the bed and opened my laptop.

Dancers, I typed. *You all deserve a rest. I don't want to risk any more injuries. Tomorrow's rehearsal is canceled. Please take care of yourselves and know that I'll be thinking of you all during the break. Have a wonderful holiday season. I'll see you in the new year.*

I changed my flight, disregarding the fee. I'd be home with Eli before noon tomorrow. It was the only thing that could soothe me.

PART II
REVELATIONS

//

DECEMBER–FEBRUARY

Now that I've ruined everything, I'm so fucking free.

—SZA, "Seek & Destroy"

CHAPTER 16

I uncrossed my ankles in the economy seat. Readjusting my legs entirely would have required a full acrobatic routine, and my seatmate had already grumbled at my shifts and wiggles. I didn't need another enemy. Not on top of Margot and the dancers. I'd tried so hard to please everyone, and it had royally backfired. Sitting stock-still in my seat, I considered every point during the last rehearsal, the last few weeks, when I might have made a change. Everything I'd done wrong. Maybe I didn't deserve to be at Briar House. To be a choreographer at all.

"Pretzels or cookies?"

The flight attendant looked angry—he'd asked more than once, but I hadn't realized he was talking to me.

"Can I have both?" I whispered.

"No."

"Cookies, then, I guess."

"Anything to drink?"

"Water." I paused. "And a coffee, please."

If I was going to have Biscoff cookies—a delicacy of the sky—I'd enjoy them properly. The internet said one cup of coffee a day was fine, and if I couldn't put my faith in the internet, what did I have left? The internet had also once told me not to drink coffee on a plane, but I couldn't recall why. Probably because it just didn't taste as good. But my standards in that moment weren't so high.

I thought of all the round-bellied girls who downed Pepsi and Flamin' Hot Cheetos in my high school's hallways—by now, their kids were on the varsity football team. My lentil would be fine with six ounces of watery coffee and a cookie. After the past few weeks, I needed whatever pleasure I could get. Joy was good for the baby too.

The skyscrapers came into view, the wheels tumbled onto the tarmac. The energy of New York blazed back. Margot had called and emailed while I was in the air. But I was on a break. On a mission. I shoved my phone in my pocket and walked quickly. It felt good, matched the energy that was simmering inside of me.

One of our older neighbors—a Trinidadian woman with thick silver hair—held open the door as I dragged my suitcase inside.

"Welcome back!" she said. All these years, and I still didn't know her name. "Your husband must be so glad to have you home!"

"It's a surprise!" I said, filled with a glee I hadn't felt in years. She gave an excited clap.

It was a hike up the four flights. At each landing, I stopped to catch my breath. When I reached our floor, I shoved the key in the lock, twisted.

The table in the entryway held board books with glossy covers. Tiny shoes lined the wall. Little hats tossed here and there. Toy trucks and dinosaurs. In the living room there were two small air mattresses covered in bright blankets, a stuffed animal on each.

The wall caught my back as I sank to the floor, my vision blurring. The world closed in around me. From the hallway outside the apartment, a child sang in French.

CHAPTER 17

When I was ten, I almost killed my cousin Bria. She'd found me in their spare bedroom watching *Rugrats,* a show that might have been about talking babies and their mishaps but felt as much a part of my life as anything. Bria chased me through the house threatening to pull down my pants—she wanted to see if I was wearing a diaper like Tommy. I didn't understand her problem. Just two years before, she'd laughed beside me in the AMC as we'd watched the gang take Paris. She'd gone through a phase where she asked her mother to put her hair in three braids so she'd look like Susie Carmichael. But Bria was twelve now. She watched *ComicView* and *Taxicab Confessions* after her parents fell asleep. She could never go back to a show whose hero was a one-year-old with a rich vocabulary and thirst for adventure. I ran through the living room—past the plaid recliner sofa where her brother and father sat watching football—defending myself. *I was only flipping through!*

Bria tired as we returned to the kitchen, with its permanent smell of frying oil. My body was used to dancing for hours on end. I had energy for days. She called me a loser and a baby between huffs and puffs.

"Being older only means you'll die first!" I said.

"Your daddy was younger than my daddy, and he dead!"

I stepped toward her, and she stepped back, nearing the open door that led to the basement. She was bigger than me, but I shoved her shoulders with all my might and sent her tumbling backward down the steps. *Clunk, clunk, clunk.* I covered my face, shocked at my capacity for violence. Bria was motionless at the bottom, face down on the concrete floor, arms bent in unnatural directions. I ran down, whispering her name. I'd said she'd die sooner, and I'd made it true.

"Bria." I touched her shoulder, the most frightened I'd ever been. "Bria?"

"Yah!" she shouted, popping up, shoving me onto the bottom steps. "That's what you get for being a stupid baby bitch."

She walked past me as I sobbed—ashamed of my anger, frightened of my power.

That was the closest I'd come to physically hurting someone, until now. My hands shook. I could throw dishes, grab Charlotte by the neck and pin her little body to the door, spit in her face, channel a fresh, hot violence that would leave everything in pieces. But even my most furious self wouldn't allow it. I'd been traumatized by the incident with Bria, and respectability was etched into my bones. When the key twisted in the lock and Charlotte and her two boys walked in to find me standing there, halfway to fainting, I looked her in the eyes and said, "Hello."

Charlotte's hands froze on the children's heads.

"Come, mes petits choux," she said, attempting to turn the boys around to head back to the hallway. "Let's go for a walk."

I liked that she feared me. That she felt the need to flee. I wasn't going to tell her to head back into the cold with two small children, but I wasn't going to stop her either. I was lightheaded, floating, watching myself from a distance.

Paolo ignored his mother and ran up to me and tapped my leg, smiling. "Mister!"

I stared at him as he continued to tap, his strength greater than he knew.

"It's Mister," he said to his mother. "'Member?"

"I remember, baby."

"Her name's Layla," said Emilio. I couldn't believe he remembered my name. He must have heard it many times since we met in the summer. What else did his little mind hold?

"Hi, Paolo," I said. I didn't know what else to do. "Hi, Emilio."

"Up," said Paolo, stretching his doughy arms toward me.

And so, I lifted him onto my hip and felt weak at the warmth of his weight. Charlotte winced. Paolo kissed his nose to mine, closing his eyes. He moved his head back and forth, smiling gently. I did the same, until tears fell from my eyes. His small hand wiped at them, but they came too quickly. I held him close as his mother, quietly crying now too, made her way to the floor and cradled the older boy in her arms.

When he finally noticed his mother crying, Paolo spiraled into a tantrum, curling himself beneath the desk in the living room. I walked away, locked myself in the bedroom. I needed to touch and feel what was mine, what I knew, to bring myself back into the world. But it was a mistake to walk back there, to be confronted with this once-sacred space. Her jewelry pooled on the bureau. Their dog-eared books beside each other on the nightstand. Her underwear folded—*folded,* psychopathic—in my drawer.

My hands shook as I called Eli, but he didn't answer. Charlotte murmured in the other room, using an adult voice now. It was clear she'd called Eli. For her, he'd answered. I ran back into the living room.

"Eli!" I shouted over Charlotte's shoulder. "What the hell is going on?"

Charlotte ended the call. She wrangled her boys and put their shoes on. Paolo kicked them off each time. I watched, hoping Charlotte would address me directly, but her eyes only shifted between the floor and the boys.

Every part of me vibrated. So I ran to the bathroom, pulled down my pants, and sat on the toilet, just to feel the cool of the porcelain on the backs of my legs.

The past few weeks sparkled. Of course, he couldn't visit me during the week we'd planned. Of course, he wasn't able to talk on the phone. *Of course, of course, of course.*

I'd never felt so stupid. So used. So basic. It was impossible to know what was real and what wasn't. What I could trust and what was a complete lie.

I called Kofi, Dahlia. But it was the middle of the day, and they were working. Why wasn't Charlotte at work? I opened the bathroom door just wide enough to shout.

"Why aren't you at work?"

"The schools have a half day," she answered, like we were only having a conversation. Like this wasn't a world-shattering crisis.

I rolled my eyes. Of course it was a half day. What a lawless existence it was to be a parent.

The phone buzzed. I closed the bathroom door. My heart jumped. It was Margot. I silenced it. She called twice more. I ignored her.

In the cool quiet of the bathroom, I took in the newness—the peppermint and chamomile soaps that filled the air, the long dark clumps of hair that coiled in the shower drain like a dead animal. By the time I'd worked up the nerve to tell Charlotte to pull the gnarly piles from the drain—she was going to clog the whole goddamn system—the three of them were gone.

I paced the kitchen, shuffling through drawers and cabinets. Dahlia called. Even as I said the words, they sounded like something out of a bad TV show. Dahlia said she'd be home in a few hours, that I could stay with her.

"I feel completely out of control," I said, opening and smelling a tin of Darjeeling tea. I'd never once had Darjeeling tea. "Like I could murder someone."

"Don't say that out loud."

"It's like I can feel everything. Every single thing."

"Did you take something, Layla?"

"No," I said, laughing as I took in the strange bags of dried beans that lined the cupboard shelves. "That's the best part. This is all me."

I walked my apartment, touching the walls, the furniture, clothing I'd never seen. Trains and tyrannosaurs, *Goodnight Moon, The Very Hungry Caterpillar, The Giving Tree.*

I crawled beneath the covers—on what had been my side of the bed—foreign scents, floral and sweat. How strange to be in the spot I'd known for so many years and smell a blend I'd never known. A blend that wasn't mine.

I cried. I opened and closed my hands, slapped my legs, clenched my fingernails into my palms, just to make sure I could feel. I was still here, alive. But nothing felt real, even as the skin broke. Even as the red seeped through.

Sleep sounded good. Sleep for a very long time. A deep, black, dreamless sleep. For days, or weeks, or years.

My cries ebbed and flowed, soft whimpers to loud, cathartic wails. The neighbor banged on the wall.

"Shut the fuck up!"

A humbling reminder that I wasn't in Vermont anymore.

I dialed Eli a dozen times. He must have been afraid.

I fell back onto the bed, stared up. There was a new, yellow-brown water stain on the ceiling that looked, appropriately, like a dying lung.

My mother answered on the first ring, and I told her plainly. She went silent. A rarity. My mother was never quiet. Then she let out a *no no no* that I'd never heard before. The sound of her cracked me in two. A mother feeling her daughter's pain from a thousand miles away, and the daughter feeling her mother's pain right back.

My fingers gripped my phone as I dialed Eli's number again and again. In the minutes in between, my eyes shifted to it anytime the screen glowed—a push notification from NBC News, a tap from my own nervous fingers.

Another neighbor caught me as I left the building—a white woman my age who'd moved in with her girlfriend two years ago. She was nice enough, but her presence enraged me now. The postal worker was on her delivery route, all the doors flung open, our truths and indecencies exposed. People were coming in and out. And here was this gentrifier, beaming at me from beneath her bike helmet, her hands gripping the handlebars.

"How's the residency? Are you loving it?" she asked, cheeks reddened, lips chapped by the winter wind. Cracked and crusty. Disgusting.

"It's going!" I shouted, louder than I meant to. "I'm having a time."

I rushed past her and out the door.

The voicemail dinged as I stepped outside. He'd called. He'd called, and she'd ruined it, wasting my time with silly questions.

The voicemail sounded like he'd been given a script. Proof of life.

"Layla. Schatzi. I'm sorry to do this to you. You mean the world to me. The truth is, I haven't felt connected to you for a while. You've been pushing me away. And really, we've both been living for you. It's time for me to figure out what *I* want. To live for *me*. I think we'll both be happier. I will never not love you. But I don't think I can be your husband anymore. That's not what you need from me. When you do figure out what that is, what you need from me, I'll be here. I want us to always be there for each other. But I don't think it's meant to be this way. We probably need some space to really figure out what this all means, so please, take your time. I don't expect you to respond to this right away. I love you."

I heard the grunts but couldn't stop them, couldn't stop my body from moving, my feet clicking down the street, past cozy brownstones just beyond our building—homes for real adults with steady lives, nailed into the city for good. I couldn't stop my fingers from tapping his name on the screen once again.

"Are you fucking kidding me?" I shouted after the voicemail beep. An old woman in a housecoat looked up from the plant she was watering on her stoop, gave me a nasty look. "What is this? What's happening? You don't want to be married? You are housing an entire family! And it's not like they're in desperate need—they're paying for fucking Montessori!"

Every part of my body pulsed. I understood how a woman could lift a car to save her baby. I felt at once near death and like the most powerful person on the planet.

"You're not happy? You're not fulfilled?" I screamed into the phone. "You don't want to be my husband anymore? Look at yourself, Eli. Consider if you'd feel this way if you weren't immediately, *immediately,* like *simultaneously,* jumping into something with a new person. You've lost your fucking mind. Call me back."

I hung up and ran down the block. A beast. Unstoppable.

I made it halfway up Nostrand before my lungs gave out and I dropped my suitcase handle, let my knees fall onto it, placed my hands on the sidewalk despite myself. People stepped over me, though one woman stopped to ask if I was all right.

"Yes," I cried, offering a thumbs-up. "Doing great."

CHAPTER 18

Dahlia held me tight on her Nostrand corner, where I was calmed by the chaos—rowdy teenagers in fur-hooded coats downing patties, an African braiding salon bursting with women getting intricate styles, the sweet smell of cigarillos from a group of men on the corner.

Dahlia was beautiful—brown curls piled on top of her head, hazel eyes that pooled with tears at the sight of me, forever sun-kissed skin, arms and hands lightly freckled with delicate tattoos, a Botticellian body. She never wore makeup other than tinted lip gloss. She fought for children in courtrooms, kept negligent and abusive caretakers at bay. The last thing she cared about was contouring.

"You can take a shower if you want," she said, which meant I ought to.

Her L-shaped studio had a shower tucked behind kitchen cupboard doors—something the apartment broker had called *charming* but that was, in fact, absurd and hazardous. I showered, then dripped onto the kitchen floor.

Dahlia sorted through her medicine cabinet. She had Ambien, melatonin, Tylenol PM, and Benadryl. A quick Google search determined a Benadryl and Tylenol PM cocktail was safe and would also help fight my allergy to Dahlia's elusive cat, Homie.

I swallowed one of each, then spiraled into sleep as Dahlia watched a reality show where the people were conventionally attractive, though puffed with filler and very, very angry. At least I wasn't them.

The sun peeked through Dahlia's thin curtains as I woke to the sound of her brewing coffee. She asked if I wanted her signature mocha-choco-latte-yaya: off-brand creamer and a drizzle of Hershey's, while she played "Lady Marmalade."

She danced around while Patti sang, grinding her hips while the cream swirled into the coffee. It was too sweet and not hot enough, but delicious still. I asked for more as the song replayed, this time the version from our youth—Christina, P!nk, Kim, Mýa, Missy there to emcee. The day before came rushing back. The impossibility of it all. The end of my life as I knew it. Another Tylenol and Benadryl. The ladies hit their high notes.

Kofi walked through the door. It was dark out again. I sneezed, the Benadryl worn off, Homie somewhere nearby.

"What are we going to do to him?" Kofi asked as I sat up, disoriented. He sounded strange, muffled, and when I looked closer, his teeth were covered in plastic.

"Do you have an Invisalign?"

"Since September."

"Oh my god," I said, a tingle in my eyes. "Everything's changed!"

"Will you relax?" said Kofi. "Statistically, someone in the group was bound to get an Invisalign."

Tears tickled my cheeks.

"Girl, I know you're going through a lot, but you really don't need to be crying over my teeth," said Kofi. "You need to focus on how to hurt Eli."

"Let's not make things worse than they are," I said, trying to mentally tally just how bad things were. These two didn't even know about the pregnancy.

"Who does this?" asked Kofi. "You're perfect! He's clearly unwell if he left his brilliant, hot choreographer wife for a squat mother of two?"

"She's not squat, she's petite," I sighed. "And she has a nose ring. And shiny hair."

"He's a man in crisis," said Dahlia. "He doesn't know what he wants. It's not your fault."

"Kevin's family has mob ties, right?" said Kofi, referring to Dahlia's on-again, off-again boyfriend. "I think we should call in a favor."

"No way," said Dahlia. "We're not seeing each other at the moment. And you know I'm not down with organized crime."

"Kevin's family?" I said. "Didn't he go to Dartmouth?"

"Mobsters can go to Ivies, Layla," said Kofi. "We're down for whatever you need. Including making Eli's life a living hell."

"As moving as this is, my head just isn't there yet. I'm angry, but also really, really sad. And so confused. It feels like a dream. Like, there's a fifty-fifty chance I wake up and none of this happened."

"It's happening," said Kofi.

"Okay, thank you. Really. Thank you."

Homie crawled out from under Dahlia's bed and gave me a suspicious look before tucking himself back in.

"There's a lot to consider here," Dahlia said. "But I think you should take him for all he's got."

"A pair of Jordans and a 2021 MacBook Pro?"

Dahlia insisted that I start to build my case. That Eli had left me at a vulnerable time. We'd made a choice as a couple to take a risk, but now, after Briar House, I'd be returning to the city with nearly nothing. No job. No income. No husband.

And a baby, I thought. It was all dizzying.

"I don't even know when it all began. In the weeks before I left? In October, when he was supposed to visit but I told him to stay and work? Like a drill sergeant!"

"Don't you dare blame yourself!" said Kofi. "Don't try to figure that man out either. You'll lose your mind. Just like he did."

"It is confusing, though," said Dahlia, "because he was absolutely crazy about you."

"He was," I admitted. "And if I can't trust him, I don't know if I can ever trust any man again."

"You can trust me," said Kofi.

I wrapped my arms around him, closed my eyes, pretended it was Eli. Their bodies were so different—Eli was tall and slim, Kofi compact and muscular, but for a moment, it worked.

Eli was less than a mile away. We hadn't seen each other in three months. Hadn't spoken in days, only the voicemails—one mechanical, one vitriolic. It was hard to believe that a few hours could shatter a marriage.

Still, it was hard to stop loving after so many years. I didn't want to be abandoned. I didn't want Eli to sabotage his own life. My mind swirled with confusion and pity. I was supposed to hate him. But he was the only man I'd ever loved. And we were on the cusp of something new.

I called him again from Dahlia's rooftop, shivering in the evening air. My body ached. I'd wanted to surprise him before, but now I couldn't bear to hold anything more inside. I gripped the brick wall when he picked up. No greeting. Silent.

"Eli?"

"Yeah."

"You answered."

"What do you want, Layla?"

There were sirens on the street below, music blasting from a bar down the block, people laughing in an apartment across the street. So much life all around. Mine was just one among many.

"I'm pregnant."

He didn't say anything. I thought maybe he'd hung up. I pressed a finger to my ear to block the noise of the city.

"You're not pregnant, Layla."

"Twelve weeks today. Almost in the second trimester. That's why I came home. I wanted to surprise you."

"You're not pregnant," he said.

I wasn't in a fighting mood.

"You're manipulative." His voice was in the high-pitched register he always found just before bursting into tears. But I didn't have to hear that part. The phone beeped. He was gone.

"Why don't you stay on my couch for a few more days?" Dahlia said. "Wallow. Gorge. You need some time to process."

"My mom needs me," I said. "Or I need her. I don't know. I just have to leave."

"You won't be here next week, for my show?" said Kofi. "Not that it's *that* important. But I do have top billing on Program B."

"She's got bigger fish to fry, Kofi!" said Dahlia.

"No, your show is a big fish. I'm sorry," I said. "I don't think I can stay that long."

"Stay for one more night," said Kofi. "Tomorrow is the Program B opening. And you're here early. What luck!"

"So lucky."

"We'll go together!" said Dahlia.

"Sure," I said, though the thought of being at BAM rattled me. But it was probably good to stay busy.

"Amazing!" said Kofi. "They're having a reception after the performance, so free booze."

I picked up my half-full glass by the stem, held it close to my chest to avoid a refill. I lifted and drank with my friends. A little bit wouldn't hurt.

CHAPTER 19

Kofi was a star—built like the running back he'd been in high school but delicate as a ballerina. He'd been reviewed in nearly every publication, with features from *The New York Times* to *Dance Magazine* and interviews on cool queer podcasts. Presenters courted him. Companies gifted him two-season contracts. Donors begged him to RSVP to their dull Upper East Side parties.

He'd been focusing on choreographing, touring the country setting works on companies big and small, and was getting tapped for music videos and commercials. Now he was finally back onstage, performing a solo at BAM.

The pre-show lobby was a who's who of the New York dance scene. This was where I'd become an adult, where I'd met Eli. It was almost unthinkable that I might one day find myself centered in this world. Tonight, I was only there for Kofi.

Kofi's show was about violence, race, and queerness. His movement was in turns languid and sharp. The twitch of his fingers was as powerful as the bounding of his legs from one side of the stage to the other. The light cast haunting shadows, and the music was perfectly calibrated with each moment. I shivered when the sound dropped, and Kofi stood onstage gesturing in what felt like a conversation with another version of himself. Little movements that told a story of pain, longing, and forgiveness. Dahlia wrapped her arm around me as I shook.

The piece was stunning, so unabashedly birthed from Kofi's experiences but artfully abstracted into movement. I couldn't believe that something like this had been crafted by one of my closest friends. I feared I might never create anything so honest.

Kofi mingled with the donors and press at the reception in the BAM café, where a light installation sparkled in the windows and respected dance artists and prominent theater actors milled about. The executive director, Michael Caspin, hugged Kofi but walked right past me—I didn't warrant his time, not in this crowd. Or maybe I'd buried my head in the crudités at the first sight of his gleaming bald spot.

My former colleague Josefina chatted with an editor across the way. When I caught her eye, she waved and mouthed something I couldn't decipher. I knew how these events went. Josefina would spend the rest of the night connecting various dots to make sure the world knew Kofi, and I was grateful. I couldn't deal with questions of how I was doing. Four days ago, maybe. But not now.

Dahlia and Kofi were precious to me. We'd grown, and learned, and failed alongside one another for nearly half our lives. They knew a version of me Eli hadn't been privy to—a girl who stayed in the campus library until closing time, surviving off dining hall granola and French vanilla cappuccinos from the machine. The girl who screen-printed Feminist Majority T-shirts, whose drink of choice for a semester was Mike's Hard Lemonade, who once performed ill-advised spoken word at an open mic night in the student center.

"That was incredible," I said as we shuffled across the reception, chasing down the cater-waiters for mac 'n' cheese balls. "I'm slightly destroyed. That was the most powerful thing I've seen in a long time. The juxtaposition of the movement with that text in the final scene. Jesus."

"And he looked fantastic," said Dahlia. "It's like he's become a better dancer in his years off. Is that a thing?"

I thought of the way my thighs burned after an hour of marking movement in the Briar House studio—movement that the dancers turned into something incredible, but barely read as dance as I fumbled across the Marley.

"I can hardly do a pirouette," I admitted, "but Kofi has turned into a Black Baryshnikov. With soul. I'll have what he's having."

He'd cracked something open within himself. There was always a piece missing from my work. It was always *almost* there, but not quite. Kofi was fully immersed in his work; he'd spent time getting lost in all its painful, ugly corners. Could I ever trust myself to fall into something so deeply?

Dahlia grabbed a drink from a passing tray as Kofi came our way. He'd been serious before, working. But as he approached us, he was *werking*. He served a strut, a twirl, a light vogue.

"That was amazing," said Dahlia.

"Compliments to the chef," I added.

"Don't bullshit me," he said. "That's what all these other people are for. Give it to me straight."

"No," I said, grabbing a carrot stick from a platter. "It was great. It made me feel like a worthless piece of shit. So, congrats."

"Aw, Layla. I love that. Thank you."

Dahlia got a text from Kevin and stepped outside while Kofi and I made our way to a quiet corner.

"Girl," he said, leaning in. "We never got to talk about Briar House. What's going on up there?"

"What do you mean?" I asked, growing hot.

"Did some shit go down?" he asked through the side of his mouth.

"How did you hear about that already?" I asked.

"This guy I'm working with for a project at Juilliard used to be room-mates with one of your dancers, and he said that things are getting sticky."

"It's such a long story," I said as we each reached for a glass at the bar, me out of nervous need to hold something, to busy my hands. "I don't even know where to start."

"There's stuff going on with funding too, right?"

"Please. Don't tell me. I'm already stressed enough. If they're going to cut me, let them cut me."

"It's not that," said Kofi.

A hand touched his shoulder. A petite, middle-aged woman with a white-blond bob. Katherine Markley, the chief dance critic for *The New York Times*.

"What a piece, Kofi!" she said in her posh English accent. "Layla."

"Hi, Katherine," I said, my face flushing.

We'd worked together for years at BAM. She was notoriously prickly and would just as soon blow you a kiss as scream in your face.

"I hear you're at Briar House," she said. "Perhaps I'll take the trip up to Siberia again, write this season's feature."

"Indeed, I am!" I let out a hiccup of a laugh.

"Kat, not sure if you know this, but Layla is one of my best friends," said Kofi, interjecting graciously. "She's an amazing choreographer. Have you seen her work before?"

"No," said Katherine. "They don't usually send me to Bushwick spaces. But very excited to see your choreography, after all these years. Quite a transition."

Katherine walked away, and I buried my head in Kofi's chest.

"She hates me."

"She hates all humans. Once she sees your work, everything will change."

"Not in a good way. How do you do it? I'm not doing what you're doing."

"You're a different person entirely. It'd be very weird if you did what I do. I'd sue you."

"You know what I mean! What you just did to all of us, it's like my raison d'être."

"Please don't speak French around me. What's the matter with you?"

"For that entire ninety minutes, I was *in it*. I was surprised, and moved, but also floating in the beauty of it all. How do I make something like that? That holds so much."

He grabbed my shoulders.

"You have to give yourself over to it completely. It has to be your entire world."

"Kofi, let's recap my world right now. I don't have an ounce left for creative intensity."

"But that's what it takes. You have to be authentic. You think you know who you are, what you want. Maybe you're still figuring it out. Maybe all this shit—this fire and brimstone—is what's going to get you there."

Dahlia and I dashed down the steps as the 4 train roared into the station. We found seats as the doors slid open, then slammed shut with the blaring sound of a hip-hop beat.

"What time is it?" shouted a voice.

"Showtime!"

A chorus I had learned to love and hate over the years. There were three of them, no older than twenty, their energy beyond anything I could imagine at this time of night.

"Not now," whined Dahlia, wiggling. She had never been a fan, but I watched with the same attention I'd give to any performance.

One of them—in baggy track pants and a sweat-stained T-shirt—jumped up, grabbed the rails, and flipped his body in one smooth motion. His friends clapped behind him, an attempt not only to get the crowd hyped but also to give the soloist what he needed—the energy that was lacking from the rest of us. He let go of the rails, landing on his feet, then kicking them back and forth in an intricate pattern before spinning to the floor, falling to his back, then thrusting himself back up to his feet. His friends went wild, clapping and cheering as the soloist let loose one of the whitest smiles I'd ever seen.

I dipped my hand into my purse as the next dancer started, a shorter guy with a baseball cap. I felt a sadness when I realized I didn't have any cash, but then the guy who'd just performed pointed to a QR code sticker on his biceps. I laughed, took a pic.

"Thank you, ma," he said as his name popped up. J'avon Martin.

I sent him five dollars, as any less through the app felt silly. These kids knew what they were doing.

The shorter guy kicked and flipped his hat, never missing a beat, never fumbling, like his whole life was in that fitted. His eyes held steady to it as it flew from his foot, his chin, his teeth, then perfectly back onto his head. Again, the friends cheered, and it wasn't for show. They were watching with held breath, hoping he wouldn't make a mistake.

Finally, the last guy started. He was tall and dark with tattoos that crawled up his arms and neck. He was ferocious in a way the others weren't, his eyes wide, grimacing as he flipped upside down, hooking his feet around the bars, sliding from one end to the other. As he passed me, I could smell his sour sweat and knew he'd been doing this all day. They all had. They wouldn't stop until they got what they needed. Until their hats were filled four times over.

He spun and jumped, flying through the air and catching the center pole, then tilting his body sideways. He moved his feet like he was swimming, then feigned blowing bubbles. Some passengers finally allowed themselves to laugh.

The train pulled into the station, and the guys thanked the crowd, then bumped fists with one another. J'avon bumped my fist too.

They walked to the next car, and I watched through the smudged glass window as the show started once again.

CHAPTER 20

My mother hated Christmas, and this year, that was the greatest gift of all. She'd grown up in the middle of seven siblings, and Christmas never meant more than a trudge through the snow to a church in rural Illinois on one of the few days of the year when their white neighbors held back their slurs. They were given plates, and silverware, and invited to enjoy a single serving in the far corner of the dining hall. They got one piddly toy each, for which they owed the church endless gratitude.

She moved to St. Louis after high school and worked at a department store—tall and slender, she'd watched enough movies to speak in a way that masked her poverty, lent her an air of sophistication. She marveled at the way ordinary people turned into monsters in December, all in the name of the lord and savior. Or Santa. None of it really tracked.

My earliest Christmas memory was from age five, waking up to find the cookies she had placed on the coffee table the night before still there, beside a stack of *People* magazines. She was supposed to eat the cookies, I explained. But it didn't matter. She didn't have to pretend. The Santa story never made sense to me—*the entire world in one night?* We never wrapped gifts, or filled stockings, or decorated a tree again. We just visited the people she loved the most and ate until we could barely breathe.

Returning to school each January always brought me anxiety. My classmates were eager to compare gifts—first toys and later brand-name jeans and sneakers, high-priced electronics. I only ever got a handful of unwrapped outfits with the clearance tags still on them—clothes that I'd wear for years, until the pants were too short, the seams burst, the zipper freed itself from the track. These items never stacked up against my classmates' gifts. They weren't well-off, but their families understood that the holiday was about spending money you didn't have, while my mother couldn't spend money she didn't have, because for us, when it was gone, it was gone.

By the time we returned from the airport, I noticed that my mother spoke in the cadence of my late grandmother, drawn-out *mm-hmm*s, stiff grunts each time she stood, shuffling steps. I loved her deeply, but I was also nostalgic for the woman she'd been—tall, dark, elegant. Hopeful.

In the kitchen, we shucked ears of corn, ripping away the green sleeves and carefully pulling the weightless silks from between the yellow teeth. She'd remodeled after retiring four years ago, and what had once been all linoleum and brown cabinets was now black-and-white-tiled, sleek, though mail was still piled on the new kitchen counter, random lids and appliance parts scattered about.

The news anchors bantered on the TV that hung on the opposite wall. The remodel had opened up the space—no more cabinets blocking the view of the flat-screen. Her shucking lapped mine as she stared at the TV, her hands long acquainted with detailed domestic work. Her silence was telling. She would rather hear the anchors' mindless holiday chatter than think about the poor already-troubled thing nestled inside me.

"How's it going in Maine?" she asked during a commercial, dropping slices of bacon into the skillet. They popped and sizzled until they were drowned by the corn kernels, peeking out only now and then from the sea of yellow.

"*Vermont*," I said. "It's okay. I'm getting a lot done. The dancers are great, and the composer and artist are very talented."

"All those people there just for you? That's really something."

"Well." I paused, considered explaining the nuances, that Jason and Amy had their own projects, but left it. No reason to burst the tiny bubble that remained.

The corn fried. I'd lost track of how many ears I'd shucked. My mind slowed when I came home. My focus drifted, my speech slipped back to the lazy lilt I'd taught myself to correct in college.

We sat down at the small table—the table where I had done my homework and flipped through college brochures before dance class, dreaming of a bigger world.

It was time to sample everything my mother had made. Greens, potatoes, dressing, fried corn, green beans, rolls, macaroni and cheese. Peach cobbler, pound cake, and carrot cake. This was how she showed her love, and I normally took that love, stuffed myself to the gills with it. But this time would be different. Besides the nausea, I was thinking about pregnancy guides—protein and folic acid.

We picked at the food. I was used to her eating with gusto, and the way she nibbled now unsettled me. We covered our plates in plastic wrap, for later.

While my mother normally spent Christmas Eve driving from house to house, dropping off cakes and pies to relatives all over the city, there was just one stop this year. Great-aunt Lula—my late grandmother's only living sibling, who was legally blind and nearing one hundred—had a houseful of people screaming with laughter, high on holiday cheer and Hennessy. Aunt Lula stood above the stove, frail but determined, sprinkling too much salt into a simmering pan of gravy. I hugged her, careful not to knock off her wig, already lopsided. I took in her scent—mothballs, frying grease, and Nivea Intensive Care lotion. I kissed her cheek, and she said, *I love you, baby,* though I didn't think she knew which one I was. Just someone's child she was meant to have affection for.

But then came everyone else. Aunts, uncles, second and third cousins. They all wanted to know how I was doing, where Eli was. *Tell me everything!*

After a half hour of smiling my way through, I locked myself in the bathroom and sat on the fuzzy pink lid. If Aunt Sheila hadn't come banging on the door claiming an emergency, I might have stayed there the rest of the day.

I rushed out to the car and stood beside it, drinking in the cold December air. My mom eventually saw the text I sent. The one saying we needed to leave. Now.

You don't want to say goodbye to everybody?

Nope.

Eventually, she made her way out, Tupperware containers filled with turkey and ham in hand. We drove out of the neighborhood, all the homes sparkling with lights, Santas waving from yards, angels twinkling in windows.

"You want to swing by Bria's real quick?" she asked.

"I need to go home."

"All right," she said, almost a question. "We can go by tomorrow."

I closed my eyes, covered them with my hands to block the shimmer of holiday lights.

CHAPTER 21

Bria and I had become close when I was seven and my mother began making regular visits to Uncle Wendell's family in East St. Louis. The reason for these new visits was unclear to me then, but I suspected it was to expose me to a father figure—though Uncle Wendell was usually alone by the grill or watching sports with Bria's brother in the living room, hardly interested in bonding with me. That, or my mother had seen something in me that set off an alarm. Perhaps I had been questioning why our vegetables were always baby-soft, why she paired spaghetti and catfish. Most of my classmates didn't eat this way. Maybe I was caught clapping on the one and three or asked her, after one too many TV episodes, why I'd never been *grounded*, only ever put *on punishment*. In any case, I quickly became comfortable in this new world of barred windows and blaring hip-hop, as long as my mother or Bria was by my side.

Bria and I made up dances to our favorite songs and crafted matching T-shirts with puffy paint, snipping off the sleeves and tying them into halters. She taught me how to lay my edges, and I taught her how to use a TI-83 Plus.

Once, I brought her to a dance at my middle school. She had never seen so many white people at once and insisted we teach a group of students a "new dance" that was completely made-up. They followed along diligently as we hopped to the right, shook our shoulders, then clicked our heels, then did the same on the left. We cried laughing in the back seat the whole ride home, imagining them showing off the move on dance floors for years to come.

That was the last year we were close. I spent my weekends with the girls in my dance classes, who lived in the stoic old homes in University City. Bria devoted her time to track and field, and to Brandon, a boy my mother had deemed a *hood rat* but who was miraculously still around. Her husband. Still devoted more than twenty years later.

Bria and Brandon lived with their kids—eighteen-month-old Imani and six-year-old Bishop—in that same East St. Louis neighborhood. As we approached the small brick house on its neat patch of grass, my mother pressed the button for the already-locked doors. Quiet places frightened me more than cities, but I let my mother exercise her internalized fear of the hood—the fear she'd been taught growing up in a rural white town. The fear of people like herself.

Bria had a fresh sew-in for the holidays and looked better than ever. Her dark skin was smooth as satin. She'd been a thick girl, sturdy enough to earn a shot-put scholarship. She sank into her curves easily now, like she'd finally arrived at the place where she'd always been headed.

We walked through the side door into the kitchen. The house had the same layout as the one where Bria had grown up. It was uncanny to see her standing behind the kitchen counter holding Imani, Bishop playing on an iPad, in the same spot where her mother used to mix Crystal Light and open packs of bologna to fry up for sandwiches. Where she pressed our curls straight, the smell of burning oil and hair thick in the air. We'd hold our breath as the hot comb neared our ears. No matter who got singed—and one of us always did—we'd both flinch.

This house had newer fixtures, a soft, clean color palette, an undeniable freshness, but otherwise, it was nearly identical.

My mother wasted no time shuffling the kids, big-eyed and late-afternoon sleepy, into the living room.

Bria started to pour me a glass of Riunite Lambrusco from a giant grocery-store bottle, but I asked for water instead.

"You're always on some health kick," she said, taking a sip. "Not me!"

My mother sat in the living room with the kids curled into her, wholly content. The room was laid out like in Bria's childhood home, but the furniture was updated. None of the African American art fair paintings her mother had favored—illustrated Black couples' nude bodies intertwined; Frederick Douglass, Thurgood Marshall, Dr. Martin Luther King, Jr., and Malcolm X playing cards.

Her mantel was lined with family photos—my favorite was a Glamour Shot of her and her mother, both wrapped in feather boas, hair intricately coiffed. Aunt Pam inexplicably wore hazel contacts. My mother always laughed about how goofy the picture was—the way their bare shoulders showed, the serious look on ten-year-old Bria's face, the fact that good money was spent on something so foolish. But I'd always wanted us to do the same. Now there was something enviably vintage about it. A time of malls, and press 'n' curls, and photographs left in the hands of professionals.

Aunt Pam had known Bishop for only a year, Imani not at all. The mantel photos were ordered chronologically, the black-and-white photo of Bria holding Imani in the hospital on the opposite end from the Glamour Shot with Aunt Pam. Even here those two would never meet.

"The kids are getting so big!" I said, sadness stirring inside of me despite the joy I was aiming for. "Imani looks just like you," I said. "And Bishop's not chubby anymore. He's a real person now!"

"They're driving me out my damn mind," said Bria. "You know *Peppa Pig*?" She said it like she was a childhood classmate. "I can't fuckin' stand *Peppa Pig*. Got these damn kids speaking British."

"Can't you just turn to something else?"

"This is how I know you don't have kids."

I shoved a fork into a salad bowl that sat in front of us. Crunched on the only leafy greens I'd seen in days.

"Enjoy your life, girl. You're doing it right. Following your dreams, kids when you're ready, blah, blah."

"Sometimes I think I am doing it all exactly wrong."

"Nah, you got a good man, and you're taking risks."

I leaned on the countertop.

"That's what's up. Crazy to think we used to be in a basement two blocks from here making up dances, and now you get paid to do that. You got all these hos dancing for you," said Bria.

"Those hos do be dancing," I said. Bria laughed her high-pitched squeak. One of my favorite sounds in the world. I'd nearly forgotten. "Honestly, I *barely* get paid."

"I'd rather barely get paid to do something I love than make ninety G's a year working for a corporate monster."

"You make ninety grand?" I said, sounding too surprised. That money went a long way in East St. Louis.

"It's not as much as it sounds like with two kids. Especially with Brandon getting laid off and Daddy's funeral last year."

That had been the last time I'd seen her. I hadn't considered the financial impact on Bria. The wake, the funeral, the burial. Both parents gone.

"I guess I'm a little lucky," I admitted. "But everything is happening so slowly. Like I've been doing this forever, and things are just starting to happen."

"This girl at my job has this saying when we're all rushing to meet a deadline. It's like 'hakuna matata' but different. It means, *take ya time, girl!* Else you're gonna fuck it up."

"Jesus."

"She's from Kenya, so—"

My mother came into the kitchen.

"What's wrong with those pigs?" she said. "Why do they talk like that?"

"They're British, Mom."

"But this is America."

Bria took another sip of her Lambrusco.

Bishop walked in behind my mother, his eyes locked on some new device, likely a Christmas present.

"Bishop," my mother said, "you're supposed to be watching Imani!" She ran back into the living room, where Imani had been left alone.

Bishop ignored her, as was his way. Every passing year pumped inches into his limbs, slimmed out his face, injected him with a seriousness neither of his parents had. We'd first met when he was two weeks old. Bria had put him in my arms, and I held my breath as I looked down at him—small and alien. He'd screeched, then quieted, sucked at her breast milk from the bottle I held for what felt like hours. They all watched, smiling. Eli right there with Bria and Brandon, my mother, Bria's parents. I wanted someone else to take the thing. It was so uncomfortable, the situation so pressurized. But they just stood there, staring. *He's not yours,* I thought. Grateful I didn't have to suffer through these early months of endless waiting. Of hoping I could keep him alive. That everything would grow properly, become more human.

Of course, everything worked out. His patchy bald head soon covered in loose curls, now in cornrows like his father. He'd become unbearably soft and round, before angling out of cuteness toward the boy he was now. Bishop was polite but resolute, interested in animals, music, and somehow, at six, coding. This was the real delight—watching him turn from next to nothing into his very own someone.

"Oh lord," my mother said from the living room. "The baby just threw up candy cane on the couch. All in the cracks."

Imani was whining, not quite crying from the other room. Bria ran in, tried to calm her down while also, presumably, determining the best way to clean the cushions.

"Wow, you just left her like that?" I said, shaking my head.

"I hopped up like somebody set that damn couch on fire. You know I can't deal with vomit."

Neither of us could. But it felt cruel to leave Bria in there with the baby and the mess. Bria was on her hands and knees, cleaning supplies on the floor, her sleek new hair now dipped in pink puke, Imani pulling at her top. The sight and the smell hit me at once. I ran back into the kitchen, where the smallest bit came up in my mouth. I spit it into the kitchen sink.

I rinsed my mouth as Bria did more than the rest of us combined, and looking better too. How was it some people just knew what needed to be done? Just handled things? There were some people who'd simply been chosen. And perhaps there was no way to know if you were one of them until the challenge was at your doorstep, in your home, pressing at the walls of your body.

Imani waddled into the kitchen, bits of something in the corners of her mouth. I brought a damp towel to her lips and wiped. She reached for me, reminded me that children were filthy and I needed to get used to that. My hands scooped beneath her arms and lifted her. She was as heavy as she looked, and it took a bit of maneuvering to get her hoisted onto my hip. But she popped a little grin that gave me some extra strength. When she placed her fingers on my face, I didn't squirm, but smiled, which made her smile more, which made me smile more. She rested her head on my chest, and I ran my hand over her hair, braided, barretted. I loved that feeling.

Brandon and his mother were on their way. His mother could keep mine playing spades for two hours, and we couldn't risk that today.

We said our goodbyes. Kissed Bria and the kids on their cheeks. Bishop flashed me a peace sign, but Imani refused to let me go. She hugged me tighter. She whined and wiggled as Bria pulled her off, tears brimming in her eyes.

"I'll see you soon, baby girl," I said. Though I didn't know when. She'd be a different person by then. Talking, running, really living life. I'd be a different person by then too. My heart sank as I walked out the door, Imani's cries ringing in my ears. The poor thing thought she knew sadness, loss. She had no idea.

My mother was at the car door when Bria called me back over. I thought we'd left something, or maybe she had something for us.

"Will you call me later?" she said.

"Of course," I said. "What's wrong?"

"I don't know," she said, looking at me. "But something is. I can tell. You were always a bad actor."

My mother and I tucked ourselves under the covers, a bowl of cobbler in my hands, a slice of carrot cake on the nightstand beside her. I ate while she flipped through the channels.

"Bria's kids are cute," she said, clicking the remote.

"You didn't seem terribly attached."

"That TV show was annoying. But the kids are sweet. Imani sat on my lap for a while. I forgot how nice a little baby feels. That warm weight."

"Mm-hmm," I said.

"That'll be nice."

My bowl was half-empty, or maybe half-full. I couldn't eat any more and rested my head on the pillow. My mother placed a hand on my back and rubbed, the way she had when I was sick as a child.

"It'll be nice," she said. "It'll be so good. You'll see."

Maybe, I thought, remembering Imani's weight in my arms. Her tickling laugh. If I could have exactly that, forever and ever, I might be just fine. Or the small boy—Mister—nose against nose. Loving even in the worst situations.

There might be a world in which I wouldn't feel the stab of betrayal every time I looked at my child. But what if I did? What if every time I looked at my child, I felt pain and regret? What if the baby was a lifelong reminder of the time when I'd been hurt the most?

CHAPTER 22

Margot picked up after the first ring. The year was coming to an end. I felt lightheaded as I opened my mouth to say the words I'd rehearsed—there was a family emergency, and I needed more time at home. Rehearsals needed to be postponed another week. I wouldn't tell her the details. But Margot was Margot, and so before a single word escaped my lips, she began.

"Happy holidays, dear! I hope you've had a restful time with friends and family, because it's about to get real, as they say!"

"About that," I said, already hating myself. Already knowing I was about to be pummeled.

"These next few weeks and months are make-or-break. I called Ava. You remember, from week one? The pretty girl. She's going to be your rehearsal assistant. Keep things under control."

"Sorry, the phone must have cut out. I think I misheard you."

"Layla, I'm worried about the piece. You seem overwhelmed. Some extra help is all you need. You'll create, and she'll keep things in order. With the preview event coming up, there's no time to lose. The board and the institute have a keen interest in this, and they have the ability to pull the plug on the show if it doesn't meet their standards. They'll love it, of course!" she said. "But you need a hand. Ava will be invaluable. She'll take some things off your plate."

As though there were anything left to take.

CHAPTER 23

The walk to the pavilion was a brutal trudge in eight inches of January snow. It looked majestic from the warmth of the house, everything blanketed, but being in it was another story—heavy, harsh, chilling.

There weren't many opportunities for escape in adulthood. That had been part of the appeal of Briar House, time away from everything—office life, my friends, even Eli. Three months of sanctioned time off is a regular part of childhood. Time to rest, explore, think, play. In adulthood, two weeks is treated like a gift from the gods. I had felt like I'd figured out a loophole when I signed the paperwork. But now—chilled to the bone, cheeks chapped, belly full, mind bent, heart broken—Briar House felt like a disaster.

Ava pranced toward me in the studio, clad, unnecessarily, in a unitard. Her hair was twisted into a perfect bun, which amplified my rage.

"Layla! Hi. I'm Ava, from—"

"I remember. Of course. Hi. I'm just"—I paused—"so confused."

"I'm really excited to be back. I was in New York and kept seeing the dancers posting all these videos and pics, and it looked like things were really coming together. I was in touch with Margot about other things, and then she let me know about this opportunity!"

"This *opportunity*?"

"That you needed a hand?"

Jade approached me wrapped in a scarf and an oversize vintage coat—sullen and glamorous. The bitterness of that final rehearsal was clearly with her now. Maybe she'd carried it throughout the entire break. She approached me, and though she was several inches shorter, I felt dwarfed by her confidence.

"Welcome back, Jade."

She turned to Ava, then back to me, waved me farther into the corner.

"The dancers are worried. This has been great for the most part—collaborative, energizing, whatever. But we were one pirouette away from a double concussion last time. And sure, Mercury was in retrograde, that was part of it, but still. Now, I don't know her," she said, nodding toward Ava, "but maybe it's not a bad idea that homegirl comes back. Keeps things in line."

"I just want to be a part of it all!" shouted Ava, walking over. "I thought you might need an extra dancer at some point too. It's perfect timing."

"Perfect, indeed," I said to Ava. "You can come relaxed, by the way." This wasn't *Fame*. I lowered my voice as the other dancers came in. "I haven't wrapped my brain around this yet. Can you just watch and take notes today? Please?"

Ava sat on a stool in the corner. "Absolutely. Check and check."

Jade stood beside me. "We're in a new moon, so I'm hopeful. But things are going to shift, so I have to say something that's been weighing me down. If you were half as worried about us as you are about Margot, things might be a lot different. I don't want to be anywhere I'm not respected. So, if I ever feel as uncomfortable as I did in that last rehearsal, I'm out."

"It won't happen again. I'm angry too. I'm sorry that rehearsal caused so much stress. I want you to trust me. I want you to feel safe. I know I can't guarantee anything, but I'm trying."

The weeks off had been the opposite of a break. I was struggling with conflicting ideas. I needed to immerse myself in the choreography, to let it be my world in order to get past what had happened with Eli. Nothing

was more important than succeeding in this. Nothing was more important than art. Except for people. The people in this room. The people in
St. Louis and New York. The person inside of me.

The dancers began to warm up. Courtney slid her hip along a foam
roller. Fresh braids flowed over her shoulders, a lumbar brace supported
her back. Her doctor had told her she'd be fine, to keep an eye on things.
Her back issues started long ago, she'd pushed through worse before. She
promised to take it easy, to rest when she needed.

"Good morning, everyone, and happy new year!" Margot didn't take
off her expensive Swedish clog boots as she stepped into the studio, trail-
ing gray droplets behind her. "I hope you're all rejuvenated after that
generous break."

The dancers looked at one another. Jade stared at Margot, her lips
pursed.

"Ava will be joining the team as the rehearsal assistant for the remain-
der of the residency. This will help things move more smoothly."

Ava smiled and waved from her stool. She'd wanted to come back, and
the dancers had wanted another figure in rehearsals, but there was a pal-
pable disconnect.

"The preview event for donors is approaching," Margot continued,
"so I encourage you to take good care of your bodies. I know there was
an injury during the last rehearsal cycle, so please, be mindful. If you ever
need to talk about anything, my door is always open."

Margot left, and the dancers' eyes followed her, then shifted to me.

"The fuck was that?" said Terrell.

"Listen," I said, meeting them on the floor, where they'd all begun to
stretch. "She's right. Take it easy, take care of your bodies. I pushed you
too hard."

"She acts like you're *trying* to hurt us," said Courtney. "We know
you're not, Auntie."

"She wants us to snitch," said Jade, turning to the dancers. "Divide
and conquer. She wants to say, 'I brought in a Black choreographer and
Black dancers once, but you know how they can be. It was just too much
trouble. Didn't work!' Let's prove her wrong."

"Exactly. If you have any concerns, please do bring them to me before

Margot. Ava is here as an extra set of eyes. She's not an informant. We're all on the same team."

Terrell gave her a suspicious once-over, still.

"I know it's been a while since we've done this," I said, "so let's take it slow."

No one jumped or lifted in that first hour. No leaps, no quick turns. It was all for spacing and to awaken the muscle memory. Most of it was there, but there were small moments of confusion. Opposing memories on certain sections. Where an arm was placed, where there was a pause. I made decisions, not because I was passionate or sure, but because decisions needed to be made. The leg was at a forty-five-degree angle, not ninety. The pause was on the seven, not the eight.

"You're getting all this, right?" I said to Ava as things began to build and solidify.

"Yeah," she said. "But you said two different things about the turn. First it was a double, then it was one and a half, so that they end facing stage right. It just depends how they should get into that *dee-dee-da* that's next. I like the way Courtney's doing it, but it's whatever you think."

I was annoyed with Ava for the specificity and relieved that she was there to catch such minutiae. For the next ten minutes, we worked on the moment, until it was sharp. Undeniable.

Maybe this was fine. A safe way to move forward. Let the dance breathe, let the movement speak. But Ava made a face each time I thought they'd gotten it right.

Margot returned to the studio that afternoon, leaned into Ava—whispering, laughing, judging. I feared they were looking for a reason to pull me from the process, slide Ava into my spot like a bootleg *Black Swan*.

It was almost unbelievable that Margot had called her back. *Almost.* Every industry was built on nepotism, and Margot had known Ava since she was a scholarship student. Ava felt chosen, and Margot probably felt like humanitarian of the year for giving her this gig. I felt like shit for being caught in the middle. For not being enough on my own.

But the rehearsal itself had an air of levity that had been lost before the break. Maybe it was the promise of marking, or the feeling that the worst was behind us. The dancers moved gently through the sections, and even without the powerhouse moves, the dance was still there. All was not lost.

Margot tipped her head, looked over the brim of her glasses, took notes. Left.

As we sat in her office, Margot said I seemed more in control. She attributed it to Ava. But I reminded her that Ava had been there for all of six hours. It was simply taking the time to slow down that made the difference. Opening the lines of communication. Making sure everyone felt heard and respected. Ava wasn't necessary.

But Margot insisted her presence would clear up mental space for me, allow me to focus on the piece. Margot mentioned *Revelations* by Alvin Ailey, *Still/Here* by Bill T. Jones, other works by contemporary Black choreographers like Kyle Abraham and Camille A. Brown. Works I loved, works that were rooted in purpose, but that had nothing to do with my approach.

What about Anne Teresa De Keersmaeker, the Judson Church crew? Experimentation, shapes, bodies. Couldn't I pick and choose when I wanted my work to mean something and when I wanted it to be about structure, or birds, or speed? Why couldn't I have that privilege?

"And Gus Solomons jr!" I said. "He ran into the same issues fifty, sixty years ago."

"Who?"

"Never mind."

"I want to make sure you're keeping an eye on the world around you," said Margot. "There's so much progress happening. The board and I have spent a lot of time over the past year talking about this very topic. BIPOCs are stepping into top leadership roles, changing the world. But also, there's so much problematic treatment of the same communities. So much violence."

I laughed, a loud, sharp yelp. As though I didn't know all this. These weren't just headlines for me. Some of my relatives had worked their way into the upper middle class through jobs in tech and business, but others had been arrested, some wrongfully imprisoned, and many more simply led stretched-thin, impoverished lives. Some artists found catharsis in creating around these issues, their work part of a larger mission. I admired that but didn't have the stomach, or the heart, or the mind for it. The more I focused on those things, the more depleted I felt. The more I was reminded of what a miracle it was that any of us were still here, pressing forward despite everyone and everything trying to crush us.

"What you're suggesting, it's just not how I work. But that's probably not helpful for selling tickets. So I guess I need to choose between making a Black Girl Magic praise dance or some sort of commentary on the state of Black America? Is that what you want?"

"Layla," said Margot, nervous, her eyes shifting around the room, searching for a DEI manual, perhaps. "That's not what I'm saying."

"Can you just be direct, then? Am I out? Am I done? Is that why Ava's here?"

"Layla, you're being very defensive. The purpose of this conversation is to reiterate that there are high expectations. You were chosen from hundreds of applicants. The board will expect something they've never seen before. Something outstanding. And I want to support you. The board can be hard to please. Especially when we take a risk."

"I'm a risk?"

"You're a different choice for us," said Margot. "Normally our artists are slightly more established, but in an effort to diversify, we expanded our vision. You're the right choice, but we need to prove that. We need to get their attention."

"If this is about attention, I don't know what to tell you. I'm making the best piece I can, and it's only January. There's time. If my piece isn't earth-shattering, if it doesn't get people buzzing, there's nothing I can do about that. Of course, I want people to be moved, but I'm done overthinking it. I'm not going to manipulate a piece for sales and clicks."

Margot leaned back, her guard down for the first time, her eyes bleary as she pulled off her glasses, pressed her fingers to the bridge of her nose. She seemed nearly as exhausted as me.

"When I started, things were a shambles. Not Briar House. Me, personally. I'd worked myself to the bone my whole career. Climbed the ladder as best I could before hitting the glass ceiling. I was ready to slow down. Arthur and I talked about having a child for years, but it was never a good time. By the time we were ready, it was too late. We tried for years before moving up here, but it didn't happen. I was too old. A woman's body has limits."

Her eyes shifted to mine. She knew.

"By the time I got up here and started taking care of my mother, I moved on from that idea. When she died, I gave Briar House everything. I could finally be in charge. In a way, I'm Briar House's mother, and I'll do anything to see it succeed."

I nodded.

"Speaking of mothers, congratulations." She smiled, though her voice remained somber. "You and Eli must be thrilled. Do you need a doctor in town? I can refer you to a friend."

Was it obvious? Or was it only clear to a woman who'd spent a lifetime watching those around her get what she'd always wanted?

Margot wrote down a name and number, handed me the paper. I thanked her, folded it, and tucked it into my bag.

CHAPTER 24

It had been four months since I'd arrived in Vermont, but I'd been too afraid to explore the land once Eli left. What was worse—a bear or his hunter? But the woods weren't far, and George was bringing firewood from the shed into his side of the house. He would hear me if I hollered. I shared my location with Dahlia and Kofi, pulled on my snow boots and coat.

Between the bare birch trees, there was a satisfying crunch with each step of my boot into the snow—clean as the day it fell.

As I walked deeper, I remembered when Bria and I were very young and got lost in the snowy woods behind our grandparents' house in the country. Bria loved everything about nature—animals, plants, the unknown—and insisted she knew the way back. But her understanding of the land was based on patterns in the soil, the way the tree roots burst from the earth. The fresh snowfall covered all that, and so we spent an hour walking in circles. One of my mittens had been lost early on, when we'd still been having fun, tossing snowballs at each other. My pocket wasn't warm enough to keep my hand from freezing. The icy ache was intense, and I cried while Bria assured me we were almost back. By the time we returned, my hand was numb. The grown folks were all playing spades in the living room, and Bria shushed my cries to avoid getting in trouble. *We'll just warm it up real quick,* she'd insisted, standing on a chair to turn the oven to a low three hundred. She pulled me up beside her and held my frozen hand inside the open oven. The instant heat against my frozen hand was a pain I'd never known, and I'd screamed at the top of my lungs, both of us falling from the chair, the adults rushing in at the sound of chaos.

I rubbed my hands together, shook them out, turned around. The blue of the house peeked between the trees. I was fine. I was safe. Gloved. Warm.

It was a windless day with an eerie silence. The slow, steady breath of chill as the sky turned a deeper shade of gray. I tried to embrace it, take in the stark beauty that surrounded me. Let my mind loosen, go where it needed.

Had I only wanted a child because I'd always been told that someday I'd be a mother? A casual brainwashing. Did that change now that I was alone? Could I let Eli back in, or would his stupidity, his gaslighting, his betrayal, end it all? My entire adult life had been tethered to him. I didn't even know who I was as a single person.

A hoot sliced through the silence. I jumped and covered my mouth. An owl—gray, brown, and white—sitting in the high branch of a tree, was looking right at me. Like an Upper East Side octogenarian in her finest fur, big black eyes peeking out beneath the hood. I turned away, hoping the owl would follow suit, let loose that enviable one-eighty head turn it was known for and mind its own business. But when I looked back, it was still staring.

"What?"

The owl blinked. Like it was waiting for me to complete my inner monologue.

I'd walked farther in than I'd intended. Farther than I should have gone on a winter evening, when dark came early. But it wasn't so deep. I could still see the house through the trees, if I squinted. My footsteps marked a clear path back.

Up in the tree, the owl blinked again. Waiting.

I felt like a coward. Not because of the owl, though that would have been reasonable—birds have been around too long, they know too much, some of them can even talk. Horrifying. No, I felt like a coward because all I wanted was to reverse course, give this all up, go back to the safety of the before.

The owl turned away. Disappointed. Or maybe this was a sign. To walk deeper into the woods.

But I would never. I trudged out, my legs heavy, nose cold, head tight with worry.

Fear was the engine behind the unsettling desire to forgive Eli everything. It had taken hold of me when he'd asked me to marry him—fear that it might be my only shot.

It had felt important to get married. And it provided entry into a different class, a different level of respect. The ring on my finger, the word *husband*. It mattered more than I'd realized. What would *divorced* mean? It was far too soon to know, we hadn't even discussed it, but my insides twisted at the thought. It was worse than being single. It was failure. I had something, and I lost it.

I smelled the burning of tinder as I walked through the final row of trees. Smoke puffed from George's chimney. A cozy sight, but not great for me or the baby.

And there it was, that other loaded term that would sneak out soon enough. *Single mother* on someone like me—how obvious and unoriginal. How expensive and emotionally draining. How intergenerational. How lonely. And if I feared being a single mother, maybe I had never really wanted to be a mother at all. Maybe the family had been the thing. The wholesome unit. Embarrassing. I thought I was worldly and cultured, feminist and progressive. But inside, I was as basic as they came.

The only thing I knew was that I needed to create. This life had not come easily. It was a most unreasonable, illogical, unrewarding thing—to be a modern dance choreographer—and yet I couldn't keep away. I had to fight for it each time.

Choreographer.
Single mother.
Divorcée.

"Divorcée," I said out loud, approaching the front door. I needed a cigarette, a martini, a slinky silk dress, ten more years, and loads more confidence, but it didn't sound so bad.

I could get used to this strange new word. This new identity.

Inside, I kicked off my boots, hung up my coat. In the bathroom mirror, I looked tired, but maybe pretty. My curls were loose and unwieldy, skin rosy from the cold, even if there were dark circles beneath my eyes. I grabbed my toothbrush between my fingers, let it dangle coolly.

"I'm a divorcée."

"I'm divorced."

"Oh believe me, I get it. I just went through a divorce!"

I hadn't heard from Eli in weeks. A cowardly move. The cheating alone would have been one thing, but the lying and manipulation, dismissing my pregnancy as a ploy—that sealed things for me. He was not a person I could return to in good faith. After nearly a decade, the person whom I'd been closest to was now the one I trusted the least.

I walked through the house turning down framed pictures of the two of us. Eli carrying me on his back at a friend's cookout in our first year. Us laughing on a beach. The black-and-white shot of us leaning into each other at our wedding dinner. He'd put them up across the living room and bedroom. It felt cruel now, but it had been a nice gesture—making this place more like home. I thought about the photos that would never be taken. His arms around my big belly, kissing me on the cheek. The two of us in the hospital, tears in our eyes, holding our baby.

I boxed up the photographs, the candles and tchotchkes. He'd really done a number on the place, overestimated my interest in bohemian trinkets and macramé.

But I left the plants. I wasn't the only one breathing this air. It was good to remember.

CHAPTER 25

The piece was finally coming together, but there were still plenty of issues. Some dancers moved with the quality I wanted—like the air was thick, made of honey—while others moved with a clean but dissatisfying sharpness. Some were a moment ahead of the pacing, others a moment behind. Ava stepped up, pointed out where things were disconnecting and how to fix them. She stopped wearing unitards, but she came dressed to dance and often fully executed the movement when we went through sections. There were times when her jumps were higher than the other dancers', her turns sharper. She made herself both invaluable and unbearable.

By the second week of January, the music was still in flux, so I had the dancers listen to the new tracks Jason had sent to determine what would work for the new sections.

They liked the first composition, a minimalist track with a Philip Glass quality. The second track was all record crackles and synths—the dancers made sour faces, but there was something subversive about it. *Maybe,* I wrote in my notes.

The last track was a plucked number with an element of twang.

"It has a hoedown vibe?" said Rebecca.

"It could work for the trio section," said Terrell. "That part is kind of slave-y."

"The Africans who were captured were *enslaved* people," said Jade, "not *slaves*."

"Doesn't it feel *enslave-y,* then?" said Terrell.

"Now that you mention it," said Courtney. "There are moments when you guys are on the ground and Rebecca is doing these aggressive but kind of sensual movements above, and it's like, yikes!"

"What? No," I said. "There's no slavery in the piece. I don't want to heighten any sense of that, so this probably isn't the best music pairing."

"What *are* you going for in that section?" asked Terrell. "It just feels"—he paused, then put on a faux-academic voice—"*historically fraught.*"

"Yeah," said Jade. "The piece isn't meant to be about race, but let's be real. Anytime you put Black bodies onstage, it's going to be about race. Especially if there's one white body doing something oppositional. I understand your resistance to making a piece rooted in history and issues, but it's kind of impossible not to. The trio is especially confusing if there's nothing specific you're trying to say."

"I'm interested in shapes and space. Texture. Movement—pure and simple. But I hear you. It sounds like everyone feels that way?" I was afraid of the response.

Courtney mumbled in agreement. Terrell shrugged. Rebecca spoke.

"I do feel weird in that section. Not when I was learning the choreography, but now that I can move through it with more emotional intention and less attention on the technicality, I kind of feel like an aggressor."

Now that they'd pointed it out, I could see the issues.

"I didn't really think twice about it," said Ava.

Of course she hadn't. Her admission didn't reassure me.

"I'm here to serve the work in whatever way you want," said Rebecca. "I trust your creative choices, and I definitely don't think it's my place to lead here. Just sharing what I've been sensing."

"Stepping back is doing *the work*!" said Terrell.

"Courtney, can you learn Rebecca's part? I think I need to swap you two out."

"Sure, but we'd have to change the section right before that, because I'm on."

"Right. Jade, can you learn it?"

"But I have the solo right after."

Ava sat up, waiting for the spotlight to find her. But I turned away.

I looked out the windows and thought of Margot—this racial subtext was precisely what she wanted. Somehow, I'd bypassed my own instincts and fed right into hers.

"We'll have to come back to this," I said. "I'll either adjust the choreography or rework the section order. It's salvageable. Regardless, no twangy music here."

"Can we talk more about this, though?" Jade said. "About why race can't be in the piece? Do you ever consider the ancestors? Your place in the world as a Black woman? Black futures?"

"Well," I said, hoping some answer would formulate in the time it took me to take a deep, exasperated breath. "If Rebecca made a piece, no one would expect that piece to be about race."

"In fact, please don't," said Terrell, turning to Rebecca, who rolled her eyes.

"So, you're thinking about race, even as you make a piece that is, decidedly, not about race?" said Jade.

"I—I don't know."

Jade threw her hands up.

"But let's say it was just us," said Terrell. "Like, just a group of Black people in the audience. Sorry, Rebecca. Then would you make a piece about race? If you knew it wouldn't be subjected to the white gaze?"

"What's the point of imagining that?" I said. "That's not what this is."

"Why not think about that possibility?" said Jade, shifting in a jolt of energy. "Why not create *into* that space? Exactly what you want. Something just for Black people."

"Like Tyler Perry," said Terrell. Courtney elbowed him in the ribs. He snorted a laugh.

"*Kind of,*" said Jade. "It's a Black man, leading his own company, creating his own content for his own people. And sure, it might be the worst thing some of us have ever seen, but for others, it's exactly what they want. His shit is, without a doubt, for Black people, through and through!"

"Who says that's what I want?" I regretted the words as soon as they came out. "I mean, it's not *not* what I want, but even if the audience were all Black, I still wouldn't want to make something about race. Besides, isn't it reductive to assume that's what all Black people want to see?"

What I didn't say was that, outside of family gatherings, I had never been in a majority-Black space. From the first moment I'd excelled, I'd been thrust into whiteness—academically, artistically, socially. Somewhere along the way, I'd started to drink the Kool-Aid, to believe that this was the best, most respected path. I'd become so accustomed to those worlds that I felt slightly out of place when surrounded by other Black people, even at family celebrations, reverse code-switching to keep up. I'd felt sick as a child the first time someone told me I was smart, or pretty, or talented for a Black girl. And while I hadn't heard those words after leaving Millwood, I'd felt their sentiment many times over the years. But rather than bristle, I'd embraced it. Now, as this truth rushed over me, I felt sick once again.

"Making work about race just isn't something I'm interested in artistically. Personally, sure. I like talking about these things. But I don't need my work to be *about* anything."

I couldn't tell them that I was confused. That their ideas, and power, and self-assuredness had sent me into a spiral in all of five minutes. My work felt wrong, empty. Like I was out of touch, crossing over into *in my day* territory. *In my day, dancers kept their mouths shut and did the steps. In my day, we smeared carcinogenic cream onto our scalps to flatten our roots. In my day, we adjusted how we talked, walked, thought, in order to be invited, to be rewarded.*

What would it have been like to grow up just ten years later, *in their day,* or even just twenty miles east? Times and places that celebrated Black people and culture for what they were.

"We'll rework that trio section tomorrow," I said. But the dancers were already grabbing their bags.

————

If my piece wasn't *about* anything, it had damn well better be tight. I focused on clarifying the shape and flow, ensuring that transitions felt natural and that any shifts in momentum were intentional. Sections were swapped, energetic moments intercut quieter ones. I bent to the circumstances, was open to change and adjustment in a way that was freeing. No more trying to jam square pegs into round holes. I carved new holes for the peg shapes with which I'd found myself.

Margot popped in nearly every day, always at a different time. She'd look over the top of her glasses, smile, squint, or squirm. Jot notes on a steno pad. She'd leave the moment I started to come her way.

One day, while I was reworking a section with Courtney and Terrell, the other dancers gone for the day, Margot brought along a woman her age whose diamonds nearly blinded me as she smiled through her substance-stiffened face. It was hard to know what she thought. The way her smile never moved sent a chill through me. Courtney and Terrell grew timid and cautious in her presence. That strange smile never left her face.

I asked Margot to please let me know if she planned to bring any other guests. She would, if she knew in advance, but certain people didn't need permission.

During the lunch break, I went to Taylor's office to vent about Margot with someone who knew her better than I did and had an equally complicated relationship. They were typing furiously and drinking what appeared to be sludge.

"What *is* that?" I asked.

"It's a smoothie," they said. "My partner and I are doing a post-holiday cleanse all month." They took a sip. "It has, like, beets and shit in it."

"Why don't you just eat beets?"

"I don't know, Layla!" they shouted. "Dammit, I don't know. But I have a stash of fancy granola in here anyway. I've been eating with a spoon. Straight from the bag."

"Been there."

"What's your trouble? You didn't come up to talk about beets and granola."

"Margot's stressing me out. There's so much pressure on this thing."

"Ah, of course. It's the institute. The 2010s annihilated the budget; the expansion had them in the red for more than a minute. Margot's been trying to crawl out ever since. They threatened to drop Briar House from their programs if she couldn't make up for the shortfall. She finally did, over the past few years, but just barely. Then the development director left last summer, hence my fake new title. I told her she can't make me ask anyone for money. I'll write the copy, but I refuse to do the begging."

"Fair."

"Besides all that, the press coverage has been mixed to bad—which is fun for me. Not that the work itself has been panned, but a lot of criticism of Briar House's *white problem*."

"Hence bringing in the cast of *Insecure*?"

"She has to hit all the marks at this point. Has to appeal to every board member, the institute, the public, otherwise they might cut off Briar House and give her the boot."

"Great. No pressure."

"Not your burden. You're here to make art. That's the beauty of your position. You do your thing, you leave and do it again somewhere else. I'm here *forever*."

"You don't have to stay. You should come back to New York."

"I don't want to live in New York. Did it for a year, didn't like it. This is better for me—it's closer to what I knew growing up in Ottawa. It's fresh and clean. I like the quiet. I like the sushi at the grocery store."

"Don't say that."

"I like the little animals and the big trees. I like Vermont! Anyway, this isn't about me. It's about you. Speaking of, the *Times* wants to do a feature on you. They're coming to the preview."

"What? Why? What did I do?" I'd pitched enough features to them to know that they didn't simply cover an emerging choreographer making a debut in Vermont. I'd sent perfect pitches—artists with incredible backstories creating works with themes directly connected to current events—that they'd declined or ignored. There was only so much space, and their pool of writers was slim.

"Your story is interesting! Seeing your name in a different context meant a lot to them. They know you as a publicist; now they'll get to know you as an artist."

"Seems like a ploy," I said.

"Marcus Greer is writing it. He's new. Never worked with him. But he's bound to be better than Katherine."

True. She'd even given Kofi a middling review, calling the piece *didactic*. At least Marcus wouldn't have any preconceptions.

In the fall, the event had seemed distant. Now it was approaching. Showing its teeth.

And there was Eli. Or the Eli-sized hole that followed me everywhere. Even in the studio, I'd think of him, wonder if he'd like this section of music or that moment of choreography. I'd check my phone anytime it buzzed or vibrated. It was never him. It was rarely anything at all—just a phantom feeling.

No one here knew my situation completely. Margot came closest. I'd gone to the clinic twice. It had been three weeks since the last visit, and the nausea had started to subside, though not completely. I hadn't yet called the doctor Margot had recommended. Something about it felt too close for comfort.

I could imagine Margot beginning to suggest names, items, brands—a crib, a changing table, a baby monitor, a collection of tiny, cute outfits. Miniature hats, the softest little socks. Would all my choices in that department be wrong too?

And then the residency would end. The baby would come. I didn't have enough money. I was barely in a place to care for myself, let alone a child who needed mini-jarred food, gentle products, and care around the clock.

My legs buckled under me, but Taylor was there.

"Do you need to sit down?"

Taylor had one hand on my shoulder and guided me back to a chair.

"Have some beet juice," they said. I looked at the purple drink, then up at Taylor again. I was lightheaded and hot. I sipped on the chalky, bitter drink. Came back to life.

"It's only a profile. This is one thing you're definitely an expert on. No need to freak out. Who knows you better than you?"

CHAPTER 26

E li picked up on the first ring.

"You answered."

I was meeting with Jason and Amy in half an hour but knew I wouldn't be able to focus until I spoke with Eli. Now that the initial shock had passed, I needed answers. Needed proof of remorse.

"You had no right to come here when you did," he said.

I'd come *home.* Three days early. He was silent as I went on about his lies, his delusion.

"And now you ignore the fact that I'm pregnant."

"You're *not* pregnant," he laughed. "It's really fucked up to try and manipulate me this way."

What was there to say? He was being completely irrational, living in a world that didn't exist. Rather than allow me to talk—because I wouldn't let myself scream in the Briar House conference room—he shouted about my rigidity. How if he'd ever mentioned being unhappy, I would have left. "That's why you went to Vermont!"

"I'm in Vermont because someone finally wanted me to do the thing I've been trying to do! I went to Vermont to choreograph. Going to Vermont had nothing to do with you!"

"Exactly! Nothing you do has anything to do with me."

"So *you* finally found something, *someone,* that had nothing to do with *me!*"

"I had something," he said. "I had my screenplays, but you made me give those up! It wasn't happening fast enough for you!"

There was no option but to roll my eyes.

"But you never took me seriously," he said. "I found your journal. Under the mattress."

"Okay," I said, grateful that I'd ripped out and shredded that page long ago. "What about it? That thing is so old."

"You were desperate for me to give up. You said I was a bad writer, that I'd be better off just sticking with a nine-to-five like a normal person."

"What's wrong with being a normal person?"

"You're missing the point, Layla!" His voice hit a high-pitched squeak. "I have to be the normal person, and you get to be the artist. That's what you decided. And you were unhappy with me for years until I gave up. You pretended things were fine, but you wanted out for so long. I don't know why you didn't just break up with me years ago."

He'd read every page. There was no denying the dissatisfaction I'd felt. How was one to know what love was supposed to feel like? How far to stretch for someone? Everyone said there would be rough patches, but how difficult was too difficult?

"I haven't written in that thing consistently since like 2023," I said.

"It's not just the journal. It's everything. You said it yourself on March tenth, 2023."

"Jesus Christ with the receipts."

"I have a lot of shit to figure out, Layla. I'm not like you. You're driven, persistent, relentless. You think I'm holding you back. So, this is me doing you a favor. Setting you free."

My hands shook as I stepped into the music studio, which was half the size of the dance studio—hardwood floors covered in worn, ornate rugs, instruments propped all around in organized chaos. Jason keyed the piano as Amy and I tried to determine what was a stool, what was a drum—Jason sucking air between his teeth. I didn't need another man tearing into me, so I pulled in a chair from another room.

Amy spoke of Jasper Johns, Merce Cunningham, and John Cage. Maybe we were the modern version. *Ailey and Duke Ellington,* I offered. *Ailey and Romare Bearden.* Our relationship wasn't organic—we'd been pieced together like a boy band. Hers was a nice idea, idyllic, but we didn't share a common sensibility.

Amy had sketched a backdrop of melting colors to complement the costume designs. Jason and I had a few good composition pairings—though he was disappointed I wouldn't be using his newer pieces. He had created them after watching some rehearsals.

I didn't know if I was annoyed by him specifically or if any straight man would have spiked my blood pressure.

Amy rolled a cigarette and stepped outside to *protect her energy.* I explained to Jason, as politely as I could, that the compositions were too on the nose for the movement, that they fit together too neatly. The complexity of his earlier work was what I'd loved, what gave the piece some dynamism. He softened at the light compliment.

"I hear you." He grabbed his guitar and began to strum. "So maybe this"—he played a series of twangy chords—"turns into this." He changed only two notes, but the entire sound shifted. "And if we add a little piano . . ." He moved to the bench and tinkered with the keys. His hands moved back and forth between the guitar and the piano, the notes dancing with one another, one moment light, the next heavy, mysterious.

"What do you think?" he asked.

"Yes," I said, surprised by how simple it was. How quickly he'd adjusted. "That!"

He tinkered with the other song and was able to pull something new from it, after a few modifications. Enviably swift and nonchalant. Making music was a sort of magic I'd never understood, but I felt the power of it deep in my core.

Amy returned, and we discussed the event a bit more before deciding to call it a night. She offered to drive me home. I hugged Jason good night, careful not to let my belly touch him, while Amy grabbed her keys.

We walked through the dark parking lot, and I felt a warmth on my back, where Jason's hand had lingered, and on the spot near my mouth where his cheek had brushed mine.

I couldn't shake the feel of Jason's breath, the brush of his hand. And so I tried to do what had been impossible for so long. It wasn't that I thought I didn't deserve pleasure, just that I'd been uninterested. For the first time in months, I craved something physical.

My body was ready, wet and warm as ever, but my mind deceived me. That had always been the trick for me in these moments, falling into my own fantasies. Even as I tried to picture Jason beneath me, I could only picture Eli and Charlotte. And it wasn't just the act but the entire scenario leading up to the moment—stolen office glances, secret texts, sneaking around, muffled mouths. I tried to think of anything else, but they kept barging in, until finally Charlotte rode him hard, Eli's fingers gripping her ass, his tongue licking at her breasts, their faces twisted in ecstasy as all three of us came at once.

CHAPTER 27

*P*retend to be a person who does this sort of thing, I told myself the morning of the preview event. *Pretend to be a successful choreographer. In control.*

We ran through the sections, refining music cues and working on transitions. There were also changes in speed, style, intention. Before, I'd told Terrell and Rebecca to dance the duet like they feared losing each other. Now I told them to dance like the other person was already gone. Before, the group section had been fueled by power. Now I wanted them to dance with heat and anger. *Your body is a flame.* They stepped up, would make this what it needed to be.

My mother texted just as we hit our lunch break.

Hope the thing goes well today.

Even if she didn't remember the details, she knew it was an important day. She'd always been a good mother in that way.

The headshot of Marcus I'd seen—a serious black-and-white photo of a slim man with a low-cut afro—was old. Now I took in his receding hairline, the sweater that hugged his round torso.

Taylor left the conference room. Marcus jumped in with questions about my previous career, my road to Briar House, my hopes for the future of my work. He asked about the cast—he'd heard they were all Black.

"Yes!" I said. "All but one. It's pretty special to be working with this particular group."

"Especially at a place like Briar House," Marcus said.

I knew what he was doing.

"They're an extraordinary group of dancers. Anyone would be lucky to have them."

He moved toward the topic of choreography. I explained that everything was born of the movement, the rest was layered on top—the music, the structure, the costuming. I liked that the audience could take from it what they would. That was the beautiful thing about art. One person saw one thing, another saw something entirely different. No one was ever wrong. They could all live with their individual stories and experiences.

"What's the hardest part about being at Briar House?" Marcus asked.

A loaded question. The thing that felt hardest about being here now wasn't what I wanted printed in the newspaper of record.

"The isolation is difficult," I said. "But it's also a gift. I probably would've created a lot more over the past decade if not for the distraction of my job and the people I love, pressure to make rent, shows and events, the cost of studio space in New York. A quiet place is a great place to make art, especially when there's a built-in support system. But unless your goal is solos, you need dancers, and most of them aren't out there," I said, nodding toward the window, where the ground was still covered in snow. "It's strange—you almost have to live in a city in the early stages of your career, when you can least afford it, before you have enough experience to earn an opportunity to focus and sharpen in a quieter place like this."

Marcus wrote quickly. I was rambling, but maybe I was making sense. He asked more questions, and I answered confidently, sure that revealing an ounce of uncertainty would send the conversation on a downward spiral.

He shoved his notepad back into his messenger bag.

"That was painless," I said, feeling lighter than I had in days.

"Not so bad, right?" He pulled on his coat. "I look forward to seeing the piece."

The dancers wore loose-fitting, jewel-toned outfits—Amy and the designer had started on the actual costumes, but they wouldn't be ready for a while. Their hair was pulled back, their faces brightened slightly with makeup. Twenty folding chairs lined the mirrors of the studio for board members, institute staff, national dance presenters, and a few writers, including Marcus.

The dancers and I marked through sections as the room filled, though I felt myself pulled away with each click of sensible heels, each shout of *Margot, darling!* from a donor.

Finally, Margot began.

"Good evening, everyone! I see we're all rosy-cheeked from this brisk evening." A few obligatory chuckles. She went on to talk about the Briar House artist-in-residence program—a spiel I assumed she gave each time. She introduced me and highlighted my past at BAM. A few nods and affirming *ah*s. There was a petite older woman with jet-black hair who had served on the board at BAM during my early time there. A young writer from *Dance Magazine* gave me a knowing smile.

Margot spoke about my work as a creation of *Americana.* I smiled through a closed mouth. If that was what everyone wanted, let them think what they would.

"I want to acknowledge the incredible work these dancers have done," Margot said. "I've peeked in here and there to see them rehearsing. Blood, sweat, and tears, let me tell you!"

The guests laughed, Ava too, loud enough to match them.

"But that's enough from me. I'm going to turn it over to the woman of the hour—the inimitable Layla Smart!"

A light round of applause from the seats, cheers from the dancers behind me.

I thanked Margot for the introduction, Briar House for the time and space, and everyone for coming out on the cold winter night.

"I won't say too much before we begin. The movement speaks for itself. It's a work in progress, so there will be many changes between now and the premiere. Mostly, I want to thank my incredible dancers. Jade, Courtney, Terrell, and Rebecca. They've been through the trenches with me. They *are* the piece. Ava has been a remarkable help as well over the last month. This work is a collaboration through and through." I turned to the dancers in the back corner of the studio and pressed my palms to my heart. A snap came from the corner.

The *Times* photographer was already capturing moments. I stepped away from the center and dimmed the studio lights as the dancers got into place. Jason and his two musicians—a guitarist and a drummer perched on chairs against the far wall—began to play. Amy clicked on the projector, casting the color abstract onto the curtains.

The piece flowed more beautifully than it ever had, each section melting seamlessly into the next. The dancers were sharp and light, full of energy and passion. The last-minute changes worked. They added depth, levels, intrigue.

There were small errors that no one else would notice, and a couple of moments that needed slight shifts of intention. All minor, inconsequential. Within these four walls, I was wholly content. Everything outside was blank space.

After the piece finished and the dancers bowed and left to change, Jason, Amy, and I sat on stools in the middle of the studio, answering questions.

"Layla," said a man in a blazer, jeans, and a startlingly long gray braid. "How did you decide to work with Jason?"

"Briar House paired us. I'm very lucky to be working with him. I fell in love with some of his compositions."

"The movement of Layla's piece inspired me in some new and interesting ways," said Jason. "It's been a fun way to create."

The man went on. "There were some songs in the piece that weren't Jason's. Will those artists perform that music live at the actual performance?"

"No, I don't think Briar House has the budget for that," I said, laughing. "Jason's compositions were perfect for some sections, other parts called for something different."

"There's nothing like live musical accompaniment," said the man.

"Okay," I said. "Well, there's some of that." I nodded toward Jason.

A woman who worked for the institute and wore a balaclava she'd either forgotten or chosen not to remove began to speak.

"I saw Trisha Brown at the Joyce in the nineties. The title was a sentence. I can't remember what it was. The costumes were kind of like these—loose, but not baggy, shirts and pants. A similar color scheme. Some parts of the movement reminded me of that piece, but maybe it was because of the costumes. Would you say this piece is an homage?"

"Not quite," I said. "I don't know what piece of hers you saw, though I do love Trisha Brown. Her movement quality is so beautiful and specific, but very different from my own."

"These aren't the actual costumes," Amy said. "We just needed a uniform look for tonight that was light and allowed you to see the dancers' lines. I'm working with a costume designer on the actual pieces for May. The backdrop will also be a proper painted canvas. Not a projection. Though we may overlay some projections."

The woman from BAM raised her hand and spoke.

"Can you talk a little about the racial tensions within the piece?"

"The piece has no themes connected to race," I said, as pleasantly as I could.

"There *are* nods to Black Lives Matter," said an older man with a gray mustache in a well-tailored suit. He'd seemed uninterested the entire time, but, apparently, he'd been paying attention. "There's the part where the two groups are facing each other, like protesters and police officers."

"When they put their fists in the air," said the woman.

My heart was doing its own dance now, knocking against my chest.

"Those moments are just movement, not symbols," I said. "The fists are more hand-tosses." I flung my hand. "Not Black Power fists." I held my fist high, staring out at the white faces, and heard the finalizing click of the *New York Times* camera.

———

Food stations stood near the stairwell in the lobby, and Mia's desk was now the bar. I was hungry, but everyone seemed intent on blocking me from the food.

"Interesting work," said the suited man. He was taller than he looked when seated and was now eating a pig in a blanket, spitting bits everywhere. He held out his hand. "Harold. Board chair." We shook. "You know, they have a robust humanities program at the institute. I bet they could pair you with some African American scholars. That might deepen your mission."

"Oh, well, maybe," I said, wondering what he thought my *mission* was.

"There might be some additional funding available if it's positioned in a certain way," he added. "All sorts of grants and the like to support work focused on marginalized groups. It's really a wonderful time to be you! And are you an LGBT?"

"I am not, as it turns out."

"Ah, well."

He gave me a tap on the shoulder and walked away.

"Powerful!" said the institute staffer who had seen Trisha Brown thirty years ago. "With a bit of work, I can see this in venues all over. Have you ever been to ImPulsTanz in Vienna?"

"No, not yet," I said. "That's the dream!"

"This could be right up their alley. I'm on their advisory council. I'm MaryAnn. Tell Margot to connect us, and we'll talk more after the premiere in May."

"Incredible, thank you," I said, shocked that someone from the institute saw the artistry within my piece and cared enough to push it forward. This room was filled with the people who mattered. I'd resented Margot's micromanagement, but maybe she *was* only trying to set me up for success.

"Bang-up job," said Arthur, who had arrived just for the reception, perhaps thinking no one would notice.

"Thanks," I said as he handed me a glass of prosecco. I took a sip. It was dry and effervescent. Calming. "Glad it's over."

"Until May," said Arthur. "When the masses descend."

"We'll see about masses."

"How's that husband of yours?" he asked.

My second sip got stuck in my throat.

"He's okay." I swallowed. "Busy."

"I expected to see him here tonight. Margot didn't suggest he wasn't welcome, did she?"

"Oh no, not at all. He just couldn't make it up from New York."

"Tell him I say he's being a bad husband!"

"Horrible, in fact!" I laughed.

"I've got to help Margot suck money out of these folks," Arthur said, lowering his voice. "She's trying to renovate the music studio, get some new equipment. Anyway, get a little drunk. You deserve it."

I wished. Alas. I walked to the bar, asked for a seltzer.

Alone, I floated through. Marcus stood in the corner taking notes. Taylor approached him now and then, and once or twice, Ava made her way over, her teeth gleaming against her red lips as she leaned in to speak. There'd been no need for her to dance tonight, so her hair was down, and loose 3b curls bounced around her face. She was obnoxiously pretty, and I couldn't understand why she was flirting so blatantly. I wouldn't have taken Marcus for her type—he wasn't rich, or handsome, or anything she could show off.

The room was emptying, and I was heading to the conference room for my things when Marcus stopped me.

"One last question." He walked with me down the hallway. "I'm wondering how you feel about your role at Briar House. They've been called out in recent years for not working with Black artists. The board is all white. The institute is very white. And tonight, it was clear they see your piece as something it isn't meant to be. There have been murmurs about shady funding and whitewashing in the past. Now they've got you and your dancers as the centerpiece. Do you feel tokenized?"

"Oh," I said, taken aback that he'd waited until now to be so direct. "I've felt very welcomed by the staff here. The whole team has really championed my work."

"But do you feel *tokenized*?" he asked again. I knew what he wanted, and I also knew what it could mean for Briar House—and my career—if I disparaged them so publicly.

"I believe I was selected for the merit of my work. If they were looking for a token, I'd imagine they'd find someone whose work addresses race more explicitly."

"Or not. An artist like that might ruffle too many feathers."

I hated that he might be right. I was nonthreatening. Agreeable. I'd been brought up on a diet of respectability politics, and I wouldn't be here without it.

"I've been given many artistic liberties here, and I'm grateful for the opportunity."

"How involved is Margot? Sounds like many of the choices—the musicians, the artist, even the dancers—were hers."

"It's *my* work," I said, careful with my words. "Every choreographic choice you saw tonight, everything that will end up on the stage, that's all the dancers and me."

He nodded, wrote in his notebook for longer than I would have liked.

"What about you?" I asked as he put his pen in his pocket. "Do *you* feel tokenized?"

"How do you mean?" he asked, crossing his arms.

"There are a handful of dance writers at the *Times*. At my last check, all of them were white. But here you are, in the middle of Vermont, no real knowledge of dance, interviewing the Black choreographer about her premiere. Why do you think that is?"

"I switched beats. This is my first dance piece, but not my last."

"I can guarantee the stories you're going to get. DEI stories."

"I enjoy covering race. I think it's important and has gone under-reported for too long."

"If you ask me, we're in the same boat."

"Sometimes you have to play the game, right?" He reached out his hand. "I enjoyed the piece, Layla. And I appreciate your time."

CHAPTER 28

The water was frozen over at the swimming hole where Eli and I had spent that final day. If it had looked cool and inviting in the early fall, it was now harsh, threatening. I put the tip of my boot on the surface but wasn't foolish enough to take the step. The ice wasn't solid. The waters weren't deep, but still, I was too far from home.

I unzipped my coat and kicked the toes of my snow boots against the doormat.

My phone buzzed. Eli.

"Layla! You're having a baby!"

"Eli, we've gone over this!"

"Your mom called."

Of course. She was bad at keeping her mouth shut, and she'd needed to talk to someone about this, the most exciting thing that had happened to her since the wedding. Nothing would ever please her more than my getting married, and now having a child. Giving her a grandchild.

"I don't have the time for this, Eli."

"Will you hold the phone to your belly?"

"For what? So I can radiate the thing?"

"I want to hear it!"

"I can't even hear it, Eli. You're not going to hear anything through the phone. What the hell is wrong with you?"

"How am I supposed to know? We've never made it this far. Is it a boy or a girl?"

"I don't know yet."

I had an appointment at the clinic Thursday morning. They could tell me the sex then, if I wanted to know.

"As long as it's healthy."

"Wow. Okay, you need to call someone who isn't me."

"I was thinking about names."

"Eli!"

"Our baby is going to need a name! That part's required."

"You can't act like this is normal! Like we're just a regular couple having a baby."

"We can be."

"Can we? How?"

"Therapy."

"Therapy?"

"Lots of therapy. I can come back to Vermont and take care of you until the residency ends. I should never have left—that was the mistake! I can be approved to work remotely for something like this."

I lay back on the couch, propped one leg up on the coffee table. The position I'd be in come June. I'd change my mind about a natural birth and shout, *Gimme the epidural!* The doctors would command me to push while sweat curled my baby hairs and I blew out rapid breaths. The sound of the screaming newborn would break the tension. Would earn a round of applause. But did I want Eli there after everything?

"I need time to think about this," I said.

"Everything is over with Charlotte."

"I don't care."

"They're gone. Back in their apartment. Her husband is back. They're trying to make it work."

"Spare me the details," I said.

"I thought you wanted to talk about all this."

"I thought you wanted to 'set me free.'"

"Can you meet me halfway?"

"Where the fuck even is halfway at this point? Imagine being me, Eli. Just imagine, for one second, what it would be like to be in my position."

Eli was chewing on the inside of his lip—a nervous habit I could hear through the phone. I considered moving the phone down to my belly, giving him what he wanted. But there was nothing to hear. The baby was still. I'd hardly felt it move.

"I'm going to give you some time," he said. "You're hurting, and it's my fault. Why don't you call me when you're ready to talk."

"If I'm ready to talk."

"Right. I'm here. I love you more than anything in the world. Same for that baby."

My heart sank. I knew it was true. He was being erratic at the moment, but if given the chance, he'd give his all to being a father. Even if we didn't reconcile, he'd make sure his child was loved, cared for, experienced a life full of delights. I suddenly felt a pang of jealousy—not of Charlotte or even Eli, but of my child. No matter what, they'd have an active, present father. Something I'd only ever imagined.

"Bye, Eli," I said, my eyes stinging for the past, the present, and the future. I hung up the phone, his last words still floating in the air. Only then did I say it back.

"I love you too."

CHAPTER 29

Taylor found me in the hallway and handed me *The New York Times.*
"That was fast!" I said. "Thanks for grabbing this."

I could tell by their face that they hadn't been expecting thanks.
They opened the door to the conference room—an invitation.

"What's going on, does he drag me?"

"Not you. Briar House. I'm meeting with Margot at ten. We have a
big call with the board and the institute. I'm sure they're polishing the
guillotine for me."

There was a triptych on the first page of the arts section. A decade-old
headshot of Margot smiling mischievously. An exterior shot of Briar
House. A photo of me and my Black Power fist. I didn't hate that this
image, though a misrepresentation, would be my introduction to many.
I looked powerful, purposeful, more assured than I'd ever been. Then I
saw the headline.

Briar House Tries to Right Its (Right-Wing) Wrongs

"A twist," I said to Taylor.

They rolled their eyes, looking like they might cry, then left the room.

Briar House has long been known as a springboard for some of the most re-spected choreographers, composers, and visual artists across the globe. But over the course of the organization's history, 90 percent of those artists across disci-plines have been white, 5 percent Asian, and only 1 percent Black. This year, they're attempting to inflate that number by hosting an Asian American com-poser, Jason Mitchell, and a Black choreographer, Layla Smart, along with a majority-Black cast of dancers. But Mitchell and Smart's presence isn't a simple case of course correction or even virtue signaling.

It has been a decade since Briar House welcomed a Black resident artist—sculptor Kwame Okoro-Cummins. This is no coincidence, but rather involves a collapsed budget, a cultural vacuum, and a $15 million "anonymous" gift to the Vermont Institute of Ideas from one of the blue state's most vocal white nationalists.

I dropped the paper onto the table and slid into a chair.

Briar House had been deep in the red five years ago, and there was a concern they wouldn't be able to keep the lights on. Margot, the insti-tute, and the board determined that the best thing to do was secure a big gift and bring in artists that would appeal to the local community. *Local* meant *white*. It wasn't all crunchy progressives with wind-chime bird feeders and a penchant for composting. Much of the area's money was in a very small conservative demographic. The Green Mountain Men.

My first day. The traffic on the highway. The Green Mountain Men's protest on public radio. Margot's late arrival. Had they been blocking her? Had they been protesting me? Mia had said the group had it out for Briar House for years—they didn't care for the organization's expansion.

Central to the Briar House–Green Mountain Men connection was Bethany "Bippy" Allen. There she was, smiling from the second page of the feature—her face plumped and pulled, her gray-blond hair coiffed into an unmovable mid-length do, her suit jacket nearly as stiff. The woman who'd watched our rehearsal a couple of weeks ago, then left unceremoniously.

Her husband was a descendant of Ethan Allen, who I'd thought was a furniture tycoon, but apparently had something to do with the Revolu-tionary War. A few years ago, when things were dire, the organization insolvent, the institute contacted Bippy. She was a known patron of the arts. The family had no connection to the chain of stores—a relief, as they truly made nice pieces—but her husband was a manufacturing magnate and the founder of the Green Mountain Men. The name was a play on Ethan Allen's Green Mountain Boys, a patriot militia that initially aimed to keep New Yorkers out of the state—ironic now—but went on to protect America from the Brits. Certainly not villains, and different from the Men, but not in the eyes of this new crew. Just like the Boys, they aimed to protect their people, their rights, their values. Bippy anonymously gifted the institute $15 million for Briar House over three years, on the condition that she have artistic oversight during that period.

Margot had been merely a figurehead for those three years, and now she was trying to make her mark. To prove that Briar House was current, progressive. That it remained one of the premier arts organizations in the country.

It was all destabilizing. The ridiculous name, the national publicity, the fact that I had been a target, a pawn. That I was, perhaps, creating the proverbial shuck and jive.

Because Briar House had perfunctory language about diversity in its mission statement, they couldn't fill their spaces entirely with white American artists for those three years. Bippy allowed for international creators. Blond Argentine choreographers, Russian composers, and all the Scandinavians rural Vermont could handle. The theater filled nicely in those years, more than the years with cumbia or Bharatanatyam. It was as though the community had stood up to announce: *Representation matters!*

But after the three-year period and enough criticism to get the board and even the institute squirming, they agreed with Margot. It was time to cleanse their palate with a Black artist. Something that spoke to the current moment. Now that Briar House had reached financial stability, they needed to show they were in step with the zeitgeist.

All this, Marcus had gathered through reviewing financial reports, piecing together old press quotes—a decade ago, Bippy had mentioned her love of seeing Briar House performances in a *Good Housekeeping* profile in which she also named Mel Gibson her favorite actor—and one anonymous source.

I didn't have time to puzzle over who the source might be. The dancers were waiting. It would have been nice to hide in that conference room for the rest of the day. But I dragged my ass to the studio.

They'd read the article and stood with their coats and shoes on. I opened my mouth, but Jade spoke first.

"We're done."

PART III
MERDE

//

FEBRUARY–JUNE

You're leaving not a trace in the world
But you're facing the world.

—Solange, "Weary"

CHAPTER 30

The dancers thought *I* was the anonymous source. Even though it was impossible to be an anonymous source in a feature about myself, a feature in which I was quoted saying something that now seemed grossly deferential about Briar House, they were skeptical.

"Fine," Jade said, giving me a once-over, then turning to Ava. "Just ride with her."

Ava smiled. She didn't have a mind for distrust. We slid into her beaten-down Honda Civic, nearly as old as she was, and followed the others.

"I'm really glad you're here," I said to Ava, feeling a strange sense of calm.

"It's fine," Ava said. "I know you didn't want me."

"That's not true. Well, it was. Before. But you're great at your job. I just wasn't expecting Margot to spring you on me with no warning."

Ava was watching the other cars, far ahead of us by now.

"We should go back to Briar House," she said. "Talk to Margot. Clear everything up."

"I don't think there's any turning back now."

"What are we going to do?" she asked.

The other cars took a sudden turn, and so did we, my body slamming against the door.

"I have no fucking clue."

The few other people at the diner stared as we walked in. We might as well have been wearing black berets over afros and toting loaded rifles— Black Panthers come to ruin their lunch.

I tried to be present in the diner but was overwhelmed by the memories inside memories it brought forth. That hungover morning after Margot's dinner when Eli brought out my double order of hash browns. Our parents' first meeting in St. Louis. This conversation was crucial, but I struggled to pay attention, only got bits and pieces.

The dancers ordered pancakes and sausage, chicken wings and fries, salads, coffees, sodas, and teas. A feast for them. Just a glass of water for me.

"Be for real," said Terrell, the mood looser now that we were settled in and eating. "How much did you know?"

"I truly didn't know about any of this."

"As many meetings as you had with Margot?" said Jade.

"Trust me, our conversations were weird. But *this* never crossed my mind. Every organization has something shady going on, but this is *a lot.*"

"Someone knew what was going on," said Jade. "Taylor for sure. A whole organization is operating under dirty money, and only one person is involved? It doesn't add up."

"Briar House is under the institute," I said, "which is a much larger beast. I don't know if it matters at this point who did or didn't know what was really going on. I think what matters is what comes next. How you all are feeling."

"Let's see," said Terrell, tapping his chin. "Bad!"

"We're striking," said Jade.

"You're not in a union," I said. "There are no protections. Besides, we've been rehearsing for months. The piece is coming together. This means a lot to me. And I'm guessing it means a lot to you too, since you all uprooted your lives to dance in Bumblefuck, Wherever."

"How are we doing?" asked the server, approaching the table from behind.

"We're great, thank you," said Courtney.

We sat quietly as she walked away.

"I think they actually prefer Crunchville, U.S.A., over Bumblefuck, Wherever," whispered Terrell.

Courtney elbowed him.

"But seriously," he said. "If we don't do this thing, they've won. Like they ultimately get to keep things as white as they were before. Isn't change the point?"

"But at what cost? What does it mean if we dance on that stage?" said Jade. "We're basically a minstrel show. I don't want to align myself with an organization that takes money from the Soft-Core Boys or whoever they are."

"Green Mountain Men *is* kind of a horny name," said Terrell.

"And they're totally inverting the name," said Ava timidly. "Ethan Allen and the Green Mountain Boys weren't even that bad. I googled it in the studio."

"This bitch," Terrell said.

"She's right, he really just fought for Vermont's independence," said Rebecca.

"Isn't Ethan Allen a furniture designer?" said Courtney.

"What the hell are y'all talking about?" Terrell shouted.

"But these Green Mountain Men," said Rebecca, "they're basically nonviolent terrorists. Despicable people. Half of them live in New Hampshire, for god's sake. I'm with Jade. We need to end this thing, and fast. I can try to connect with the local ACLU and NAACP chapters."

"They don't have any CPs here, how they gonna have an NAA?" said Terrell.

"Not in this town, but they're here. Around. And there are organizations to support diverse communities," said Rebecca. "I was starting to make some connections when I was working at the ballet academy. Trying to diversify our student body. I'll do some outreach. I'm happy to work on that."

"*Okay,*" said Courtney. "Somebody's been reading up and following social justice influencers!"

We passed the plates, ordered refills, debated the best course of action. We agreed that the work deserved to be in the world, we just didn't know what that meant yet.

There'd be no rehearsal that day. We needed time to process everything. Tomorrow, we'd reconvene at Briar House. They had the space, and we'd need time to determine a cost-effective alternative. To plot things out. Maybe even throw Margot and the leadership off course.

I spread out on the couch and wondered what to do, no clear idea fully forming. My phone had been buried in my bag all day, and now I pulled it out, watched it buzz and vibrate with calls, texts, and emails. Everyone knew. Everyone was speculating. Everyone needed to talk to me. Now.

CHAPTER 31

A mandatory-meeting email from Margot. A public statement from Taylor. A good-luck-and-Godspeed email from Josefina at BAM— I looked great in the *Times* photo, by the way, but what was happening? What did I need? If only I knew.

The press hadn't hesitated. It must have been a slow news week. *Dance Magazine, The Washington Post,* local TV and radio producers. Everyone wanted a statement. I'd keep quiet for now. I knew how easily words could be misinterpreted.

There were texts from Kofi and Dahlia, old BAM co-workers and friends. A voicemail from Beth, Eli's mother. Beth who lived in a bubble. Who wouldn't know *The New York Times* if it smacked her pickleball paddle out of her hand. Beth who thought she knew just how a life ought to be lived. God, and family, and easy money. She said I should talk to Eli. And she and I should talk, *woman to woman.* I blocked her.

Many of my phone's vibrations were from social media—apps I checked only occasionally. But now there were comments of all sorts from people across the country beneath the Briar House preview photos, even more beneath the *Times*'s Instagram post.

Turns out Layla Smart is not very smart.
Black Lives Matter.

Minstrelsy at its finest.

The master's tools will never dismantle the master's house.

GET. OUT.

People messaged to tell me I was a race traitor, to remind me that *all skinfolk ain't kinfolk.* Some sent me words of encouragement, commended my efforts to "bring about radical change." One woman offered to represent me if this went to court. Would I have to go to court?

It was shocking that strangers felt the need to speak to me. How much they knew about me. How much they felt about me.

It took everything in me not to engage. Not to explain myself, that I *did* care about race, but it wasn't what this work was about. It wasn't what I'd come here to do. I gave to mutual aids back in Brooklyn all the time! I'd donated a bag of clothes to a Black trans liberation fund just last year. I read Saidiya Hartman and Hanif Abdurraqib. I was good and progressive, proud to be Black. But none of that had anything to do with my choreography. Still, I knew how this went. It was better to say nothing at all.

"Layla!" said my mother. "Bria sent me that article."

"I can't do this right now."

"They didn't say *you* were racist. I don't think they did, I didn't get through the whole thing. It was so long. You looked cool in that picture, though. Reminded me of Wendell back in the day. He used to go to all the marches. That was never really my thing—"

"You had no right to call Eli."

She grunted as she wiggled in her seat, the way her mother—my grandmother—used to.

"Someone had to tell him about the baby."

"I told him weeks ago! And this is my baby, not yours."

"His too."

"I called him in December, and he didn't believe me. He doesn't care about me or this baby. If he did, he'd have been there for me rather than her."

"Maybe you weren't there for him?"

I threw the phone against the wall.

"Bitch," I said when the phone was face down on the other side of the room, like one of my white middle school friends who'd shocked me as they cursed their mothers over curfews or cold pizza rolls. I saw the appeal now. A sizzling pleasure.

The call had ended, but my mother called me back.

"I heard that," she said.

I could hate my mother. And I had.

In my early years, it hadn't seemed possible. But when I was twelve, it all came rushing in.

My father had been gone for as long as I could remember. A car accident had ripped him from our lives when I was four, or so I'd been told. But one summer afternoon, while Bria and I sipped Crystal Light in front of the floor fan in her house—our relaxers sweated out, our spaghetti straps pulled down, dangling against our shoulders—Bria told me my father had never been around. Yes, he died when I was four, but he was gone long before that. Bria was two years older, so she knew all the family secrets.

His picture sat stoically on our mantel—a handsome man with a thick mustache and glimmering eyes. I remembered him feeding me ice cream samples at Baskin-Robbins, flying me like an airplane around our backyard, rapping to Tupac in the car and nudging me to bounce along.

"Mighta been with the Tupac," Bria said. "But Daddy's the one used to take us to Baskin-Robbins and fly us around this backyard. You loved that—used to laugh until you cried!"

Maybe Bria was still angry from the push years ago, or maybe she simply thought it was unfair to keep the truth from me. She had no real reason to lie.

She had concrete memories. I had images and feelings, but I'd been so young, it was hard to know whose hands had lifted me into the blue sky, handed me the pink spoonful of cookies 'n' cream, tapped on my leg to "Changes."

For my entire life, I'd carried around an amorphous sadness for my father, but in that moment, it shifted into something more solid. Tragedy hadn't taken him from me. Choice had. That truth—abandonment—began to aggravate me, keep me up at night.

I'd never thought of myself as typical, had always stood out everywhere—at my poor white school, in my dance classes, and among my cousins, who spoke with a lilt and cadence, moved with a cool ease that evaded me. But my father was absent long before he was gone for good, and in my world, there was nothing more typical than that.

Then there was the question of my mother: Had I ever really known her? She taught me, without meaning to, to judge women who'd been left behind. She led me to a vision of a man who didn't exist. She allowed me to believe my father had been good and worthy of reverence, when he only flitted in and out of our lives. What had she been trying to prove? Exactly what I had come to believe—that I, that we, were better than the people around us. That Bria's parents—Uncle Wendell and Aunt Pam—weren't the only two who could make it last. *Till death do us part.*

Who was I now that my father hadn't been good, as my mother had led me to believe? He'd only been a man. The truth of this hit me in waves. When my middle school plastered the hallways with flyers for the father-daughter dance. Years later, when Uncle Wendell walked Bria down the aisle. Anytime I heard Stevie Wonder's ode to his daughter, "Isn't She Lovely." Some children warranted a whole song. Others nothing at all.

My mother regained my trust in time—helping me draft scholarship essays for summer programs, researching college grants, encouraging me to eat real food after noticing I'd consumed nothing but hundred-calorie packs for a month during my junior year. She was a good, supportive mother. But I represented something to her, and if *I* failed at marriage, *she* failed.

I couldn't worry about what she wanted. What Eli wanted.

What *I* wanted was to be alone. Truly, completely, unconditionally alone. No Briar House. No Green Mountain Men. No Bippy. No Margot. No dancers. No Mom. No Eli. No baby.

CHAPTER 32

A limp crowd of protesters circled outside the Briar House entrance. The all-white group, mostly people Rebecca had contacted, held uninspired signs and rattled off stale chants as they stomped in their L.L.Bean boots. *Hey hey! Ho ho! Racist funds have got to go!* They smiled as I passed, but I looked straight ahead, ignoring whatever they were giving—support, or judgment for crossing enemy lines.

Mia met me at the door, only to shut it swiftly once I was inside.

"I went to high school with two of those girls," she said. "They're the worst."

The worst could have meant a lot of things—slut-shaming bullies, self-righteous do-gooders. Mia could have been out there with them, but maybe they were different flavors of liberal. Or perhaps she was merely disaffected, not progressive.

"They can't be that bad. They have more integrity than Margot."

"Well, good news: Margot's not here. But everyone else is. Conference room."

The board had jumped on Margot's meeting. Some of the dancers had been hesitant to attend but ultimately decided that change couldn't happen without conversations.

Half the board was crammed into the conference room along with the dancers, Amy, Jason, and Taylor. Pastries and coffee lined the table. I was the last to arrive, perhaps for the first time in my life. My mother had warned me about CP time from a young age, and so I hustled every moment of my life to arrive everywhere early. To prove that I was reliable, organized, trustworthy. But today, whatever fucks I had were folded into my underwear drawer in Brooklyn, shoved into the barrel of Bippy Allen's family rifle.

"Perfect timing!" said Harold, the board chair. He wore a suit over his lanky frame and had a napkin tucked into his collar to protect from the Danish he was waving in front of himself. "Layla, we just did introductions, but I think you know everyone."

I remembered the names of only a couple of board members, but that didn't feel like a priority at the moment.

"Up here, dear," said Barbara, the woman I recognized from the BAM board, gesturing to the seat beside her. She wore a kente cloth collared shirt tucked into expensive jeans and a massive diamond ring.

I'd hardly slept all night between anxieties about Eli and Briar House, the sharp pains and overwhelming heat. I got up every half hour to drink water, then sit on the toilet, trying to press something out—make more space inside myself. I tried to calm down by reading into another world, but each word might as well have been in another language.

The board had nothing real to say. Harold apologized for the way everything had unfolded. He had not been the chair at the time Bippy's money was approved, but he had been a board member. Many of those here had. They were all disappointed, but it had been a matter of Briar House surviving or not. Margot pushed for the gift, as did the development director at the time, and Margot threatened to step down if the board voted to deny it, said there was no way she could do her job without the funds. They panicked. But we should rest assured—the board planned to make a donation to the ACLU on behalf of the organization.

"I only joined the board this year," Barbara said. "One of the first things I said was we need more BIPOC programming!"

This must have been where Margot learned the term—the region's foremost DEI expert, Barbara. She spoke intensely, her eyes shifting from me to the dancers, who slouched in various states of apathy and confusion.

"As I'm sure you know, Vermont's motto is 'Freedom and Unity,'" said Harold.

A collective held breath.

"We intend to embrace that motto," Harold went on. "It's important that we support diverse artists like yourselves. That we remain united in this stance."

The other present board members sat there like robots as Harold and Barbara went on about how they were here for us. How Briar House was intent on remaining at the forefront of arts innovation. A quiet chuckle from Terrell. A groan from Jade.

"Margot will be out this week," Harold said, as if announcing a death. "At least."

"Is she being fired?" asked Jade.

"Well," said Harold, nervous. "I don't know. We can't really say right now."

"But you approved the decision too, right?" said Jade. "With the funding?"

"Not me!" said Barbara. "I wasn't here yet, and I would have had a thing or two to say about that, to be sure!"

"The institute forced us into the decision," said Harold. "Margot had us in a corner. She and Bippy were close. Once those conversations started, there was nothing we could do."

"But didn't the institute have *Margot* in a corner?"

Jade couldn't stand Margot. A month ago, she would have fired Margot herself if given the chance. For her, this wasn't personal. It was about justice.

"Briar House's survival hinged on that funding," said Harold. "It's complicated."

"We're no strangers to complications," Jade said. "I'd love to understand the nuances of the situation. And while we're at it, I'd also love to know if there have been discussions about diversifying the board, which is totally white, in case you haven't noticed."

I felt like the floor had fallen out from under me. Like I'd set a natural disaster in motion. I grabbed half a bagel from a plate and shoved it, dry, into my mouth.

"We've discussed everything under the sun," said Barbara. "Perhaps one day you'll be on a board, dear, and then you'll understand. This particular situation, it's a rather lengthy explanation. Lots of footnotes and such. It would take quite a while to detail here, so we'll write it all up for you."

"Please do," I said, startled that the words from my head were now on my lips. "We'd love to have as much information as possible before we determine next steps."

Barbara turned to me, offered the slightest forced smile.

"Some of us have to get to work. I volunteer at the women's shelter on Tuesdays, so that's where I'm off to," she said. "Taylor wants to talk to you about public statements, so you should stick around. And finish these pastries!"

The board members stood and pulled on their coats.

"Take care, then," said Harold.

"Be well," said Barbara, pressing her hands together in front of her chest.

The other suits offered farewells, as though we'd just had a normal, pleasant meeting.

"Was that wildly disrespectful, or is it just me?" said Courtney.

"They think we're naïve," said Jade. "Thing is, we're very not."

Slowly, we made our way to the studio, though Ava and Rebecca shuffled to the restroom, one of them, it seemed, in tears.

The dancers leaned into one another, picking at the leftover pastries. Ava and Rebecca returned, their faces splotchy.

"Taylor," I whispered. "What the fuck? Did you know about this?"

"Obviously not," they said. "Though I should have figured something was up when the development director unceremoniously quit last summer with no explanation, nothing else lined up. This is bad. Real bad. And she knew."

"What's really up with Margot? Is she getting the axe?"

"They're having a vote of no confidence later this week," they said. "The funding was already a sore point, and the *Times* piece just put a spotlight on everything."

Taylor was on edge, but was committed to speaking to the dancers directly. To clearing the air.

The dancers were circled up on the floor. A few curled into the fetal position.

"Everyone," I said, "Taylor has something to say."

"This whole thing is wildly fucked up," said Taylor. "You may not believe me when I say I'm on your side. But I've experienced microaggressions from Margot and the board. I just want you to know, off the record, that I can't stand those assholes either. The tricky thing is I work for Briar House. Which means, technically, I have to protect the organization. It means, technically, I have to ask you all not to do any interviews with the press."

Taylor looked between all of us, their eyebrows raised. "I have to advise you against posting about any of this on social media. Your contracts have language about defamation. If you're accused of libel or slander, you'll be released from your contract, kicked out of dancer housing. Technically. So, I'm going to *technically* recommend that you review your contracts to make sure you're entirely clear on what you *are* and *are not* allowed to do. I'm also going to give you all my personal cell, in case you need to talk about anything offline."

"Wait," said Courtney. "What are you saying?"

"I'm not saying anything right now," Taylor said. "But if you call my cell, I might have more to say."

"But we should stick around, right?" said Ava. "Make our stance clear, of course. But hold on to the space and funding. Our paychecks. It's a lot to lose."

"I'd rather lose money and a performance opportunity than my integrity," said Jade.

"I say we bounce and see what happens," said Courtney. "I can't imagine being in this place with these people for three more months."

"I will pretend I didn't hear that," said Taylor. "I've written a statement to share with the press. 'Briar House is deeply ashamed of the choices that were made in the past, and we denounce white supremacy no matter what shape it takes. We're working closely with the artists in our community to determine what steps need to be taken for everyone to feel safe and respected.' And, basically, we're sorry. We're really fucking sorry."

Rebecca and Courtney nodded. Terrell and Jade rolled their eyes.

"I'll send the official statement around later."

Taylor started to leave the studio, but I ran over, grabbed their wrist.

"Can we schedule a meeting with the board? Just you and me?"

"I'll see what I can do, but getting them together today was a nightmare," they said before stepping out of the studio, closing the door behind them.

When I turned around, the dancers were staring at me, looking at once defeated and restless.

"Are we just gonna sit here like a bunch of losers," said Jade, pressing herself up to standing, "or are we gonna dance?"

Terrell hooked his phone up to the sound system as they began running the energetic group section. My mind was useless, Ava was too overwhelmed to lead, so the dancers took rehearsal into their own hands. They moved through the group section with flight and flash, and while I'd set it to one of Jason's compositions, the dancers needed something different. Turned out the group section also worked to Solange, and Kendrick Lamar, and Megan Thee Stallion.

The energy in the room shifted as the music blasted louder than ever before.

Made this song to make it all y'all's turn.

For us, this shit is for us.

The dancers spun and jumped, gliding through the air like they were being carried on strings. They improvised—replaced leaps, turns, and jumps with glides, pops, and jerks. They were living and giving.

I got power, poison, pain, and joy inside my DNA.

I got hustle, though, ambition flow inside my DNA.

They shouted at one another as each took the center for a solo moment.

"Go off, Courtney!"

"I see you, Terrell!"

It wasn't my dance anymore, and it certainly wasn't Briar House's. It was theirs. There were no more stilted moments. It was all honey. They locked eyes, slapped one another on the back as they passed. They sank deep in their pliés, hips rocking, bodies rolling, shoulders loose, eyes closed in ecstasy. If the dance hadn't been Black before, it sure as hell was now.

We ended rehearsal early that day, but not before agreeing on one thing: We would not perform at the Briar House theater. We'd break our contracts at the end of the month—Briar House covered our housing, so we'd need to figure out our next move before leaving in March. Three weeks away. Two months before the show. We'd find somewhere to perform. We had to.

"Black Lives Matter!" a pair of protesters shouted as we walked out that evening, their faces pink with cold and anger. I offered a thumbs-up. Ava kept her head down.

Ava offered to give me a lift home, but the drive was painfully slow. My house was close but had never seemed so far away as we drifted forward in silence, until we pulled off onto my road.

"It was me," she said, looking straight ahead. "I told the *New York Times* reporter about the money. I knew."

CHAPTER 33

Ava sat on my living room couch, knees pulled into her chest. I handed her a cup of tea and kept the other for myself. She blew away the steam, tugged at the string. Finally, she spoke.

Ava grew up in Yonkers. She'd taken the Metro-North into the city three times a week for classes at the School of American Ballet. She earned a scholarship at age ten—a much more metropolitan version of my own experience. Margot was on the board and noticed Ava the moment she saw her in class. Margot advocated for Ava throughout her time on the board. When Margot moved to Vermont, Ava's scholarship money dropped from 100 to 60 percent, which her mother couldn't afford. Margot funded the difference for the next few years. She believed in Ava's potential, thought she might be a major success. The next Misty Copeland, with the right guidance. She wrote her recommendation letters to dance programs across the country, which—along with her undeniable talent—landed Ava scholarships to prestigious summer programs and ultimately Juilliard.

Childhood loyalties can be hard to shake. It's why so many people have trouble skipping the songs they loved growing up, even after learning that they're listening to the voice of a bigot, a rapist, a monster.

When Margot visited the city, she'd take Ava out to lunch or a Broadway show. They'd go back to Margot's pied-à-terre and gossip. Ava always thought she'd spend a season at Briar House after Juilliard, but Margot discouraged her. Ava couldn't understand why, but eventually Margot explained what was happening. It was the first year of Bippy's funding. Better for Ava to stay away for now. Audition in New York. Try to land somewhere big.

"Why, after all that bullshit, did you still come this year?" I asked, taking a sip of my cooling tea.

"She was only trying to protect me. I danced for some small companies in those three years, but Briar House was always on my mind. Maybe I wanted it even more. I figured things would be different now that the funding was over."

"Didn't it bother you that they accepted the money in the first place?"

"I didn't really think about it too hard. It seemed like the sort of thing that happens. How was I supposed to know how anything actually works?"

Things did tend to be opaque. I'd worked in the industry for a decade, and much was still a mystery to me.

"But then, you came, hated it, and left? After three years of anticipation, one day with me was enough to send you running?"

"No!" she said, straightening up. "I liked you. The movement was challenging, and it's hard for me when I don't get something immediately. I wanted to try, but something just felt off. It was my first time being around Margot in years, and between getting stuck with the movement and knowing that this whole thing was being orchestrated to look like something it wasn't, I wanted out. Margot pulled me aside after the first day to see how things were going. She knew I wasn't quite feeling right. Or she wanted me to go. I'm not totally sure. In any case, she made it easy for me to leave. There was an audition for a touring Broadway show the next week, so it just made sense to go back to New York."

"And now you're back, because?"

"I can barely carry a tune, I bombed the audition! And the next three. My head wasn't in it. But also, Margot promised me a choreographic residency in a few years if I helped out with your piece. At the bare minimum, she wanted it to be sharp as a tack, and knew I'd be able to get it there."

This was a stab to my ego, but I didn't interrupt.

"I was angry that I wouldn't be dancing, but that was part of the deal. I had a new perspective too. I knew I could handle it this time. And then the guy from the *Times* came, and he recognized me. I couldn't believe someone at *The New York* freaking *Times* knew my name. That means a lot, you know? He knew about Margot being on the SAB board, and he asked if I knew about the funding from Bippy. My face gave me away. I took drama in high school, but I'm a very bad actor. Probably another reason I didn't land those gigs. I didn't say anything to him at first, but he had his answer. He said I could be an anonymous source, and that didn't sound so bad."

"Why didn't you tell me?"

"Everything happened so fast. I guess I didn't realize it would snow-ball like this. Besides, you and I were never exactly friendly. But now Margot knows. No more choreographic residency for me here. If she talks as much as I know she does, probably not anywhere."

Our tea was cold. George's pickup pulled into the driveway. He hauled tools from the bed to the shed. I watched him through the living room window while Ava watched me. Waiting.

"I have so many more questions," I said, my mind muddied. "But go home. It's late."

Ava walked to her car. I closed the door, then my eyes, fell back on the couch, placed my hands on my hard, round belly. And then I felt a pain—sharp as a razor slicing through me.

CHAPTER 34

There are loads of books, movies, and articles on what to expect when you're expecting—most of them fronted by thin white women with enough money and sense to keep the real secrets to themselves. And yet still, it was all utterly indecipherable. Every aspect of the process felt like a devouring from the inside out. And there were the external stressors eating away at me too.

So, how was I to know?

The doctor's face on that third clinic visit told me there was a problem. Her tone was different from before. And she had so many questions. It felt like a pop quiz.

When did the pain start? What about the headaches? The swelling?

"What swelling?"

"Your face," she said. "Your hands as well."

She grabbed one, turned it over, let me marvel at its fatness. There wasn't a mirror in the room, but in the window, I could see my reflection in the February darkness. I'd noticed a few weeks ago that my nose looked wider, like Bria's had when she was pregnant with Bishop and Imani, but I now saw that everything seemed slightly bigger—like someone had placed an air pump between my lips and given it one gentle puff. Enough that a doctor who'd seen me only twice before knew it was more than post-holiday bloat.

"I wish you'd come sooner," she said as the nurse practitioner pulled out the gel and wheeled over the ultrasound machine.

It didn't feel good to be shamed, and I was only a few weeks behind in my appointment scheduling. People around the world and for all of time had given birth to healthy children without visits scheduled to the day. Without supplements and special exercise classes. Without aggressive advice about what they should or should not be ingesting.

"I had to leave town. And it was the holidays, so I couldn't see my regular doctor at home. This was the earliest appointment I could get."

"Okay," she sighed. "Well, your weight has gone up."

"I'm pregnant!"

Suddenly, I felt embarrassed. Everyone must have noticed. Some might have simply thought I'd put on weight, but there must have been more who could see the truth in my body. More than just Margot.

"This is quite a lot since your last visit. Could be water weight. Lie back for me. Let's see how Baby is doing."

She rubbed the cold gel on my stomach, and I squirmed. The tool rolled over my body, and I turned away from the screen before the projection appeared, afraid of what I might see.

"Baby is looking healthy for now," she said, her voice tilting downward. A hesitation.

"But?"

Before, she'd asked if I wanted to see. This was meant to be the visit where I'd learn the sex. But this visit wasn't a celebration. She placed the tools down, wiped her hands, and pulled the gown back over my stomach.

They needed to do more tests, but my symptoms and blood pressure pointed toward preeclampsia.

"But I'm drinking less than a cup of coffee a day. I've been eating only pasteurized cheeses. One glass of wine since I found out. *Maybe* two. In France they drink a lot more than that!" I tried to laugh. "I haven't been perfect, but I'm doing my best."

"You haven't done anything wrong. And Baby is fine right now, though that could change. Your risk for stillbirth increases by a lot with preeclampsia, and some babies born to preeclamptic mothers develop long-term disorders and disabilities. *But* many babies are just fine. Right now, I'm more worried about you than Baby. This condition is dangerous, and it's not uncommon in African American women."

Of course. Everything was more common for us. It was a miracle any of us survived into old age given the way the world whittled at us. The way trauma was etched into our cells.

"What do I need to do?"

She took off her glasses.

"We'll need more tests. You're just past twenty weeks. If you were further along, say thirty-seven or more, I'd suggest an emergency induction or C-section. Now, that comes with its own risks. But it would be an option, once you get to that point. You could try and get through these next ten weeks, eliminate any stressors, just rest and care for yourself. And then we'll reassess the situation."

"There's nothing I can do now?"

"It's too early. Right now, this situation is putting you at a high risk for several things, including stroke and potential heart failure."

There was nothing to say to that. No clever quip. No questions. I knew what those words meant. Had seen them take out my family members for decades, though none as young as me. My mouth opened. Maybe an attempt to say something, or to cry. But my body betrayed me here too.

"We also need to keep a very close eye on Baby, make sure there's enough blood and oxygen flow. If that's compromised, things change. If you want to get through these next months and consider early delivery, we'll monitor you closely. We'll put you on a very strict regimen, and you'll have to eliminate any stressors."

"Is that my only option—to wait it out and hope I don't die?"

"Like I said. We need to do some more testing to understand the safest course of action. If the tests reveal this is, in fact, preeclampsia and your health is severely at risk, and/or the risk starts to rise for Baby, an abortion would be an option."

A muffled conversation happened in the hallway, two women laughing.

"I'm going to send you down the hall for blood work. You'll have the results in a day or two. Take a few days to think about it. But I'd urge you to decide quickly, to reduce your own risk. In the meantime, take it easy. Drink lots of water. Eat well. Sleep as much as you can."

Nice ideas, all.

I sat up, rubbed my belly. Closed my eyes.

When the results came back two days later, there was no question about what I had to do.

CHAPTER 35

I slept, and woke, and slept again.

My mother arrived.

We wept.

I told Eli.

He wept.

I called Dahlia and Kofi. Bria. Told them everything I'd kept secret. They apologized for all they hadn't known.

My mother drove me to the clinic.

She drove me home.

She fed me foods I hadn't eaten in years. Foods I thought I didn't like anymore, until I ate them and remembered. Salt and fat could heal.

I pressed a cold compress to my weakest parts.

My mother left.

Then it was just me.

CHAPTER 36

Ava led rehearsals while I took the week off. The dancers needed to continue creating, planning, commiserating. But my mind and body were maxed out. I called them each over the phone to explain my absence, my reality—that I'd been pregnant, and now I wasn't. By the third call, I was used to the gasp, the sympathy, the sighs, the silence. They were all so sorry to hear it. I knew when to jump in, to assure them that I was still here and would be back soon.

Jade was becoming a doula, something I'd learned that first day but forgotten. She was trained in birth, but also in miscarriage and abortion.

She drove over, her car filled with blankets and pillows—beautiful soft things to cushion my every part.

"I'm not certified yet," she said. "Just for transparency."

"You can't possibly do me any harm at this point."

She spread out the blankets and pillows, and we lay on the floor. She asked if I'd like her to hold my hands. *Yes.* She asked if she could touch my back. *Yes.* She turned on gentle instrumentals. We breathed. We meditated. When I asked her to hold me, she did. We curled on the blankets together, her tiny body wrapping mine, and she stroked my hair—dry, uncombed, flaking at the scalp—while I cried.

She brought me cucumber water. Fed me bowls of vegan stew. We talked about death and grieving. The precarity of life. We talked about ourselves and our pasts. About her abortion at fifteen. How it had changed her life, expanded her empathy, created a path forward.

Each day she checked on me, listening to whatever I had to say. Catering to my requests for breath work, or talking, or silence. When she came over, she brought me food or cooked the items left behind by my mother—I didn't yet have the capacity to hold a knife, to turn the knob that ignited heat. When she didn't come, she called, asked what I'd eaten. She promised not to destroy my digestive system again with that vegan stew. I had forgotten the sound of my own laughter.

What would it be like to enter the rehearsal space with her again? Would it be possible to return to our previous dynamic, complicated though it was? Would she see me as the person she'd known before rather than the empty person she'd just wrapped her arms around? On that first day back, she hugged me tight and long. If things had changed between us, it was only an upward track, a deepened understanding.

Jade had always seemed so serious. So intense. Judgmental and harsh. But that wasn't the case at all. This was how her love manifested. She cared deeply. Completely.

The other dancers hugged me too, and I soaked up their energy. Then, we danced.

Still in a daze, I allowed Ava the pleasure of continuing the rehearsals.

"Lead with your solar plexus!" she'd shout, while I sat against the mirrors, taking it in. "Gorgeous, Jade! Just keep your momentum going after the jump." Ava was born for this.

Soon, I was more solidly in my body and the world. I saw the work with new eyes, began to live inside of it. I read it like a book, examined its curves and angles like a sculpture, listened to its rhythms like a song. The more time I spent within the choreography, the less time I had to think about my life. It felt good to give myself over to the piece, to be vulnerable to my art, even if it might never see the light of day.

This meant rethinking every moment. Sections shrank and expanded.

Dancers shifted roles. Some created their own movement that exploded everything I'd imagined—and how could I deny where their bodies led them, after all these months?

Eli called to make sure I was all right. I was—much better than I'd been before. He wanted to visit. I'd insisted he not come up for the procedure. The miscarriage had burrowed into us, still lived under our skin. He wanted to come take care of me, help me readjust. And to make sure things were fine with Briar House.

"You don't need to come here, Eli."

"Are you sure?" he asked.

I was resolute, had a newfound clarity.

He hung up, and a vibration moved through my body. The next time we spoke, it would be to discuss divorce. I could hang on by a thread forever, or I could snip it. Let go.

Before our trip to Berlin three years ago, I'd considered ending it. Things weren't awful, but they were going nowhere. Eli had been aimless. I worried his projects wouldn't get off the ground. That his dreams were merely wishes. He was growing sullen in his stagnancy, and I was growing anxious in turn. We loved each other, but we were wearing each other out.

I thought maybe things would change after a week traipsing through foreign streets, eating street food, drinking wine at corner cafés. Berlin might enlighten him or remind me of how happy we could be. If nothing changed—no lightning-bolt moment—I'd break up with him once we got back to New York.

Something did happen in Berlin, though. Unintentionally, we arrived on the one night of the year when the city's museums were open all night and musicians played in the streets. We danced a tango in Potsdamer Platz. We didn't know how to dance tango, but dozens of older couples around us did, and the air was warm, so we held each other close, then pulled away, following the others, twirling in a way that felt right and romantic.

Inside the bright museum at midnight, we lingered in front of paintings we didn't understand, grasping for language, seeing who could go the longest without laughing. In the early morning, we walked over bridges that covered sparkling black water back to our Kreuzberg Airbnb. It started to drizzle, and Eli dropped to one knee. I didn't think twice. Gone was the idea that this would be our last trip together—it was only the beginning. I bent down and kissed him where he knelt, crying. I pulled him in and said, "Yes, yes, yes."

What if I had not let myself be taken by the moment? What if I had trusted the doubt that crept in as we walked back into our Brooklyn apartment? Maybe I'd be living with roommates in Bed-Stuy, or married with a child in a London row house, or on my own and in demand, setting work on companies around the world.

I had quieted my instincts in those post-Berlin days, afraid of what would happen if I backtracked off the path of certainty. Afraid of changing my mind. But now I'd learned my lesson. I'd ignored my instincts with Eli, but Briar House was ripe. I could walk away politely, or I could blow it all up.

CHAPTER 37

The press release was written. My emails were queued up—pulled from a press list I'd downloaded in my final week at BAM. Our month's pay was pending in our accounts. The dancers were in the studio, teeing up their social media posts. An open letter demanding that Briar House diversify its board and staff was drafted, and Rebecca had preemptively secured the support of a few local social justice groups— their names the first of many we hoped would sign. I sat in the conference room reviewing the release obsessively. Once I hit send, it could be either the beginning or the end of everything we'd worked toward.

Our coats were on, our bags were packed. At twelve-thirty, we would announce that we were leaving Briar House over a disagreement with the leadership that they had failed to adequately address. They'd ignored our requests to meet again. We were searching for other spaces to present our work.

At twelve-fifteen, I emailed Harold and Barbara, a separate note to Margot—whom no one had heard from since she was forced to resign a week after the article.

Jade popped her head into the conference room.

"We're ready to go out here," she said. "You all set?"

"Sure am," I said, smiling.

She came in, gave me a hug, a kiss on the forehead.

It happened in an instant—my press release, their posts.

"Bye, Mia," we said as we walked past the front desk.

She was whispering on the phone, confused to see us all leaving just as our afternoon rehearsal was set to begin. The other phone line began to ring as we made our way through the front doors and into the fresh silence of Vermont at midday. The only sound was the rush of wind. The protesters had given up weeks ago.

The dancers rented a four-bedroom Airbnb—a renovated farmhouse twenty miles north of Briar House, surrounded by two acres of pasture. There was a big finished basement to rehearse in until we found another home.

Bria and I had spent hours in her basement working on choreography to Destiny's Child songs. We did it for ourselves, feeling cute as we shook our hips and sang off-key, striving for the high notes, failing. We had no audience to think of. Untethered from Briar House, my work with the dancers didn't feel so different.

George said I could pay him directly once Briar House stopped sending him checks for my stay. Part of me still worried he was a secret Green Mountain Man. That after all these months, I'd learn I was sharing a home with a conservative militia member. After all, he drove a pickup truck and blasted country music. But when I told him what was happening, he offered a swift *fuck those assholes* and invited me to join him for an evening toke. I declined but was grateful for confirmation that he was on the right side. That I wouldn't sleep in fear like I had the night the driver picked me up from the Rusty Rail. The way my mother and her siblings had for so many years after integrating the area school, much to their neighbors' chagrin.

By the time I got home, I'd missed a call from Margot and two from Harold. Katherine from the *Times* wanted an exclusive. It felt powerful to have her reach out to *me,* but I wasn't interested. Marcus was who I wanted.

Interview requests flooded my inbox, some people sharing links they'd already posted. Links that included the dancers' social media posts, by turns emotional and joyful—carefully crafted statements from some, clever dance videos from others. But nothing from Marcus. I'd included him on the press release blast, but I'd guessed at his email address, and the *Times*'s formatting was inconsistent. Taylor had handled all previous communication, and his contact info wasn't online.

Until I heard from him, I wouldn't respond to anyone. Patience was the key. Haraka haraka haina baraka.

The dancers sent me videos of the Airbnb. They danced across the expansive country kitchen, pirouetting around the island. They bounced on the plush beds, tried to figure out how the sauna worked. I'd see the place tomorrow, when Jason drove me up.

I was standing in my own small kitchen, reminding myself what it felt like to make a meal—it had been so long since I'd chopped garlic, turned on the stove, fed anything to myself other than what was edible and within arm's reach—when my phone rang from across the room. By the time I reached it, a voicemail pinged. It was Harold, asking to talk with me on behalf of the board. I thought of pretending it didn't exist, but an email came through from him soon after. It was clear I wasn't getting rid of him, so with a churning stomach, I called him back.

"Ms. Smart!" he said. "Thanks for returning my call."

"Yes," I said, unclear on what was happening. "That's what I'm doing."

"Are you aware that you're in breach of contract? We were trying to help you. And the dancers. We were going to keep things going for you if you only let us."

"Then you should have responded to our emails. We felt very uncomfortable with the whole situation. If that much came out in the article, I can only imagine what else is happening behind the scenes."

"You have to trust the board," said Harold. "Briar House, the institute. You have to trust us all."

How could I after this? We needed to separate ourselves from it all, I explained. It was detracting from the work.

"You think making a big stink about it is going to help?" asked Harold.

"We're not making a stink. We're exercising our freedom and informing people."

"Informing people? My daughter saw a social media video with the dancers singing, 'Middle fingers up!' And they were all putting their middle fingers up. In front of Briar House!"

I hadn't seen that one, though the "Break My Soul" video Terrell had posted—boasting about having just quit his job, and about how we were looking for a new foundation (he'd tagged Mellon and Ford)—was spot-on.

"They're artists. We all are. We express ourselves through language and movement."

"I'm a businessman. And I express myself through paperwork and fine print. And the fine print says if you're not on contract with Briar House, you can't remain on our property. So, unless we figure this out, you have to vacate your lodging. That house belongs to Briar House."

"George owns this house. He already said I could pay him directly and he'd talk to whomever to make sure that happened. Do you have a pen? I'll give you his number."

"If you don't leave, you and the dancers could be sued."

"What?" I said. "That makes no sense! George owns the house!"

"Well, I own *you*," said Harold.

Even the birds who'd been chattering in the trees outside my window quieted their chirping.

"I didn't mean it like that," Harold said.

"You don't own me," I said, my voice low, slow. "No one fucking owns me."

"What I meant," said Harold, speaking slowly too, carefully, "is that we own any work that was created at Briar House, so you're prohibited from performing anything created here on an outside stage."

"The choreography is our intellectual property."

"Dance can be copyrighted," he said. "Mia looked into it."

"Glad Mia can google. But that only works if you'd already copyrighted the dance beforehand, and you didn't. I read my contract. I'm not a moron."

"You have twenty-four hours to have a comprehensive conversation with us. Otherwise, our lawyers will be in touch."

"But we've been trying to schedule a meeting for weeks!"

He hung up before I could finish, but it was a half-hearted slam of the receiver. If anything, he was slightly shaken by his gaffe. Unsure of how bad it really was—of how far was too far.

CHAPTER 38

The dancers wore sneakers to protect their joints from the unforgiving concrete beneath the Berber carpet of the basement, moving full-out as they dodged a column in the middle of the space. Committed and completely present, they were unearthing something within the dance.

With each passing day I grew more nervous that no venue would want us—that all this dedication, sweat, and pain was only an exercise. Still, I worked with the dancers like it was a sure thing. Maybe I knew that if I stopped for just one moment, I would fall apart.

The press continued to roll out. Even though I hadn't done any interviews, some of the dancers had, adding a bit of spice to an otherwise quiet period in the dance world. I had no objections to the publicity, though it added to the pressure I was already feeling.

Regardless of where we ended up, I needed the dance to be as tight as possible. We were close, but something was off. Not with the dancers, but with the way it came together—like a puzzle with a handful of pieces in the wrong spaces. I stripped away the sound and ran sections in random order, watched from the barstool in the corner, pen and notebook in hand. Their minds were as fatigued as their bodies, their emotions rattled by all that had gone down. But they were willing. They wanted to get it right too.

"Mark everything except for partnering," I instructed. If one person marked during the partner section and the other didn't, there would be drops and crashes—career-ending injuries that I didn't need on my conscience. "This is just for my brain. You all are doing great."

They were with me as I struggled through, calling *group, second transition, solo, trio, second transition again, duet, first transition, group again.*

Finally, we settled on the order of the sections and the music pairings. The piece would close with the full group exploding into a finale set to Aretha, or Doechii, or whatever loud, familiar song moved us most to our collective core by showtime.

Jade's section was the only one where the music was unclear. We stayed late in the basement one evening, at her request, to work through different options—everything from Jason's compositions to ferocious rap verses. It all sort of worked, but nothing felt perfect. I sat thinking back to those early days in the studio. Thought back to my early days in every studio, let my memory take me as far back as it could.

"Can we try something weird and possibly a little silly?" I asked.

"I'm totally here for weird," said Jade—exhausted, sweaty, eager. "And maybe even silly. Depending on the flavor."

I pulled out my phone and searched for something. To my surprise, I found it.

"This time, do it as slowly as you possibly can," I said. "Jumps and turns can be quick, but the rest, really milk it. Hold the pauses forever, painfully long."

Jade nodded.

The crack of the audio rang through the silence of the basement. An inhale came through at the start of the track, and Jade began to move, circling her foot along the floor and stepping onto it as a melodic moan came through the speakers. Her movement was supple and raw against the lyrics, sweet and powerful at once—haunting without backing music.

It sounded like a different song stripped down this way—a poetic personal essay about obstacles and loss, perseverance and hope. It looked like a different dance too. Jade moved, the somber stillnesses eerie against the boom of Whitney's voice. She froze, her leg bent behind her, her arms draped over her head, her eyes closed.

'Cause your love is my love.

Her body pressed through the choreography, whipping around itself, flying and falling, occasionally catching the wave of lyrics perfectly, other times resisting them. The chorus returned at a moment of pause, and Jade crouched on the floor, her fingers pressed into the carpet like she was ready to pounce, tears streaking her cheeks.

It would take an eternity to break us.

As Jade danced, the tears rolled, but she only danced more deeply. She leaped higher, her arms flung behind her. Each turn got an extra rotation.

When the solo finished, just shy of the end of the track, Jade crumpled onto the floor, sobbing. Lying down beside her, I asked if I could touch her back, and she said *yes*. I asked if she wanted to be held, and she said *yes*. I pulled her in close—such a small, delicate thing.

CHAPTER 39

BAM wanted us. Josefina was moving from publicity to the programming team and had convinced the artistic director to give me their small black box theater for the first week in June, just a week after the original show date.

"This is going to be big," Josefina said. "Full circle."

She'd known me when I was practically an infant. The twenty-two-year-old who'd walked into the nonprofit offices on that first day in slacks, a blazer, and sensible heels—like a middle-aged real estate agent. She'd known me when I worked late Friday nights, finalizing photo approvals with prickly company managers, finishing weekend press-ticket requests, and tying up loose ends. She'd known me when I ate rice and veggies from an old yogurt container every day for lunch, desperately awaiting an email announcing leftover pizza or sandwiches in the kitchen.

"You deserve this," she said. "That Briar House bullshit, totally unfair. This is meant for you."

Talking to Josefina made me nostalgic for before times. For Eli. What if I could go back to my full-time job, to my status as an unknown choreographer showing at crumbling outer-borough venues? Would it be worth it for the comforts and consistency I'd known with him? Picnics in Prospect Park, long breakfasts together on Sunday mornings, reading side by side at night? A life I'd loved, in most ways.

"Don't be gross," I said aloud, with a shake of my head. "Don't be an idiot."

Dahlia had recommended a handful of attorneys—for the divorce and the potential Briar House lawsuit—so I reviewed their websites. In another time, I'd have panicked about all that loomed. But the worst was behind me. The rest was all paperwork and fees. And perhaps my reputation, if the show bombed. But nothing was life or death.

Jason and his musicians joined us for full run-throughs at the Airbnb the week before the show. Their energy lifted the dancers, and we could make sure things were synced. Amy brought her delicately painted backdrops and new costume ideas—we no longer had access to the Briar House wardrobe manager, but Amy had enlisted Courtney, who was effortlessly chic and knew her way around a sewing machine, to help her craft light, elegant looks from fabric bolts and thrift-store finds.

It was electric seeing it all come together. Jason's compositions and the recorded music, the blocking, the elegant flow of the costumes over the dancers' bodies. The way one element melted into another, and another, and another.

Marcus finally called—two days before I was set to leave for New York. He wanted to do a feature on our departure. But he needed the anonymous source to go on the record. It would give the story its juice.

I pulled Ava aside at the top of the basement stairs. Since the piece had come out, she'd become quieter, focused on sharpening the work rather than putting her stamp on it, even making her way in. Now she wanted to fade into the background.

"How would you feel about talking to Marcus again?" I asked. "On the record this time."

Her eyes shifted. "I don't know. It's too risky."

"What, you think Margot is going to come for you?"

"Not just Margot. It involves so many people. The School of American Ballet. Juilliard. My mother! She called when she found out about the piece. Her friend saw Margot's picture in the paper, asked if that was the lady who used to give me money. She started cursing in Spanish through the phone."

"She should be proud of you!" I said.

"It's not that simple, Layla. What I said *anonymously* has already stripped away opportunities from me. If I go on the record, who knows? It's like everything I've built was a lie. Like I'm only where I am because of Margot. Like I don't exist. Fuck, I'm going to end up in nursing school like my brother. It's what my mom wanted anyway."

"Ava, you'd be a terrible nurse. And trust me, you definitely exist. I have felt your existence, deeply, since you came back. If you speak to Marcus, you'll help to bring the truth to light."

"I'll also end my career. Choreographers and directors will recognize me at every audition. And not in a good way. They won't trust me."

The dance world was full of dirty secrets, and the last thing most leaders wanted was a whistleblower in their midst. Her fears weren't unfounded.

"Maybe you can be a part of something big," I said. "Maybe you can ignite change. People need to be held accountable, don't you think?"

"I don't want to be the face of that," said Ava. "I'm not an activist. I'm not *Jade*. I just want to dance. You and my mom are the only people who know—and she's been going to mass twice a week on my behalf. She's even got me praying again. Insurance, sort of. Besides, what about the other dancers? What'll they say if they find out I knew the whole time? That I was involved."

"Do you care that much what people think, Ava?"

"Layla, be serious. Our entire lives hinge on what people think."

The basement was so thickly protected that none of us heard the storm booming. After rehearsal, I stood on the porch, shielding myself from the rain. Jason quickly stubbed out a cigarette he was smoking with his shoe, like a kid who'd been caught.

"I don't usually smoke," he said. "Just a little stressed."

"You were smoking when we first met."

"Touché. Stressful few months, I guess."

"Does driving calm you?" I asked. "I could use a ride home."

"Come on," he said, tossing me his flannel to cover my head. We ran out, the rain pelting us.

Inside his car we shook like wet dogs. His own music played through the speakers, and he quickly turned it off, then drove up the windy roads in the pouring rain.

"I know this has been a tough process," Jason said. "With all the money stuff coming out."

"'Money stuff.' That's one way to put it."

"Everything, I mean. I'm here if you ever want to talk."

"Thanks. I'm okay at the moment. Between the dancers and friends from home, it's been manageable."

"And Eli."

"Well." I sighed. "Eli died."

"What!"

"I mean, he's dead to me. We split up."

"Holy shit," said Jason. "You can't say that." The patter of the rain on the hood was like acrylic nails on a countertop. "But I'm sorry. That really sucks."

"It does really suck," I said. "But in new and exciting ways every day."

"I get it. My girlfriend and I broke up at Christmas."

"No way!" I said. "I mean, I'm sorry to hear it, but misery loves company."

"We could have drowned our sorrows at the Rusty Rail had we known!"

"We can have a drink at my place?" I said. "Once you drop me off. As long as you'll still be fine on the road?"

"Best idea I've heard all day."

———

We ran through the torrent to my front door. I held his flannel above my head again, the musk of his body cutting through the smell of fresh spring rain.

"I'm going to change," I said, running up the stairs. "I'll bring you down some of Eli's clothes. He left a bunch of stuff here."

I washed up quickly over the bathroom sink, rinsing away the day's sweat, the rainwater. After brushing my teeth and putting on clean leggings and a sweatshirt, I grabbed a pair of Eli's sweats. They still smelled lightly of his fir-and-spice deodorant, still held strands of his smooth hair.

Downstairs, I tossed the clothes at Jason and went into the kitchen for wine and beer—untouched since the fall.

"Nice place," Jason shouted from the living room.

"Thanks," I said. "I can't take credit. Most of the stuff was here when I arrived. Eli got the plants, which probably helped keep me alive."

Jason stepped into the kitchen in the sweats that were a size too small. I handed him one of the beers Eli had left in the refrigerator, then twisted open a bottle of Cabernet Sauvignon.

"To breakups!" Jason said.

"That's bleak," I said. "To new beginnings?"

"Sure, to new beginnings!" he repeated.

We clinked, drank.

"I have a couple of auditions coming up in the summer. There's a small ensemble in New York, so I'll let you know when I'm there. Philadelphia Orchestra is the big one."

"Look at you!" I said, jealous that his future was starting to peek at him from behind the curtains of this project.

There hadn't been a chance for me to get there. To think beyond my current circumstances. I had applied for a couple of programs in the fall, before everything had started closing in, but all the big ones had fallen off my radar, their deadlines now months behind me. We were weeks away from the end, and I had no idea what was next.

The sky darkened, and the rain kept on.

"Hopefully it'll ease up soon," said Jason. "I can get out of your hair and leave you to your evening."

"Don't be silly. The rain is clearly making a scene out there. Just chill."

We relaxed. I made pasta and laughed at the way Jason swirled it into a spoon, like he'd learned to eat spaghetti from cartoons. He claimed it was efficient. I kicked him beneath the table, and he brushed my leg with his foot. I'd forgotten about this feeling. That brief, charged period of time when anything at all can happen if you let it.

He had seconds and I did too, my appetite strong. I took away his spoon, and he marveled that he was able to eat without it.

The rain eased. Jason thanked me for letting him hide out, for feeding him. He grabbed his things.

"You can stay if you want," I said.

He looked at me, his face serious.

"It's really dark and still drizzling. Besides, you've had a few drinks."

"I'll be fine."

"The couch is comfy. I can bring you pillows and a blanket."

"Okay," he said.

It was just that easy.

I thought I heard him call my name, but when I peeked down from the top of the stairs, he was only walking by with another beer, scrolling on his phone.

For an hour, I lay in bed, listening for a creak on the steps, for the sound of his voice. But there was nothing aside from the eventual hum of his snoring.

There was a pleasant pounding in my chest. A drumbeat that told me I was alive. That I could feel again. All the way up here in this isolated town, there was possibility. The world was vast. There were so many places. So many people I hadn't yet met. So many experiences left—things I couldn't even imagine.

CHAPTER 40

Fort Greene had changed so much over the years—some streets were lined with classic brownstones and quaint cafés, but now many views were blocked by half-empty high-rises with generic ground-floor restaurants. Tech bros had infiltrated, pushing lifetime residents deeper into Brooklyn, out into the far reaches of Queens or the Bronx, or out of the city altogether.

Rather than stay at the studio BAM offered blocks from the theater and feel depressed about a neighborhood that wasn't even mine to mourn, I booked a hotel room. My mother was flying in for the show, and we both loved the sterile luxury of hotels. We deserved a treat.

The room was wonderfully clean and sleek with robes and high-end products, endless cable options and overpriced room service. I wanted to iron and steam things for no reason, to use the hair dryer and look up the local recommendations in the place where I'd lived for a decade. But Taylor called just before my scheduled interview with Marcus.

"Marcus reached out to me about the anonymous source," they said.

"He asked me too, but the source didn't want to be identified."

Whether Taylor knew about Ava, I couldn't be sure, but I assumed they'd started to put the pieces together.

"He tried a bunch of people," said Taylor. "I told him I had nothing aside from what he already knew. No way was the board going to get involved in this. But he must have called the front desk at just the right moment. He got Mia."

"Okay?"

"She mentioned Rebecca."

"What about Rebecca?"

"She was here last year. Didn't you know?"

"I'm sure she didn't realize what was going on," I said.

Taylor paused. "She's Rebecca Allen."

"I know."

"Rebecca *Allen,* Layla. She's Bippy's daughter."

"Hmm," I sighed. And then again and again, until they were like hiccups or hysterical laughter. "Hmm hmm hmm hmm hmm."

"It's going to be in the piece," they said. "I wanted to tell you ahead of time."

"What am I supposed to do with this? The dancers get here tomorrow, we're about to tech, then we have dress rehearsal the next day."

"I'm only the messenger. And for what it's worth, they're estranged. She apparently stopped speaking to her parents after January Sixth."

"Jesus, her parents were at the Insurrection?"

"I doubt it. I can't imagine they'd want to be around that many working-class people. It may have just felt like the right time?"

"Wow," I said. "Perfect. Thank you for this."

"I just wanted to tell you first. Don't be mad!"

"You could have told me months ago! You said you didn't know any of this."

"I *didn't* know! I'm just learning this too. Apparently, Mia knew more than me this whole fucking time, which feels great."

"Okay, well, Marcus is calling me, so—"

"So—"

"Bye."

"Hi, Marcus," I said, prepared for the worst. I hoped he couldn't hear how newly shaken I was. But he wanted to know how I felt about being at BAM—if it felt like a homecoming. This couldn't be his endgame. I wanted him to cut to the chase.

"Listen," I said, "I know you got some info from the assistant at Briar House."

"There was one person who didn't want to give a comment on record, but they've seen some communication. They've facilitated some activity. They know of some interesting connections. In the end, they unintentionally gave several comments."

"I know you can't tell me too much at this point. I guess I'm just wondering if you know where in Brooklyn I can get some Valium before your story comes out."

He chuckled. "It's not that bad, Layla. The anticipation is always the worst part."

"I used to believe that."

"I mean it. I shouldn't tell you this, but trust me. You have nothing to worry about. I wouldn't do that to you."

Said the reporter. Said the husband. Said the mother.

"Anyway," he continued, "how are you feeling about premiering at BAM? About coming home?"

That evening, a new Vermont number flashed on my phone screen. That heart-dropping feeling returned. I lay flat on the bed to keep myself intact until the ringing stopped. Until I knew if it was Harold, or his team of cutthroat lawyers, or a Green Mountain Man out to take me down.

The voicemail played.

"Hi, dear. It's Margot. Home phone. Sorry about all this mess. They're making a mountain out of a molehill, the press. The institute. The board! Harold's quite high on his horse. I hear you're at BAM, which is fabulous. Tell Michael I say hello."

There was a pause. I paced around the room.

"I also wanted to check in and see how you're doing. Dr. Klein said you never reached out. I hope you found someone good and that you, that everyone, is healthy."

I hadn't thought about the baby in nearly a week—the longest stretch so far—had nearly forgotten Margot had known. That section of pain had been cordoned off.

What a strange cocktail for her to serve: compassion and passive aggression, warmth and a quietly threatening chill. It was unclear what Margot really wanted, how she really felt. If all this mess was her fault, the board's, the institute's, or all three. I could call her back, tug at her, see what was really going on. But I was done looking back. I had to move forward.

I dialed Rebecca.

She picked up on the first ring.

"Hi," she said. "I just got off the phone with Taylor."

"Mm-hmm," I said.

"I didn't do this on purpose. I don't talk to my parents, and I don't believe in anything they stand for. I just wanted to dance."

I laughed.

"Please don't tell the other dancers."

"The story comes out this week, Rebecca," I said.

"I know, but," she sighed. "I'm so sorry."

"Don't worry about coming to New York with the rest of the dancers tomorrow," I said.

"What? Layla. That's not fair! I shouldn't be punished for my parents' crimes."

"You had months to say something! Everything could have been different had you just told the truth."

She whimpered, defended her choices. Tried to explain that she was *doing the work.*

"Best of luck to you, Becky."

I dropped my phone on the bed and threw my arm over my face to block out the light through the curtains. Not a minute had passed before I heard the click of the key card at the door and that exasperated sigh I'd known all my life.

My mother and I ordered room service and watched old movies on her bed. I picked from the french fries that came with her burger, and she let my salmon kale salad be. She unwrapped a slice of pound cake she'd flown up from St. Louis, and we shared it. She didn't ask me about anything. She said I seemed tired. Grown. I told her everything was hard. Everything was exhausting. She kissed my forehead. She knew.

CHAPTER 41

On the Monday before opening, I met Josefina and Michael Caspin at BAM. My time in the administrative offices would be quick—lingering too long would result in catch-up conversations that would eat up my whole day and require more personal explanations than I was ready for. Last everyone knew, Eli and I were happily married.

Still, it felt good to sit in Michael's office, where I'd been only a handful of times. His chairs were big, ugly leather things, too comfortable for productivity unless you were an old man whose sole job was to sit and ponder. Even Michael had to do more than that. I sank into mine as Josefina, who sat beside me—her long dark hair streaked with gorgeous new grays, her lips their signature red—passed me the paperwork.

We chatted for a few minutes, and I was grateful that there wasn't a Keurig in sight. Michael was a strict patron of the coffee shop down the block that slung overpriced cortados and cold brews strong enough to kill a small mammal.

My show had a four-night run, and sales were decent so far. The news had piqued people's interest. The Briar House situation had made me rethink everything I'd ever known about myself, about the dance world.

And so I'd mentioned an idea to Josefina the week prior that I brought up again now.

"I'd love to do a Black Out performance," I said, pushing myself up in my seat. Making myself taller, bigger. I forced myself to look Michael in the eye. "Just one show with discounted tickets, only for Black ticket buyers. I think it'll open the door to dance for a lot of new people."

"I don't know if that's legal," said Michael. "Could we run into discrimination issues?"

"Other theaters have done it," said Josefina before I even had a chance to open my mouth. "I love the idea."

"Well, Josefina, if you can figure it out with marketing and the box office, I'm fine with it."

"I really appreciate it, Michael," I said. "And the wider community will too. Just think of it as a little sprinkle of reparations."

Josefina and I were in the hallway, out of earshot of the rest of the staff, when she asked me about Eli.

"You two used to be such little nerds running out on coffee breaks, hanging out in the copy room like no one knew what was going on."

"You knew?" I said, nostalgic for those simpler times. For the smell of warm paper.

"Girl." She faced me. "You turned bright red whenever he came by your desk. Came back from your breaks with this goofy smile on your face."

"We thought we were hiding something."

"It was clear you were hooking up."

"Not at work! We'd go on walks to get yogurt from the market by the park."

Josefina looked disappointed.

"Yogurt? I don't understand your generation," she said, shaking her head. "In my day, we used to fuck in the supply closet!"

"I was scared of getting fired for printing more than the suggested daily allotment. No way was I going to even kiss anyone on the premises. But anyway, no more yogurt. Definitely no sex. The asshole left me."

Josefina's face fell. She'd watched us since the beginning. She was shocked. She was sorry. She didn't know what to say.

"There's not much that needs to be said," I assured her. "Just one of life's curveballs."

"This is wild," Josefina said. "I mean the split, sure, but the instigation—unbelievable. You were always too good for him. Wasn't he really into fedoras for a while?"

"He did have a short-lived fedora phase! Nipped that one in the bud."

"Fuck that guy. Not even worth our breath. Truly. Promise you'll let me know if you need anything." She raised her eyebrows. "I mean it. Anything truly means anything."

She pulled me in. "I missed you."

"I missed you too," I said. It was true, I just hadn't realized. Sure, work was work. But work was life too.

One last time, I walked those familiar hallways, passed a dozen offices and corners that awakened memories. Spaces where I had been young and believed that anything was possible. I walked onto the street, a sense of hope rushing in all directions.

The redbrick façade of our apartment building had a classic New York feel, now that I was really taking it in. Our unit was in the back, our windows facing the opposite street. I almost expected Eli to appear—in a stranger's window, in the lobby, anywhere. Thank god he didn't.

I wandered the neighborhood, soaking in the early evening, passing the bodega where Eli and I had gotten late-night sandwiches, the boutique where we bought expensive handmade candles. As cafés switched out coffee mugs for wineglasses, I wondered if I'd ever walk this neighborhood and not think of him. It might take time, but the more I walked alone, the better the chances were I'd gain a different understanding of the neighborhood. Of the world. Soon, I'd have months' worth of memories without him. Then years'. Maybe one day, our relationship would feel like a different lifetime.

But it was fresh still. I grabbed my phone and dialed.

"I'm in town. We should talk."

"Hey!" he said. "It's good to hear from you. Why don't you come to the apartment tonight? I'm on my way home from work. I'll swing by the store and get some stuff for dinner."

As though it were that simple.

"Maybe we can get a coffee or something tomorrow."

"I don't mind making dinner."

"I'd rather just have a chat out somewhere."

"Someone in my therapist's office does couples therapy. We could try that."

"You're going to therapy?"

A suggestion of mine he'd ignored for so long.

"Where are you staying?" he asked. "Stay here."

"I'm staying at the Wymore. I have my show at BAM this week."

"You have a show at BAM? Layla, why didn't you tell me? That's amazing!"

There was no way he didn't know. He still had friends there. If random internet people knew I was at BAM—liking their announcements, following me, sharing my posts, offering their encouragement—surely Eli knew too.

"Things are coming together even faster than you thought they would. I'm so proud of you."

"Thanks. Well, let me know if you're free tomorrow," I said. I hung up quickly so that I wouldn't say something I regretted—like I couldn't have done it without him.

I walked over to Dahlia's and ran into Kofi in the lobby. I was exhausted but relieved to see him. We walked up together, and Dahlia met us on her floor looking unusually cheery.

"Look at that face!" I said. "Tell me something good."

Dahlia smirked, her hands pressed against the band of her jeans.

"Guess who's having a baby?"

It wasn't just that Dahlia's relationship with the guy she'd been seeing for the past few years had waxed and waned with the moon. It wasn't that Kevin had barely spent any time with us, or that Dahlia was bisexual and had tended toward women in the past. It wasn't that she'd been the president of Feminist Majority and had led safe-sex workshops for years. It was that I'd never seen her so much as smile at a child. She *cared* about them—her work demanded it—but she didn't seem to *like* them. I waved at toddlers on the subway, picked up any child that was placed in front of me. Dahlia had always been indifferent. But now she was elated.

"I'm sorry," Dahlia said as Kofi grabbed champagne flutes. "I wasn't sure how or when to tell you. I wasn't sure how you'd feel."

"I'm happy for you! Really. I just can't believe you're having a baby with Kevin from Hinge!"

"We'll see how it goes. With Kevin, I mean. I'm pretty jazzed about the baby."

She was so cool and calm about what was a relatively complicated scenario.

"Doesn't he live in Bushwick?" I asked. "Long-distance co-parenting?"

"Bushwick?" said Kofi. "Where will you store the baby, Bed-Stuy?"

"That *would* be the midpoint," I said.

"Well, this studio is too small, so I'll, *we'll,* move in there. At least to start. His place is pretty great. Two bedrooms, high ceilings."

"Oh my god, you're having a baby *and* you're moving?" said Kofi.

"Relax," said Dahlia. "I'm keeping this place. Who knows what's going to happen with Kevin. But we figured we'd try out this *partner* thing for a little while at least."

"Cheers to being a chill, progressive mom," I said, popping the bottle of cava. I poured her just a splash, but she grabbed the bottle, filled her flute a bit more after confirming the number of ounces allowed.

We wouldn't discuss what I'd planned on—how to get my things from Eli, make sure the BAM opening went smoothly, and not get sued by Briar House. Those things were important, but nothing is bigger than a baby.

Dahlia folded her legs under herself, and I thought of Josefina. She and her partner had tried for five years. She'd spent more on IVF treatments that hadn't worked than I'd ever earned in a year. They broke up. Josefina had taken a six-month leave of absence to be with her family in Colombia. To mourn all she'd lost. All she might never have. She seemed clearer when she returned, but not quite the same. A shift I understood.

Kofi asked if I was all right. I assured him I was.

"Dahlia and I are like ships in the night, that's all."

As soon as I left the world of the pregnant and coupled, she joined it. It would have been nice to be there together, to raise our children side by side, spread out a blanket in the park and chill with the guys while the kids ran wild. It would have been a dream.

But Dahlia deserved nothing more than joy and celebration. So I poured myself another glass, enjoying it now that I could. It was after my third glass, as Kofi and Dahlia chattered on, that I grew hot. I went to the bathroom and locked the door.

The due date would have been near. A week away. I sat on the toilet and let the tears rush for just a minute—a popcorn shower. Kofi and Dahlia laughed in the living room. I did my best to keep it down. This was her night.

In movies, people splashed their faces with cold water, but that always seemed dramatic. A cool washcloth would do the trick. I placed it on my neck, took deep breaths, felt my feet on the floor, my hands on my thighs. I was safe and whole.

I squeezed in between Kofi and Dahlia on the couch.

"Everything is changing so fast," said Kofi, holding me.

"Too fast," I said. "First your Invisalign, Kofi, and now this."

He kissed me on the cheek, then smiled his big, plastic smile.

"All our worlds are completely different than they were at this time last year," I said. "I don't even know if I'm coming back to the city. I can't afford it on my own. I am *not* living with roommates again. But I'm also not moving back to Missouri with my mom. That would definitely send me off the deep end. I just. I don't know what to do."

"Why don't you stay here?" said Dahlia. "When I move into Kevin's place."

"That could be an option, I guess. Though I don't really like showering in the kitchen."

"Speaking of kitchens," said Kofi, "what produce is your baby?"

"It's an avocado now."

"Yum!" I said.

"They grow so quickly. Soon he'll be an artichoke."

"What size even is that?" said Kofi. "I've only ever had it in dip."

"It's like this," I said, holding my hands apart. "I had it whole at a restaurant but didn't really know what parts to eat. Was kind of like chewing on leaves."

"It'll be a grapefruit a little while after that."

"Ick," said Kofi. "I hate grapefruit."

Dahlia looked offended.

"It's not like your baby is going to taste like a grapefruit," said Kofi. "I just don't get why people love them so much. Grapefruits, not babies."

"But you love palomas," I said to Kofi.

"Palomas are alcohol. My mom was on a grapefruit diet for like two years when I was a kid. It was depressing."

"I bet that's why you hate them," I said.

"So that's all about the baby?" said Dahlia.

We turned to her.

"Listen," said Kofi. "My sister has two kids. There will come a time when you wish you had the opportunity to talk nonsensically about fruit with your friends for five straight minutes."

"Thanks, Kofi. I can't wait for the day when I don't care about my baby."

"You'll always care about your baby!" Kofi said.

I slid my head down to Dahlia's stomach and held her around the waist, pressing my ear close, listening for the life inside.

"*We'll* always care about your baby," I said. "We care about your baby now, and we'll care about it when it's the size of a hundred avocados."

CHAPTER 42

The opening was in two days. The dancers had just arrived from Vermont, and I couldn't let them hear about Rebecca's family from the *Times*. As they made their way into the backstage area at BAM—navigating around the giant cherry picker beside the stage door, wooden stools and scattered benches, ink-marked folding tables cluttered with porkpie hats and costume jewelry—I waved them over to the wings.

They gasped. They shouted. They ran through the wings, lapping the stage, rolling on its freshly Marleyed floor. I waited patiently while they got it all out.

No surprise, Ava was ready to go when I asked her to step in.

"I think I may just be a size smaller than Rebecca," she said later that morning, grabbing her costume from the rack Amy had just rolled in.

"Of course you are," I said.

"Nothing a few pins won't fix."

"I'll get to you after I finish with Courtney," said Amy, making alterations based on what she'd learned from a YouTube video.

Terrell leaned against the exposed brick wall.

"You really waited it out, girl. Over there taking notes for months and stayed snatched too. I know that's right!"

Ava let a nervous smile peek through. She was finally part of the group. It was possible she'd known about Rebecca, but she clearly hadn't anticipated the extent of the fallout. The two of them weren't so different. They craved an easy world—a world in which they could simply dance, despite where they came from and what people expected of them.

Amy stepped back to look at her work.

"I think this is good, Courtney," she said.

Courtney did a light twerk, the fabric flowing, somehow, elegantly. Courtney, who on the first day had arrived in a leotard and tights. Courtney, who'd spent her life studying ballet in Boston. Courtney, who had never been in the company of more than one other Black dancer at a time.

"Yeah," she said, one hand on the ground, the other on her butt, "this is perfect."

"Ava," said Amy, "you're up."

"It's a little tight in the bust and loose in the waist," Ava said, twisting her top.

Amy fidgeted with the pins while I took them all in—dancing, laughing, stepping into something new.

There was only one day for tech and another for dress, thanks to a rental that had only loaded out of the theater the day before. During tech rehearsal, I sat in the theater seat where I'd sat many times over the years, two rows behind photographers there for a photo call, always ready to yank one back from the director's sight line, ready to ask the dancers to hold their bow lineup so that the photographers could ID everyone—no cases of mistaken identity in the career-altering reviews to come.

This was the least majestic of BAM's three theaters—not the grand Opera House with its ornate molding and glittering lights, or the romantically rustic Harvey that had welcomed nearly every major Shakespearean from the last century, but the more intimate Fishman black box space. Sleek and flexible, two hundred and fifty seats.

Perhaps this was what kept the overwhelm and intimidation at bay. I'd always preferred baby steps to big leaps. I was familiar with the space, the way sound echoed. I had called in my own lighting designer—a friend of Kofi's who knew how to light dark skin and was willing to do it in exchange for an additional BAM credit on her résumé. She would make the dancers shine, certainly better than whoever Briar House had, who'd probably never conceptualized Black people onstage.

Finally, now, with all of these elements—choreography, costumes, music, lighting, design, a home—the piece felt whole.

Eli met me at a buzzy coffee shop in Clinton Hill—it had replaced a soul food restaurant during my time away. It was filled with the most beautiful multiethnic mix of people that could fit into seven hundred square feet—all tattoos, shag haircuts, and vintage jumpsuits.

"You look good," he said.

I wondered if he meant it. I hoped so, despite myself.

"You too," I said. He did—neatly trimmed, clean and casual. "I figured we should start figuring things out before too long. Get the ball rolling on the divorce."

He squinted. A face of condescension and skepticism. He told me I was wrong, I was still hurt. He reminded me of everything that I'd already reminded myself of. How much easier things would be if we just tried again. But I'd arrived there first, weeks ago, and was no longer susceptible to nostalgia. He hadn't thought anything through and was coasting on delusions.

"I'll start filing after the show," I said, finishing my coffee. "We can do uncontested, since we don't have any major assets. It'll be quicker and cheaper that way."

He held his mug so tight I thought he might crush the ceramic. Bleed and bleed.

I pulled out my credit card.

"This is on me."

CHAPTER 43

Marcus's feature was tucked into the second page of the arts section of *The New York Times*. It further confirmed the connection between Briar House and the Allens, the way things had fallen to pieces, the covert infiltration. A finance department composed entirely of contractors, feigned ignorance from the institute, a community pleased with productions that reflected what they wanted to see. A new anonymous source, Mia, had detailed the NDA Margot had her sign when she started (a waste, it turned out). The way Margot had strategically outsourced certain accounting work to keep things outside of the organization.

While Marcus hadn't spoken to Rebecca, Mia had given him all he'd needed. Rebecca was the "estranged" daughter of Bippy Allen and had been paid twice as much as the other dancers—more, even, than me. Marcus had gotten ahold of a recent ballet school colleague of Rebecca's, who confirmed that she had been called back to Briar House after our first rehearsal day to quell threats from the Green Mountain Men. Bippy and her husband promised to keep the group quiet if Margot gave their daughter one more gig—enough to beef up her dance résumé and get her onto larger stages. To give Bippy something to brag about.

Those early days—the public radio story, Margot's delay, Ava's sudden departure followed by Rebecca's immediate arrival. It all seemed so obvious now.

The piece went on to detail the work the dancers and I had done since leaving Briar House, the way the entire group had worn every hat in order to spread the word about what was happening and pull things together, even if it meant losing it all.

And then there were my words.

I've always said that I don't create work about race, and nothing has changed. I believe artists should create in whatever ways inspire them and feel true to their vision. Still, there's no denying I'm a Black woman, a minority in this field. So maybe I am thinking about my race more in this context and asking more questions of myself and those around me. How can I change the systems? How can I open pathways to dance for more people like me? I don't have all the answers just yet, and maybe I never will. But I'm thinking. I'm trying.

There was a line about the twenty-dollar Black Out matinee that was now sold out.

Marcus had spoken not only to Mia and me, but also Kofi and Jade. *She's able to extract something from deep within each dancer,* said Jade. *Something we didn't even know was there. That's her gift.* This praise and faith in me kept me upright. So much had gone wrong over the past nine months, but it was these words that kept me going. The voices that mattered most.

The backstage door swung open.

"Happy opening!" my mother said. She'd buttered up the security guards with cakes and cookies yesterday, and they no longer followed the protocol that dictated I had to come sign her in.

"Did you see you're in *Essence*?" she said, holding up her phone. "Bria sent it to me."

"You know it's only online," I said, "not in the magazine."

The two of us used to sit in the salon decades ago, holding the magazine as our scalps burned with relaxer, carcinogens seeping in, sores crisping under the hood. Becoming beautiful. Nothing would ever be bigger for her than *Essence*.

"People only go on the Web now anyway," she said. "It's amazing. You're a real hotshot!"

She kissed me on the forehead.

The dancers filed in, wishing me a happy opening and saying hello to my mother. She'd been sitting in on rehearsals, pestering me with her questions, but also caring for me in a way only she could.

"Good morning, Mrs. Smart!" said Terrell, hugging my mother as though he'd known her forever.

It had never felt strange to hear her called Mrs. Smart until now. My father, her husband, had left her thirty years ago, yet she still clung to the name, didn't think twice. I was grateful I hadn't taken Eli's. Johnston. I'd never even imagined that name as mine—not even in my most lovestruck early days. It simply didn't suit me. Now I wished I had my mother's maiden name. That we both did. Monroe. Less piercing than Smart, but something of our own. Almost. There were, of course, names connected to me that I'd never know—names from hundreds of years ago, thousands of miles away. Names that had been ripped away, forgotten.

My mother was showing everyone the *Essence* piece, but I worried about where this would lead.

"There's going to be a lot of press coming out in the next few days," I said. Their eyes were all on me, and I felt the same nerves that had rattled me on that first day in the studio. "Please don't read anything other than, I don't know, Jade's tips in Refinery29 for staying healthy on a budget."

"You can make your own oat milk with just oats and water!" she said.

"Hard pass," said Terrell.

"Dancer spotlights are great, but anything else—just avoid it until after the run."

They nodded. Terrell and Courtney hadn't seen the *New York Times* feature. Of course Jade had. She was in it. But I knew she'd keep mum.

They made their way to the stage, where Courtney began to lead the warm-up. I leaned into Ava as she followed the others, waved her toward me.

"Did Margot force you to leave?" I asked. "On that first day. Did she give you an out or did she push you out?"

"I—I don't know."

Her eyes darted around.

"I think she let me leave. That's what it felt like. Like she was allowing me to go if I wanted to."

She shook out her wrists, let her head fall. I pulled her in, rubbed circles on her back.

"I'm sorry," I said. Because someone owed her an apology. It might as well be me.

CHAPTER 44

In the hotel room, my mother stood beside me, a black knee-length dress hanging from her soft, lived-in body. A bob wig sat snugly on her head, looking just right.

"Hot tamale," she said as I adjusted the strap of my white silk pants set with delicate beading around the hems. I wore simple gold jewelry and had untwisted my hair so the curls sprang boldly around my face. I'd always straightened my hair on special occasions, but things were different now. My hair might as well be too.

"This time next year, we'll be headed to Broadway," she said.

She kissed me, leaving a maroon stain from her beauty-supply lipstick on my cheek. It was the same shade she'd worn since I was a girl.

After circling up with the dancers backstage—holding hands, syncing our breath, saying an almost-prayer for this, the night we'd been building toward for so long—I squeezed between Josefina and my mother, who sat in the orchestra holding their programs. I looked down at mine, high at the sight of my name in that distinct typeface I'd seen all those years. All my favorite companies had appeared in this print.

"Revival" by Layla Smart and Dancers

The sound dropped from my ears as the piece began and the lights lowered. My head and body felt light—like I might float above the audience and watch it like a ghost. Or an angel. The curtain went up.

Jade stood center stage, a spotlight on her, smiling softly. The musicians were in the corner, in shadow. Jade's eyes took in the audience, and she let out the smallest laugh, unrehearsed, as her hands gestured near her body in rhythm with the steady chime of the piano keys, the rest of her body still. Until her hip jutted out for just a moment, her gestures growing, so that it wasn't just her hands now but her arms, swinging, swimming, bending, and dropping in quick sync with the chords. Her hip jutted again, and then her opposite knee bent, a sudden snap that collapsed the depth of her movement. Now she moved in levels, hands, arms, shoulders, neck, back, hips, knees, feet. Everything elegantly gliding, in turns jerky and delicate, on fast-forward. She stopped at the very moment the music picked up, the ensemble coming in, and the full lights rising to reveal Courtney and Terrell moving just behind her—so close it seemed impossible that they hadn't been visible a moment ago. Their movements were explosions of hers—what were once arm-swings now lifted the dancers into the air, then down to the earth, where they held the landing for a moment before swiveling into a turn that took them to the ground, never a moment of discrepancy between them. Jade joined back in, the three of them thrusting their bodies through the space, rotating positions as the piano dropped, leaving nothing but drums as they danced harder, their breath now another instrument in the score. They all made their way to the back of the stage, then ran forward, stopping just before arriving at the edge to tip back into a smooth roll that landed them on their knees at the moment the musicians stopped. It was quiet for a moment, the dancers staring into the audience, the audience staring back. Everyone waiting. Waiting. And then a rupture of applause before the blackout.

When the lights came up, Ava and Terrell stood side by side. Terrell curved around her, holding her waist, his body floating effortlessly off the floor as she lifted him, spinning slowly before letting him go, so that he glided through the air, landing in a quiet roll. She moved above as he did below, sweeping arms, gentle leaps, until they were back together again. Terrell scooped Ava up by her hips, their faces close, swung her up, then back, so that her legs then wrapped around his waist, where they remained for a moment before he let her go, catching the hook of her arm just in the nick of time, taking her for an effortless spin. They went on like this, a magnetic force always pulling them back together. Like it was the last time they'd see each other—like nothing mattered more.

I wasn't religious, but something like the holy spirit took over me. When the theater went dark again, the crowd still rowdily clapping, I crawled over my mother to stand in the back, near the doors, where no one could see me move.

Jade's solo began, and I stood still, watched as her dark body swam in bright light, moving through the silence—during dress rehearsal she determined that this had been the issue all along. We'd been seeking music, but the solo wanted no sound at all. The choreography was all hers, and tonight it was different from what she'd danced in the basement—the sprung floor allowed her leaps to bound, the width of the stage let her grapevine the movement, expand horizontally, stretching her drags and turns in all directions. It had felt so contained before, but now she was bursting out, her dynamism all the more striking when juxtaposed against unexpected freezes, where not so much as a finger twitched. I was too far away to look directly into her eyes, but even from the back of the house I could feel her tears. The silence was deafening—I could have heard a joint creak, an eye blink. Jade's movements intensified, her pauses more agonizing. She let out the same small, sad sounds that had escaped her lips that day in the basement. A glorious release.

Individual dancers reentered the stage, repeating phrases they'd done before, but reversed, inverted, retrograded—until nothing looked the same. Each dancer was the star of their own universe, where gravity and time and space operated on a different plane. The musicians' playing swelled as the complete group of dancers filled the space and everything snapped to black with a final, vicious violin stroke.

Now they were at the finale. The musicians gently complemented the pulsing recording that came through the speakers as the energy picked up, the dancers shouting at one another, egging one another on. The jumps were buoyant, the floor work earthy and rooted, the leaps like bursts of joy. I found myself moving fully now and couldn't keep from shouting with them. As the audience clapped and cheered along—parents and friends letting out joyful shouts and whistles—I ran into the lobby and around to the backstage door. I arrived at the wings as Ava bounded off Terrell's back and through the air, landing in Courtney's arms just in time to be swung around and sent off into the other wing.

"Yes!" I screamed from the sidelines, thrilled at the perfection of the moment. Of all these moments strung together.

Jade and Courtney caught my eye as they neared the final moments of the piece.

"Come on!" shouted Jade from the stage, waving for me to join in.

Before I had time to second-guess myself, I kicked off my shoes and was onstage with them, dancing under the heat of the stage lights. The audience clapped and hollered as we leaped to one side of the stage, then slid to the floor, crawled forward, and bounded up to standing. The movement was simple now, and so I wove through the dancers, making eye contact with each one. My body was impermeable and light.

Five and a six, hold, and eight, we spun, then held for a beat before hinging into a ninety-degree tilt, their legs pointed skyward, mine as far as it would go. The beat rolled—a soulful track punctuated by Jason's band—and we picked up our knees, jumped from side to side, slid nearly down to split, before stopping, just as our hips hovered above the floor, then melted into a side roll. We pushed ourselves up, and I sighed at the rush of air on my skin. We ran, jumped, spun, kicked. We shouted for one another through it all and slipped into a light groove as the music neared its end, as the lights faded, the curtain fell.

In the darkness, I opened my arms and let the dancers fall into me, sweating on me.

The dancers ran to their places for bows, and I ran to the wings. They held hands, bent at the waist, moved forward and back in the way we'd rehearsed, before they gestured toward me. Only then, stepping back onto the stage as myself, not as Layla the Dancer, did I feel the wave of embarrassment that should have kept me in my seat minutes before. But it faded as I clasped the dancers' hands and the crowd rose.

Jason and his musicians clumsily joined us for a bow. Amy came out from the wings too. The audience was on their feet, a full house, cheering. All those real people, just for us. We stood onstage, fingers intertwined, arms up, and in one motion, we bent. Once, twice, three times. *Thank you, thank you, thank you.*

If Kofi's reception had been a who's who of the New York performance world, mine was more of a who's that? The lower lobby was filled with families and friends of the dancers, along with younger dance writers, bookers from a few presenting organizations, and BAM regulars. Josefina introduced me to people, and I smiled, answered their questions, tried to be competent and charming, drained though I was.

Finally, my friends grabbed me. Kofi knew what it was like, that I physically needed to be stopped, slowed, brought back to a human state.

"Nice choice with the white," he said, taking in the sweat and stains that covered my outfit. "Very matrimonial."

"I didn't think I was going to go up there. Obviously." I grabbed a passing glass of seltzer and dipped a napkin into it, dabbing at one of many spots.

Michael walked over, hugged Kofi, then me. He was impressed with the night, the crowd, the work. He had to head home to pack for a flight to Tokyo in the morning, the poor thing, but wanted to talk later in the summer.

Like a splash of cold water, Katherine from the *Times* appeared. She kept it brief.

"Nice work. Shame about all the Briar House nonsense, but good to know the right people in the right places, I suppose!"

"I appreciate it," I said, ignoring her hint at nepotism. She wouldn't ruin my night.

It was midnight when my mother and I crawled into our adjacent beds. I was reaching for the bedside light switch when my mother spoke.

"Chickadee." She paused. "I'm so sorry."

"For what?"

"For lying to you."

I thought about her phone call with Eli, how angry I'd been.

"Technically it was more betrayal than lying. Convenient omission."

"Oh. That. Yeah, that too. But I'm talking about your dad."

"Why would you bring that up now?"

"I can tell you're still hurt. Now, that's one where I really *did* lie. But I knew you knew, at a certain point. And watching your dance tonight, I thought, *Wow, there it is.* All those feelings from decades ago. Or maybe new feelings mixed with the old. As soon as the curtains went up and that first girl started moving. All jerky and mixed-up. I said, *That's her. That's me. That's what we been feeling.*"

"Mom," I said. But that was it. Before I could say another word, I heard a catch in the back of her throat. My least favorite sound in the world—so distorted and helpless. I crawled into her bed and held her, her body oddly both bigger and smaller than I remembered. As she cried, I rubbed her arm, uncertain if her tears were for the pain she'd felt, the guilt she'd carried, or the fact that she hadn't been held in thirty years.

A part of me didn't know what she was talking about, couldn't determine how anything she'd seen that night connected to my father. But when something is on your mind, bigger than anything else, it's impossible to disconnect it from everything around you.

We both flipped around, and she cradled me like she had so long ago. Maybe this was the thing she'd been craving. The thing we'd both missed.

The pillow was wet with tears. I couldn't be sure which of us they'd come from. At a certain point, it was all the same salt water.

CHAPTER 45

The opening night reviews were lackluster at best. There'd been so much attention on the work after the Briar House fiasco that some of the major critics—who would never have come to the Vermont show—were underwhelmed. Katherine from the *Times* most of all.

She praised the dancers, Jade especially—an *ethereal powerhouse* who *glided through a suite of emotions* during her solo—but deemed the choreography *standard "emerging artist" fare,* the expansive BAM stage underutilized. Never mind the fact that we'd encountered that stage, double the size of Briar House's, just a day before the premiere. She liked Jason's original compositions but found the musical selections overall to be erratic, inconsistent. She pointed out the convenience of my past at BAM, the connections I still maintained there, suggesting that I'd skipped the line. As though I hadn't been working toward this for a decade. *And after the racial tensions exposed by the Briar House debacle, the piece was hardly even interested in the topic. In fact, it was meandering and formless, seemingly about nothing at all.*

These words shouldn't have hurt me, but I'd learned to trust these people, not because they were always right, but because they were the world's guide to the work. Now anyone who read Katherine's review might doubt me. Might pass on seeing the show. Might spend their money on something tried-and-true. Might deny me a future spot in their program, on their stage.

But as the run continued, there were more and more writers who appreciated the piece. Writers for smart dance blogs and Black outlets. They connected with the fragmentation, the frenetic energy, the confusion, the doubt, the celebration. They appreciated the minimalist stage—no set pieces or extravagant lighting, just an abstract backdrop of colors bleeding into one another that took on the shifting tones of the light and simple jewel-toned costumes that flowed and showed the dancers' lines. They were impressed with how the dancers filled the space with their bodies and energy, and their words above all aligned with what I'd wanted—*elegant, explosive, supple, playful.*

One reviewer even likened Jade's solo to *Cry* by Alvin Ailey. Not the triumphant finale that often came to mind when people envisioned the dance—a woman bounding powerfully across the stage as a choir sang, "Right on! Be free!"—but the more pained early sections. *Like the dancer in* Cry, the reviewer said, *Freeman's movement is a marriage of anguish and elegance. While there is something wilder, less polished here, the inspiration is undeniable as she spins like a dervish before springing into the air, then coiling into herself, where she rests, facing away from the audience, like a punishment. A protest.*

I read on, waiting for the other shoe to drop. But it was only praise to the highest degree. I might have wept had my mind not drifted to Margot—she might not have gotten her *Revelations* redux, but it looked like I had a little Ailey in me, after all.

Thankfully, the audiences were with this fresh crop of reviewers. Each performance was transformative. I could feel the held breath of those around me, could see their smiles, their sadness, their total commitment to what was happening before them. Whenever Katherine's words came to mind, I reminded myself that it wasn't about her. It was about this.

As the week went on, more familiar faces appeared. My first New York roommate, Ashley, hired a babysitter and came down from Connecticut with her husband—a squat, balding man, much different from the guys she used to bring home, who seemed to love her very much. College classmates and former BAM colleagues. Though I was wise enough not to go onto the stage after that first night—my opening-night star turn had, in fact, resulted in a mildly pulled hamstring—they still cheered for me when I took the stage during bows, humbled each time.

The night before closing, Bria and Brandon were waiting for me after the show in the lobby.

"Aye! That's my cousin!" Bria shouted from across the way.

"Are you serious?" I said as she ran up to hug me. "You came all the way up just for this?"

"My mama got us standby tickets," said Brandon. "She's watching the kids." Of course—his mother was an airline gate agent.

"That was the best dance show I've ever seen!" said Bria. "Even better than 'Beef. It's What's for Dinner.'"

We fell into each other, laughing, while Brandon tried to figure out what was so funny.

My mother gave Bria a hug.

"You always look so pretty," she said. "Hair always laid so nice."

"We get it," I said. I'd lazily pulled my curls into a messy topknot that my mother hated.

Bria had made a reservation for us at a restaurant near the theater— a new tapas spot on the ground floor of one of the half-empty high-rises. My mother and Brandon complained about the tiny plates while Bria and I shouted over the blaring hip-hop.

"I'm sorry to hear about everything with Eli," she said.

I was grateful she knew. It was painful to relive everything each time someone asked how he was. At one point, I'd considered drafting a press release, just to streamline things.

"I guess maybe it was inevitable," I said, tapping my glass of watery sangria.

"Yeah, he was nice, but also kind of a little bitch." She took her drink down in one gulp. "You need someone mean like you."

"What?" I laughed. "I'm not mean!"

"Yeah, you are!"

The waiter passed, and she mimed pouring to get another pitcher. "You fully pushed me down the stairs when we were kids. And that was after you told me, with a straight face, that I would die first!"

"You did insult my dead dad in the meantime. Besides, I was ten!"

"Exactly," she said. "That fire's been in you for a long time. You tried to tamp it down and it blew up in your face."

The waiter came by with a fresh pitcher. Bria grabbed the empty one and scooped the fruit into her glass as he poured for the rest of us.

"Damn," I said. "You flew all the way up here to drag me, I guess."

"Girl, ain't nobody dragging you. That's your superpower. You don't play."

I blushed. I'd thought of myself as careful and meek for so long, but maybe she was right.

"I been scared of you for years," she said, raising her glass for an unnecessary third round of cheers. "And you know if I was, that fool must have been terrified."

The Black Out show was a Saturday matinee—the audience loud, wild, gorgeous. It was incredible to watch them all flow into the lobby. Couples wearing matching Air Forces. Friends tipsy after brunch, their curls big and bright. Parents holding the hands of their young children. I thought of the first time I'd seen Alvin Ailey American Dance Theater on a special trip with my dance group at ten—how my eyes had grown wide at all those beautiful Black dancers. The most skilled I'd ever seen—then and maybe even still. These kids lived in New York. They probably saw Ailey and Dance Theatre of Harlem, Complexions and Ballet Hispánico all the time. This experience probably wouldn't be for them what that one was for me. But maybe, for just one, it would be.

And after the show, in the lobby, I saw them. The guys from the subway. The day Michael green-lit the idea, I'd found J'avon on Venmo, and after much deliberation about how weird it would be, how much I could afford to pass off with no guarantee any of them would come, sent him forty dollars and a link to the show. And they had come. *My* showtime. They'd covered the difference for the third person on their own and seemed as happy in that lobby as they had on the train. I tried to make my way to them through the post-show crowd, but my eyes lost them. They were gone.

A few minutes later, my phone buzzed. A Venmo notification.

Thank you so much, ma! That was dope.

After the final show, I stayed in the theater once the dancers had left, after the stagehands struck the space, ripping up tape and Marley so that it was bare for whatever came next. There was a closing-night party, but I'd get there when I got there.

Now, in the empty space, I let myself enjoy a bit of peace.

A theater was never as still as in those final moments. Aside from the bodies moving around and through one another—jumping higher than in the studio, because the prospect of being seen brought new appreciation for the space above—there was the lighting designer moving keys up and down the board, the stage manager adjusting her headset and calling cues. There was the wardrobe assistant mending ripped seams, the theater manager ensuring that the stage door was locked, that front of house looked neat. There was the creator who could not keep her legs still, could not keep her hands from gesturing each movement, could not stop her lips from mouthing the choreography. There was the fog that slithered through rays of light—rolls and rolls.

All the while, a loud buzz of electricity went unnoticed because of all the other sound, all the motion. It was so persistent that its presence was as natural as the way a tongue rests between the teeth and roof of the mouth. Nestled. No one noticed the incessant sound until the very end, when the last person was preparing to leave. They flipped the switch and the sound dropped. It was only real once it was gone.

Everyone stood when I arrived at the party—clapping, stomping on the floor, clinking glasses with forks.

"Speech! Speech!" chanted the dancers.

"Be serious, I'm not gonna give a speech," I said, dropping my bag on a chair. "I'll just say that this was an amazing experience. I don't know where I'd be without each and every one of you. And . . ." I paused, looking around, rolled my eyes. "I love you all very much." The group let out a collective *awwww,* but I waved it away.

Everyone was light now that the weight of the show had been lifted. I wished we could have more of this, but most of the dancers would be going home—wherever that was for them now—while Jason, Amy, and I went back to Vermont to pack up our places. I was sure I'd see the dancers often, even the ones who didn't live in the city. There was always one reason or another for a dancer to be in New York. Amy was headed to MacDowell in the fall—perhaps I'd pay her a visit. Taylor might end up swinging through the city. Maybe Jason would get the Philadelphia Orchestra job he was auditioning for in a week—or maybe he'd end up on the other side of the country. In any case, there was no need to be sentimental.

That's how endings are—you convince yourself they aren't final. That they're just a *see you later,* then years go by, and someone posts a photo in the same city where you happen to be, just for now, and you find time to grab a drink. You tell each other about the years in between. All the things that are the same, and everything that's different. So much is different. You don't quite pick up from where you left off—how could you? It's been so long. But you feel light and comfortable. And you're both doing well. Better than before. You can't believe that time in your lives. *So wild! Who were we then?* And it's good to see each other. You don't want to wait that long until the next time. You make promises. And you go on. You forget again.

But we were all together in that moment, for one last time.

Amy pulled a stack of sketches from her bag. Gifts for the dancers that had been in the works for so long. Amy handed each dancer their rendering, hugging them all, lingering with Jade just a little longer.

There was one last sketch in her hands. In it, I was expansive, legs and arms outstretched, my face open and proud. I looked powerful, in control.

"You didn't have to do this," I said.

"It's not about what we *have* to do," said Amy, her eyes welling.

We hugged, and I feared I might cry too. But a song came on that made all the dancers holler, and so I found my way to their circle. Kofi, Dahlia, and my mother came too. And as the beat dropped, we twisted, and shook, and bounced.

CHAPTER 46

I t was a strange dismantling—to walk through the house with my mother, packing up items that had come with me or found their way here over the past nine months, unearthing all the trinkets and photos Eli had brought and I'd hidden away. I carefully packed each plant, some of which I'd replanted in larger pots because they'd overflowed. If they could thrive here, they could thrive anywhere. I ran my hand along the bedposts, envious of all the sex the colonial settlers had no doubt had here. I tucked the Homer Simpson nesting dolls into one another, then— remembering the delight and confusion I'd felt upon seeing them that first day—into my backpack. George certainly wasn't keeping inventory.

My mother took a break, sat on the couch, her hip aching, sweat beading at her temples. I told her to rest for once. I'd take care of everything.

It was nice to be with her in the quiet of the Vermont house with no outside obligations, no family or friends to visit. She fried pork chops, conveniently forgetting that while it had been my childhood favorite, I didn't eat pork anymore. I conveniently forgot too, slicing through the crunchy crust to the tender meat inside. Everything slowed as the simple flavors and textures melded. It was the best thing I'd eaten in months.

I had spent all afternoon packing boxes, calculating the specific geometry of books and tchotchkes until everything fit just right. I found Jason's clothes from the rainy night he dropped me off, and texted that I'd leave them in a bag on the doorstep tomorrow morning. He told me he could come by tonight to get them. But that wasn't necessary. Packing had been tiresome in every way. I wanted to spend time with my mother finishing up these last few things. I didn't need to say another goodbye.

Jason might be in New York next month auditioning for the city's chamber orchestra. I told him to break a leg, but that I was really pulling for his Philly audition. A place was not the same as an opportunity. New York would always be there.

Are you sure I shouldn't just come by tonight for the clothes?

I was. He said he'd miss me. I said goodbye.

After dinner, my mother and I loaded the rental car. My mother leaned against it, out of breath after a couple of trips.

"You okay?" I asked.

She nodded, looked up at the sky.

"Just old."

"You're not *that* old," I said, looking up now too, thinking how strange it was that I hadn't taken in the night sky since my first week here. The glimmer was overwhelming.

"Pretty," she said. "Reminds me of the sky out in the country when we were kids."

"Same sky, I guess."

"Funny how time works."

"That must feel like such a long time ago now."

"But also like yesterday. What I mean is the stars. How what we're seeing now is in the past."

"You an astrologist now?"

She gave me a smug glance.

"I think you mean *astronomer,* smart-ass." She shouldered me, and I covered my face, embarrassed. "I just *remember* things. When I was young, we had to *remember.* We couldn't look everything up on our phones."

"Enlighten me, then. The stars are in the past?"

"It's the way time and distance work or something. Give me a break, I learned this stuff more than fifty years ago. But a lot of the stars we see are dying. Some are already dead."

I wrapped my arms around my mother, nestling into the soft of her. In the sky I searched for the constellations we'd learned about in elementary school, inside a blow-up planetarium in the school gym. I spotted Orion's Belt, moments later the Big Dipper. Guiding lights. The rest was a mystery—a story to someone else, but for me, just shapes and sparkle. A dream.

"Whatever's happening," I said, "they're very pretty."

"Strange what it takes to make some things shine."

From my bedroom window, in the cold, gray morning, behind the rolls of fog, I saw Briar House. I imagined it crumbling beneath the weight of its sins, leaving nothing but a mound of rubble and sweat. But it wouldn't go anywhere. What was immoral wasn't necessarily illegal. A scandal wasn't a sentence. Briar House would go on as it always did, would soon be filled with artists based on what the numbers dictated, what looked good for the moment.

Downstairs, my mother gathered a pile of mail.

"Don't forget all this."

Junk, promotions, a large envelope from a law firm in Bennington. Harold. The board. What was inside that envelope might ruin my life. Or at least try to. That was their job. To wear me out, make me suffer. But my skin had grown thick since arriving. I wasn't afraid of work, of time, of administrative attacks. I stuffed it into my bag.

George was gardening in a small patch near his front door.

"Layla!" he said, standing. "It was so nice having you here."

"Thank you for everything," I said. "You're a real one."

"You are! The next person has big shoes to fill. The only shame is that I didn't get to see your show. But maybe one day I'll make my way down to the big city. From all the coverage, sounds like you have a bright future ahead."

We hugged, and he smelled as he always did—wood, and paint, and working man's musk. I was flattered, hadn't considered that he might read the articles. But why wouldn't he be a reader, a citizen of the world?

I dropped my shoulder bag into the back seat, on top of what remained of my life. My mother was slowly making her way back from a distance, something dripping from her hands.

"What in the world is that?"

"You got this beautiful sugar maple right outside the house."

She held out a piece of bark as she licked watery syrup from the other hand. It dripped onto my fingers too, and I gave a quick lick—it was just sweet enough.

"We had one just like this about a mile from the house, growing up."

For all my time here, I had walked right past the tree without knowing its capabilities. Now, as its leaves waved goodbye with the blow of the breeze, I saw that it was just like the picture on the bottle—big and beautiful and bursting with sugar.

My mother would stay with me for a week in Brooklyn before I'd pack my things up to spend the summer with her in St. Louis. I needed to save up. Reassess. Eli was with his family in Iowa for now. His mother had demanded he come home for a visit, and he couldn't say no.

"You know, he's really sorry," she said as I backed the car out of the driveway and onto the road that led to the highway. "He was going to come opening night, but I told him not to. I thought that might upset you."

"You were right. But I'd prefer if you didn't talk to him anymore, Mom."

"He's a good guy. He's trying."

"He's trying *something*."

"Lots of people cheat. It happens."

"You know how he treated me. He lied to me for months. Gaslighted me. He threw eight years out the window. And the pregnancy." I sighed. I had a lingering feeling that he'd contributed to my body's revolt, but it wasn't fair to put that on him. It didn't make sense to place blame. It was just something that happened. "Remember when we used to watch Ricki Lake, and you said you never understood why women begged for their cheating men back?"

"But Eli's not those men."

"Eli's not *Eli*, Mom. You have this idea of him, but it's not real."

She groaned, frustrated by my stubbornness and ready to change the subject. My pain had transferred easily to her, but she had buried it deep. She couldn't recognize that I was moving forward. She held on tight, even while I was letting go.

A ping came from my phone. I'd silenced it for much of my time in Vermont, thanks to a Pavlovian anxiety that took hold with each call. I'd turned the sound on this weekend, now that Briar House was over, and in case I received a call from the lawyer Dahlia had connected me with. I wanted to take care of things as soon as possible.

I asked my mother to check my emails as rain spat on the window.

"Bonjour, Madame Smart," she read.

"Sounds like spam."

She was quiet for a moment.

"It's from a college in Canada."

"Delete."

"Collège Dufort, in Montreal," she said in an awful attempt at a French accent.

I tried to look at the phone, then quickly back to the road, my whole body buzzing.

There was a sliver of time in the fall when I'd begun to apply for post-residency programs. Dufort—a small but respected college that had welcomed some of my favorite choreographers over the years—was one, though I'd failed to share a list of references. I'd thought Margot might be one at first, but that quickly changed. So I'd left it. Forgotten it. Submitted it incomplete.

"What did they say? They need me to complete the application?"

She continued reading. "We are pleased to offer you a position as choreographer-in-residence for the Fall 2026 semester at Collège Dufort in Montreal, Quebec. We were impressed by the breadth and artistry of your portfolio. Additionally, Canada Council for the Arts advisory member Taylor McMillan submitted their enthusiastic nomination for you, highlighting your talent, passion, and leadership."

Of course. Taylor was the one who'd recommended the residency to me in the first place.

"They want you to start at the end of August, through December."

It wasn't the most high-profile program, but it was a strong one. The idea of leaving the country for a bit appealed to me, as did the idea of engaging with students—scrappy and energetic, eager to exhaust me.

"So, what do you think?" my mother asked.

I nodded. Exhaled.

"I could finally try poutine," I said.

My mother laughed.

"I'd like to try some too."

As we approached the state border, my mother pressed the radio button.

"These stations up here are terrible," she said. "That's one way to keep us out—only offer classic rock, country, and talk radio."

The rain picked up as she scanned through stations. She finally found one playing an old soul song, turning up the volume and rocking in her seat as the horns blared.

"We used to have a dance to this song," she said. "When we were little."

"You all made up dances? Like Bria and me?"

"Of course we made up dances! You think you invented making up dances? Wendell was the best. He had all this fancy footwork. But the girls, we used to do a little shoulder-roll, hip-pop. Shoulder-roll, hip-pop." She showed the movement as the song went on. I joined in with her, smiling even as I gripped the steering wheel. "Makes sense you ended up being a choreographer," she said. "It's in your blood."

Another old soul song came on as the clouds broke, the sun peeking through. Conveniently, my mother and her siblings had made up a dance for that one too—it seemed they had one for every hit from the sixties. This one was a love song—she put one hand in the air, then placed it on my chest, over my heart.

"Go on, you do it too. We did it so everyone's hand was on the chest to their right, then did it again on the other side."

I lifted my right arm and put it on her chest, felt the thump of her heart. There was a shoulder-bounce, a head-turn to the left, a nod. After that, a little freestyle moment, where they danced around, snapping, bumping hips. That part was looser. It didn't really matter how it looked, only how it felt.

ACKNOWLEDGMENTS

There are far too many people to thank them all in these pages, but I'll do my best.

First, I must begin with my mother, who is the reason for everything. Thank you for encouraging me to pursue my passions, to dream big, and for only making me feel like every choice I made was the right one (except when I quit dance for a moment at age four; somehow you knew). Thank you, also, to my aunt Dorothy, who is like a second mother and has taught me so much about life and all its prickly parts.

To my friends who were with me (together apart!) when I first began to conceptualize this novel and it was just as big a mess as I was—thank you is not enough. Heather Day, Laura Snow, Kate Enman, and Raja Feather Kelly, I can't imagine what I'd do without you.

A double thank-you to Raja, as well as everyone in the feath3r theory, for bringing me into the fold and allowing me to immerse myself in your rehearsal process for a brief but wondrous moment.

A huge thank-you to my immensely talented cohort from the Helen Zell Writers' Program at the University of Michigan: Dur e Aziz Amna, Laurie Thomas, Catalina Bode, Anna Majeski, Maya Dobjensky, Drew Nelles, Kashona Notah, Matthew Wamser, Kelsey Wiora, Julia Argy, and Connor Greer. Your brilliant feedback helped make this book, and your care got me through those chaotic, Covid-y MFA days. Thank you also to the phenomenal HZWP faculty, especially Peter Ho Davies and Julie Buntin. And to Naima Coster for your incredibly insightful early reads and endless encouragement.

Blanche Boyd, thank you for being the first writing instructor to give me the confidence to keep going back when I was a shy little teenager at Connecticut College.

Many thanks to the good people at Tin House, Aspen Words, and Kimbilio for giving me the time and space to hone my writing over the past few years. And to the friends I made along the way—I'm so grateful for all of you.

To my agent, Jenni Ferrari-Adler, words are not enough. You believed in this novel from the beginning, and I am so grateful for your time, patience, and guidance.

A massive thank-you to my wonderful team at Random House, beginning with my editor, Miriam Khanukaev. You are nothing short of a gift, and this book would not be in the world without you. And to the entire team—Erica Gonzalez, Carla Bruce-Eddings, Maria Braeckel, Madison Dettlinger, Cara DuBois, Hasan Altaf, Elizabeth Eno, Sam Wetzler, Rebecca Berlant, Cassie Vu, and everyone else involved—I will forever be grateful.

And Andrea Walker, thank you for seeing this book (really *seeing* it), guiding me through its revisions, and changing my life. I hope one day we can dance together.

To my colleagues at Dutton, Plume, and Tiny Reparations Books, thank you for making my transition to the publishing world seamless. I'm so grateful to work with such a smart, thoughtful, supportive team.

To my friends and family at BAM and Alvin Ailey American Dance Theater, thank you for teaching me about art from the inside out and for allowing performance to thrive. I will be in the audience forever and always.

Thank you to my dance teachers from the very beginning, especially the late Lee Nolting, whose memory is all over these pages.

Dance has shaped my life, and I must thank the late greats Katherine Dunham, Alvin Ailey, and Judith Jamison, just to name a very small few, for making this a space where so many of us could see ourselves.

Thank you to David for encouraging me to pursue my MFA and believing in me even when I didn't.

Finally, thank you to everyone who read this book, especially those of you in that purgatorial part of life. Sometimes you have to change everything to change anything. So, don't overthink it, just take it from the top. Five, six, seven, eight.

ABOUT THE AUTHOR

LAUREN MORROW studied dance and creative writing at Connecticut College and earned an MFA in fiction from the Helen Zell Writers' Program. She was a Kimbilio Fellow and an Aspen Words Emerging Writer Fellow and is the recipient of two Hopwood Awards, among other prizes. Her writing has appeared in *Ploughshares* and *The South Carolina Review.* She worked in publicity at the Brooklyn Academy of Music (BAM) and Alvin Ailey American Dance Theater and is now a publicity manager at Dutton, Plume, and Tiny Reparations Books. Originally from St. Louis, she lives in Brooklyn.

laurenmorrowwrites.com
Instagram: @lomo_bk